CW00823457

1 MONTH OF
FREE
READING

at

www.ForgottenBooks.com

By purchasing this book you are eligible for one month membership to ForgottenBooks.com, giving you unlimited access to our entire collection of over 700,000 titles via our web site and mobile apps.

To claim your free month visit:
www.forgottenbooks.com/free458138

ISBN 978-0-483-76601-3
PIBN 10458138

Afield and Afloat. By Frank R. Stockton xxxxx

Charles Scribner's Sons
New York ~~~~ 1900

NERVOUS MAN LYING ... ... THE WATER BUT THE HEAD AND NECK ON A
ROCKS AND THE HEAD AND SHOULDERS OF THE MAN.

Afield and Afloat. By Frank R. Stockton

Charles Scribner's Sons
New York 〜〜〜 1900

Copyright, 1900, by

Charles Scribner's Sons

TROW DIRECTORY
PRINTING AND BOOKBINDING COMPANY

INTRODUCTION

By land or sea; from old-time mansion; from far afield or afloat; from inland waters, or the distant seas, these stories come together and form a company which will proceed, whether on wheels or keels, into that vast region marked " Unknown " on the maps of good and bad fortune.

These stories wear no uniform, and although they stand together, each in its appointed place, they have no common purpose except to make a book. They are related only by the bonds of love or water, for those tales, the interest of which does not rest on the fate of lovers, deal with the fortunes of the brave folk who float on stream or ocean.

For the moment it was thought that it might be well to give the book the title of " Love and Water," for there is but one story in it, and that a little one, which does not deal with one or the other or both of these two great sources of romance. But as it was deemed unwise to designate the tales by a title which might be construed to indicate diluted affection, this idea was quickly set aside.

There are a great many Bullers in this world, and perhaps an equal number of Podingtons, who find that while there is joy afield and happiness afloat, it is dangerous to forsake a chosen element and to do that which may give an amphibious nature to one's experiences. The two friends in the opening story are not the first to find out that a mixture of land and water makes mud.

But in " The Mule-Car " the happy lovers care not whether it is on land or water that they sit together and hold each other's hands. Love to them is everything, and whether it be tossing wave or ragged rocks of which the world around them is composed, they care not. Their Cupid bears no bow, but he wears upon his neck a tinkling bell.

It is to the troublous storms which of late have swept the Spanish main that a Governor-General of an eastern isle, a Spanish captain, and a Yankee skipper, owe their places in this group of tales. War is stern and grim, no matter how we look at it, but on the edges of the most dreadful precipice fair vines and blossoms often grow, and we are lucky if we can pick the flowers without tumbling into the deep ravine.

The holiday story belongs to the land. Although Christmas comes to those who sail upon the seas, and the New Year begins upon the ocean on the first of January, as it does on mountain or on plain, Santa Claus was never known to come sliding down a mast, nor is it likely that the New Year was ever asked to come in through an open hatchway. The true Christmas revel demands the warm hearthstone and the sheltering roof.

So, too, the ghost; the great staircase and the lofty halls of the olden times best please his fancy, and although the spirit of a departed mariner might appear on quarter-deck, in cabin, or even at the wheel, it would, most likely, present a dim and watery aspect. The true ghost, though of no weight whatever, demands solid ground to tread upon, whether said ground be tradition or old oaken floors.

The boomerang does not always hit its mark, and it often fails to come back again in the manner and direction which was expected of it, but to the onlooker a devious course and unexpected deflections may be more interesting than a commonplace flight direct to its object, and an ordinary return to the hands of the hurler.

A well-tied "sailor's knot" has nothing Gordian about it. It may appear difficult, or even impossible, to untie it, but, if one knows how to give it the proper pull, the thing is done; the knot disappears. Thus it is in the story in which Captain Brower ties a knot which it would appear no man could loose; yet, in spite of all this subtle ingenuity, old Captain Lopper finds a hidden end of a rope, and, although it may be said that he uses his teeth, the knot was pulled apart and Love's restrictions fell away.

Love has nothing to do with "The Ghosts in My Tower," and there is no water in the story. Like the tower, this little tale stands up alone; as for the ghost, he hated water, and, as far as was possible, avoided contact with the land. Thus, although steadfastly keeping its place in the line, this story is not unlike an unarmed Esquimo marching into China with the International marines.

"The Landsman's Tale" came into existence in a fashion somewhat odd. It was first told to a company of salt-wrinkled Cape Cod captains, all with memories laden with wild doings of the winds and waves, and rocks were never so hard and stern as were the countenances of these old mariners, while listening to the tale the landsman told. But not one word was heard in deprecation. If a traveller from afar had told them that he had seen a turtle of Galapagos playing upon a violoncello, they would have regarded him with the same silent, stony stare with which they gazed upon the landsman who presumed to tell a story of the sea.

With the rippling of water; the rumbling of wheels; the tinkling of a bell; the booming of cannon; the silent footsteps of ghosts; the crash of timbers, and the roar of a hurricane, these stories now go on, and good luck go with them.

CONTENTS

LIST OF ILLUSTRATIONS

THE BULLER-PODINGTON
COMPACT

THE BULLER-PODINGTON
COMPACT

"I TELL you, William," said Thomas Buller to his friend, Mr. Podington, "I am truly sorry about it, but I cannot arrange for it this year. Now, as to *my* invitation—that is very different."

"Of course it is different," was the reply, "but I am obliged to say, as I said before, that I really cannot accept it."

Remarks similar to these had been made by Thomas Buller and William Podington at least once a year for some five years. They were old friends; they had been school-boys together and had been associated in business since they were young men. They had now reached a vigorous middle age; they were each married, and each had a house in the country in which he resided for a part of the year. They were warmly attached to each other, and each was the best friend the other

3

had in this world. But during all these years neither of them had visited the other in his country home.

The reason for this avoidance of each other at their respective rural residences may be briefly stated. Mr. Buller's country house was situated by the sea, and he was very fond of the water. He had a good cat-boat, which he sailed himself with much judgment and skill, and it was his greatest pleasure to take his friends and visitors upon little excursions on the bay. But Mr. Podington was, desperately afraid of the water, and he was particularly afraid of any craft sailed by an amateur. If his friend Buller would have employed a professional mariner, of years and experience, to steer and manage his boat, Podington might have been willing to take an occasional sail; but as Buller always insisted upon sailing his own boat, and took it ill if any of his visitors doubted his ability to do so properly, Podington did not wish to wound the self-love of his friend, and he did not wish to be drowned. Consequently he could not bring himself to consent to go to Buller's house by the sea.

To receive his good friend Buller at his own

house in the beautiful upland region in which he lived would have been a great joy to Mr. Podington; but Buller could not be induced to visit him. Podington was very fond of horses and always drove himself, while Buller was more afraid of horses than he was of elephants or lions. To one or more horses driven by a coachman of years and experience he did not always object, but to a horse driven by Podington, who had much experience and knowledge regarding mercantile affairs, but was merely an amateur horseman, he most decidedly and strongly objected. He did not wish to hurt his friend's feelings by refusing to go out to drive with him, but he would not rack his own nervous system by accompanying him. Therefore it was that he had not yet visited the beautiful upland country residence of Mr. Podington.

At last this state of things grew awkward. Mrs. Buller and Mrs. Podington, often with their families, visited each other at their country houses, but the fact that on these occasions they were never accompanied by their husbands caused more and more gossip among their neighbors, both in the upland country and by the sea.

One day in spring as the two sat in their city office, where Mr. Podington had just repeated his annual invitation, his friend replied to him thus:

"William, if I come to see you this summer, will you visit me? The thing is beginning to look a little ridiculous, and people are talking about it."

Mr. Podington put his hand to his brow and for a few moments closed his eyes. In his mind he saw a cat-boat upon its side, the sails spread out over the water, and two men, almost entirely immersed in the waves, making efforts to reach the side of the boat. One of these was getting on very well—that was Buller. The other seemed about to sink, his arms were waving uselessly in the air—that was himself. But he opened his eyes and looked bravely out of the window; it was time to conquer all this; it was indeed growing ridiculous. Buller had been sailing many years and had never been upset.

"Yes," said he, "I will do it; I am ready any time you name."

Mr. Buller rose and stretched out his hand. "Good!" said he. "It is a compact!"

Buller was the first to make the promised

"GOOD!" SAID HE, "IT IS A COMPACT."

country visit. He had not mentioned the subject of horses to his friend, but he knew through Mrs. Buller that Podington still continued to be his own driver. She had informed him, however, that at present he was accustomed to drive a big black horse which, in her opinion, was as gentle and reliable as these animals ever became, and she could not imagine how anybody could be afraid of him. So when, the next morning after his arrival, Mr. Buller was asked by his host if he would like to take a drive, he suppressed a certain rising emotion and said that it would please him very much.

When the good black horse had jogged along a pleasant road for half an hour Mr. Buller began to feel that, perhaps, for all these years he had been laboring under a misconception. It seemed possible that there were some horses to which surrounding circumstances in the shape of sights and sounds were so irrelevant that they were to a certain degree entirely safe, even when guided and controlled by an amateur hand. As they passed a piece of meadow-land, somebody behind a hedge fired a gun; Mr. Buller was frightened, but the horse was not.

"William," said Buller, looking cheerfully around him, "I had no idea that you lived in such a pretty country. In fact, I might almost call it beautiful. You have not any wide stretch of water, such as I like so much, but here is a pretty river, those rolling hills are very charming, and, beyond, you have the blue of the mountains."

"It is lovely," said his friend; "I never get tired of driving through this country. Of course the sea-side is very fine, but here we have such a variety of scenery."

Mr. Buller could not help thinking that sometimes the sea-side was a little monotonous, and that he had lost a great deal of pleasure by not varying his summers by going up to spend a week or two with Podington.

"William," said he, "how long have you had this horse?"

"About two years," said Mr. Podington; "before I got him, I used to drive a pair."

"Heavens!" thought Buller, "how lucky I was not to come two years ago!" And his regrets for not sooner visiting his friend greatly decreased.

Now they came to a place where the stream, by which the road ran, had been dammed for a mill and had widened into a beautiful pond.

" There now! " cried Mr. Buller. " That's what I like. William, you seem to have everything! This is really a very pretty sheet of water, and the reflections of the trees over there make a charming picture; you can't get that at the sea-side, you know."

Mr. Podington was delighted; his face glowed; he was rejoiced at the pleasure of his friend. " I tell you, Thomas," said he, " that———"

" William! " exclaimed Buller, with a sudden squirm in his seat, " what is that I hear? Is that a train? "

" Yes," said Mr. Podington, " that is the ten-forty, up."

" Does it come near here? " asked Mr. Buller, nervously. " Does it go over that bridge? "

" Yes," said Podington, " but it can't hurt us, for our road goes under the bridge; we are perfectly safe; there is no risk of accident."

" But your horse! Your horse! " exclaimed Buller, as the train came nearer and nearer. " What will he do? "

" Do? " said Podington; " he'll do what he is doing now; he doesn't mind trains."

"But look here, William," exclaimed Buller, "it will get there just as we do; no horse could stand a roaring in the air like that!"

Podington laughed. "He will not mind it in the least," said he.

"Come, come now," cried Buller. "Really, I can't stand this! Just stop a minute, William, and let me get out. It sets all my nerves quivering."

Mr. Podington smiled with a superior smile. "Oh, you needn't get out," said he; "there's not the least danger in the world. But I don't want to make you nervous, and I will turn around and drive the other way."

"But you can't!" screamed Buller; "this road is not wide enough, and that train is nearly here. Please stop!"

The imputation that the road was not wide enough for him to turn in was too much for Mr. Podington to bear. He was very proud of his ability to turn a vehicle in a narrow place.

"Turn!" said he; "that's the easiest thing in the world. See; a little to the right, then a back, then a sweep to the left and we will be going the other way." And instantly he began the manoeuvre in which he was such an adept.

"Oh, Thomas!" cried Buller, half rising in his seat, "that train is almost here!"

"And we are almost—" Mr. Podington was about to say "turned around," but he stopped. Mr. Buller's exclamations had made him a little nervous, and, in his anxiety to turn quickly, he had pulled upon his horse's bit with more energy than was actually necessary, and his nervousness being communicated to the horse, that animal backed with such extraordinary vigor, that the hind wheels of the wagon went over a bit of grass by the road and into the water. The sudden jolt gave a new impetus to Mr. Buller's fears.

"You'll upset!" he cried, and not thinking of what he was about, he laid hold of his friend's arm. The horse, startled by this sudden jerk upon his bit, which, combined with the thundering of the train, now on the bridge, made him think that something extraordinary was about to happen, gave a sudden and forcible start backward, so that not only the hind wheels of the light wagon, but the fore wheels and his own hind legs went into the water. As the bank at this spot sloped steeply, the wagon continued to go backward, despite the efforts of the agitated horse to find a footing on the crumbling edge of the bank.

" Whoa! " cried Mr. Buller.

" Get up! " exclaimed Mr. Podington, applying his whip upon the plunging beast.

But exclamations and castigations had no effect upon the horse. The original bed of the stream ran close to the road, and the bank was so steep and the earth so soft that it was impossible for the horse to advance or even maintain his footing. Back, back, he went, until the whole equipage was in the water and the wagon was afloat.

This vehicle was a road wagon, without a top, and the joints of its box-body were tight enough to prevent the water from entering it immediately; so, though somewhat deeply sunken, it rested upon the water. There was a current in this part of the pond and it turned the wagon down-stream. The horse was now entirely immersed in the water, with the exception of his head and the upper part of his neck, and, unable to reach the bottom with his feet, he made vigorous efforts to swim.

Mr. Podington, the reins and the whip in his hands, sat horrified and pale; the accident was so sudden, he was so startled and so frightened, that, for a moment, he could not speak a word. Mr. Buller, on the other hand,

was now lively and alert. The wagon had no
sooner floated away from the shore than he felt
himself at home.. He was upon his favorite
element; water had no terrors for him. He
saw that his friend was nearly frightened out
of his wits, and that, figuratively speaking, he
must step to the helm and take charge of the
vessel. He stood up and gazed about him.

"Put her across stream!" he shouted;
"she can't make headway against this current.
Head her to that clump of trees on the other
side; the bank is lower there, and we can
beach her. Move a little the other way, we
must trim boat. Now then, pull on your starboard rein."

Podington obeyed, and the horse slightly
changed his direction.

"You see," said Buller, "it won't do to
sail straight across, because the current would
carry us down and land us below that spot."

Mr. Podington said not a word; he expected every moment to see the horse sink into
a watery grave.

"It isn't so bad after all, is it, Podington?"
continued Buller. "If we had a rudder and
a bit of a sail it would be a great help to the
horse; this wagon is not a bad boat."

The despairing Podington looked at his feet. "It's coming in," he said in a husky voice. "Thomas, the water is over my shoes!"

"That's so," said Buller. "I am so used to water I didn't notice it. She leaks. Do you carry anything to bail her out with?"

"Bail!" cried Podington, now finding his voice. "Oh, Thomas, we are sinking!"

"That's so," said Buller; "she leaks like a sieve."

The weight of the running gear and of the two men was entirely too much for the buoyancy of the wagon body. The water rapidly rose toward the top of its sides.

"We are going to drown!" cried Podington, suddenly rising.

"Lick him! Lick him!" exclaimed Buller. "Make him swim faster!"

"There's nothing to lick," cried Podington, vainly lashing at the water, for he could not reach the horse's head. The poor man was dreadfully frightened; he had never even imagined it possible that he should be drowned in his own wagon.

"Whoop!" cried Buller, as the water rose over the sides. "Steady yourself, old boy, or you'll go overboard!" And the next moment the wagon body sank out of sight.

But it did not go down very far. The deepest part of the channel of the stream had been passed, and with a bump the wheels struck the bottom.

"Heavens!" cried Buller, "we are aground."

"Aground!" exclaimed Podington, "Heaven be praised!"

As the two men stood up in the submerged wagon the water was above their knees, and when Podington looked out over the surface of the pond, now so near his face, it seemed like a sheet of water he had never seen before. It was something horrible, threatening to rise and envelop him. He trembled so that he could scarcely keep his footing.

"William," said his companion, "you must sit down; if you don't, you'll tumble overboard and be drowned. There is nothing for you to hold to."

"Sit down," said Podington, gazing blankly at the water around him, "I can't do that!"

At this moment the horse made a slight movement. Having touched bottom after his efforts in swimming across the main bed of the stream, with a floating wagon in tow, he had stood for a few moments; his head and neck well above water, and his back barely visible beneath the surface. Having recovered his breath, he now thought it was time to move on.

At the first step of the horse Mr. Podington began to totter. Instinctively he clutched Buller.

"Sit down!" cried the latter, "or you'll have us both overboard." There was no help for it; down sat Mr. Podington; and, as with a great splash he came heavily upon the seat, the water rose to his waist.

"Ough!" said he. "Thomas, shout for help."

"No use doing that," replied Buller, still standing on his nautical legs; "I don't see anybody, and I don't see any boat. We'll get out all right. Just you stick tight to the thwart."

"The what?" feebly asked the other.

"Oh, the seat, I mean. We can get to the shore all right if you steer the horse straight. Head him more across the pond."

"I can't head him," cried Podington. "I have dropped the reins!"

"Good gracious!" cried Mr. Buller, "that's bad. Can't you steer him by shouting 'Gee' and 'Haw?'"

"No," said Podington, "he isn't an ox; but perhaps I can stop him." Then with as much voice as he could summon, he called out: "Whoa!" and the horse stopped.

"If you can't steer him any other way," said Buller, "we must get the reins. Lend me your whip."

"I have dropped that too," said Podington; "there it floats."

"Oh, dear," said Buller, "I guess I'll have to dive for them; if he were to run away, we should be in an awful fix."

"Don't get out! Don't get out!" exclaimed Podington. "You can reach over the dash-board."

"That's under water," said Buller, "it will be the same thing as diving; but it's got to be done, and I'll try it. Don't you move now; I am more used to water than you are."

Mr. Buller took off his hat and asked his friend to hold it. He thought of his watch and other contents of his pockets, but there was no place to put them, so he gave them no more consideration. Then bravely getting on his knees in the water, he leaned over the dash-board, almost disappearing from sight. With his disengaged hand Mr. Podington grasped the submerged coat-tails of his friend.

In a few seconds the upper part of Mr. Buller rose from the water. He was dripping and puffing, and Mr. Podington could not but think what a difference it made in the appearance of his friend to have his hair plastered close to his head.

" I got hold of one of them," said the sputtering Buller, " but it was fast to something and I couldn't get it loose."

" Was it thick and wide? " asked Podington.

" Yes," was the answer, " it did seem so."

" Oh, that was a trace," said Podington; " I don't want that; the reins are thinner and lighter."

" Now I remember they are," said Buller. " I'll go down again."

Again Mr. Buller leaned over the dash-board, and this time he remained down longer, and when he came up he puffed and sputtered more than before.

" Is this it? " said he, holding up a strip of wet leather.

" Yes," said Podington, " you've got the reins."

" Well, take them, and steer. I would have found them sooner if his tail had not got into my eyes. That long tail's floating down there and spreading itself out like a fan; it tangled itself all around my head. It would have been much easier if he had been a bob-tailed horse."

" Now then," said Podington, " take your hat, Thomas, and I'll try to drive."

Mr. Buller put on his hat, which was the only dry thing about him, and the nervous Podington started the horse so suddenly that even the sea-legs of Buller were surprised, and he came very near going backward into the water; but recovering himself, he sat down.

" I don't wonder you did not like to do this, William," said he. " Wet as I am, it's ghastly! "

Encouraged by his master's voice, and by the feeling of the familiar hand upon his bit, the horse moved bravely on.

But the bottom was very rough and uneven. Sometimes the wheels struck a large stone, terrifying Mr. Buller, who thought they were going to upset; and sometimes they sank into soft mud, horrifying Mr. Podington, who thought they were going to drown.

Thus proceeding, they presented a strange sight. At first Mr. Podington held his hands above the water as he drove, but he soon found this awkward, and dropped them to their usual position, so that nothing was visible above the water but the head and neck of a horse and the heads and shoulders of two men.

Now the submarine equipage came to a low place in the bottom, and even Mr. Buller shuddered as the water rose to his chin. Podington gave a howl of horror, and the horse, with high, uplifted head, was obliged to swim. At this moment a boy with a gun came strolling along the road, and hearing Mr. Podington's cry, he cast his eyes over the water. Instinctively he raised his weapon to his shoulder, and then, in an instant, perceiving that the objects he beheld were not aquatic birds, he dropped his gun and ran, yelling, down the road toward the mill.

But the hollow in the bottom was a narrow one, and when it was passed the depth of the water gradually decreased. The back of the horse came into view, the dash-board became visible, and the bodies and the spirits of the two men rapidly rose. Now there was vigorous splashing and tugging, and then a jet black horse, shining as if he had been newly varnished, pulled a dripping wagon containing two well-soaked men upon a shelving shore.

" Oh, I am chilled to the bone! " said Podington.

" I should think so," replied his friend; " if you have got to be wet, it is a great deal pleasanter under the water."

There was a field-road on this side of the pond which Podington well knew, and proceeding along this they came to the bridge and got into the main road.

" Now, we must get home as fast as we can," cried Podington, " or we shall both take cold. I wish I hadn't lost my whip. Hi now! Get along! "

Podington was now full of life and energy, the wheels were on the hard road, and he was himself again.

When the horse found his head turned toward his home, he set off at a great rate.

" Hi there! " cried Podington. " I am so sorry I lost my whip."

" Whip! " said Buller, holding fast to the side of the seat; " surely you don't want him to go any faster than this. And look here, William," he added, " it seems to me we are much more likely to take cold in our wet clothes if we rush through the air in this way. Really, it seems to me the horse is running away."

" Not a bit of it! " cried Podington. " He wants to get home, and he wants his dinner. Isn't he a fine horse? Look how he steps out! "

" Steps out! " exclaimed Buller; " I think I'd like to step out myself. Don't you think it would be wiser for me to walk home, William? That will warm me up."

" It will take you an hour," said his friend. " Stay where you are, and I'll have you in a dry suit of clothes in less than fifteen minutes."

" I tell you, William," said Mr. Buller, as the two sat smoking after dinner, " what you ought to do; you should never go out driving without a life-preserver and a pair of oars; I always take them. It would make you feel safer."

Mr. Buller went home the next day, because Mr. Podington's clothes did not fit him, and his own out-door suit was so shrunken as to be uncomfortable. Besides, there was another reason, connected with the desire of horses to reach their homes, which prompted his return. But he had not forgotten his compact with his friend, and in the course of a week he wrote to Podington, inviting him to spend some days with him. Mr. Podington was a man of honor, and in spite of his recent unfortunate water experience he would not break his word. He went to Mr. Buller's seaside home at the time appointed.

Early on the morning after his arrival, before the family was up, Mr. Podington went out and strolled down to the edge of the bay. He went to look at Buller's boat. He was well aware that he would be asked to take a sail, and as Buller had driven with him, it would be impossible for him to decline sailing with Buller; but he must see the boat. There was a train for his home at a quarter past seven; if he were not on the premises he could not be asked to sail. If Buller's boat were a little, flimsy thing, he would take that train—but he would wait and see.

There was only one small boat anchored near the beach, and a man—apparently a fisherman—informed Mr. Podington that it belonged to Mr. Buller. Podington looked at it eagerly; it was not so very small and not flimsy.

"Do you consider that a safe boat?" he asked the fisherman.

"Safe!" replied the man. "You could not upset her if you tried. Look at her breadth of beam! You could go anywhere in that boat! Are you thinking of buying her?"

The idea that he would think of buying a boat made Mr. Podington laugh. The information that it would be impossible to upset the little vessel had greatly cheered him, and he could laugh.

Shortly after breakfast Mr. Buller, like a nurse with a dose of medicine, came to Mr. Podington with the expected invitation to take a sail.

"Now, William," said his host, "I understand perfectly your feeling about boats, and what I wish to prove to you is that it is a feeling without any foundation. I don't want to shock you or to make you nervous, so I am not going to take you to-day on the bay in my boat. You are as safe on the bay as you would be on land—a little safer, perhaps, under certain circumstances, to which we will not allude —but still it is sometimes a little rough, and this, at first, might cause you some uneasiness, and so I am going to let you begin your education in the sailing line on perfectly smooth water. About three miles back of us there is a very pretty lake several miles long. It is part of the canal system which connects the town with the railroad. I have sent my boat to the town, and we can walk up there and go by the canal to the lake; it is only about three miles."

If he had to sail at all, this kind of sailing suited Mr. Podington. A canal, a quiet lake, and a boat which could not be upset. When they reached the town the boat was in the canal, ready for them.

"Now," said Mr. Buller, "you get in and make yourself comfortable. My idea is to hitch on to a canal-boat and be towed to the lake. The boats generally start about this time in the morning, and I will go and see about it."

Mr. Podington, under the direction of his friend, took a seat in the stern of the sail-boat, and then he remarked:

"Thomas, have you a life-preserver on board? You know I am not used to any kind of vessel, and I am clumsy. Nothing might happen to the boat, but I might trip and fall overboard, and I can't swim."

"All right," said Buller, "here's a life-preserver, and you can put it on. I want you

to feel perfectly safe.   Now I will go and see
about the tow."

But Mr. Buller found that the canal-boats
would not start at their usual time; the load-
ing of one of them was not finished, and he
was informed that he might have to wait for
an hour or more.   This did not suit Mr. Buller
at all, and he did not hesitate to show his an-
noyance.

"I tell you, sir, what you can do," said one
of the men in charge of the boats; "if you
don't want to wait till we are ready to start,
we'll let you have a boy and a horse to tow
you up to the lake.   That won't cost you much,
and they'll be back before we want 'em."

The bargain was made, and Mr. Buller joy-
fully returned to his boat with the intelligence
that they were not to wait for the canal-boats.
A long rope, with a horse attached to the other
end of it, was speedily made fast to the boat,
and with a boy at the head of the horse, they
started up the canal.

"Now this is the kind of sailing I like,"
said Mr. Podington.   "If I lived near a canal
I believe I would buy a boat and train my
horse to tow.   I could have a long pair of
rope-lines and drive him myself;   then when

the roads were rough and bad the canal would always be smooth."

" This is all very nice," replied Mr. Buller, who sat by the tiller to keep the boat away from the bank, " and I am glad to see you in a boat under any circumstances. Do you know, William, that although I did not plan it, there could not have been a better way to begin your sailing education. Here we glide along, slowly and gently, with no possible thought of danger, for if the boat should suddenly spring a leak, as if it were the body of a wagon, all we would have to do would be to step on shore, and by the time you get to the end of the canal you will like this gentle motion so much that you will be perfectly ready to begin the second stage of your nautical education."

" Yes," said Mr. Podington. " How long did you say this canal is? "

" About three miles," answered his friend. " Then we will go into the lock and in a few minutes we shall be on the lake."

" So far as I am concerned," said Mr. Podington, " I wish the canal were twelve miles long. I cannot imagine anything pleasanter than this. If I lived anywhere near a canal— a long canal I mean, this one is too short— I'd——"

"Come, come now," interrupted Buller, "don't be content to stay in the primary school just because it is easy. When we get on the lake I will show you that in a boat, with a gentle breeze, such as we are likely to have to-day, you will find the motion quite as pleasing, and ever so much more inspiriting. I should not be a bit surprised, William, if after you have been two or three times on the lake, you will ask me—yes, positively ask me—to take you out on the bay!"

Mr. Podington smiled, and leaning backward, he looked up at the beautiful blue sky.

"You can't give me anything better than this, Thomas," said he; "but you needn't think I am weakening; you drove with me, and I will sail with you."

The thought came into Buller's mind that he had done both of these things with Podington, but he did not wish to call up unpleasant memories, and said nothing.

About half a mile from the town there stood a small cottage where house-cleaning was going on, and on a fence, not far from the canal, there hung a carpet gayly adorned with stripes and spots of red and yellow.

When the drowsy tow-horse came abreast of

the house, and the carpet caught his eye, he suddenly stopped and gave a start toward the canal. Then, impressed with a horror of the glaring apparition, he gathered himself up, and with a bound dashed along the tow-path. The astounded boy gave a shout, but was speedily left behind. The boat of Mr. Buller shot forward as if she had been struck by a squall.

' The terrified horse sped on as though a red and yellow demon were after him. The boat bounded, and plunged, and frequently struck the grassy bank of the canal, as if it would break to pieces. Mr. Podington clutched the boom to keep himself from being thrown out, while Mr. Buller, both hands upon the tiller, frantically endeavored to keep the boat from the bank.

" William! " he screamed, " he is running away with us! We shall be dashed to pieces! Can't you get forward and cast off that line? "

" What do you mean? " cried Podington, as the boom gave a great jerk as if it would break its fastenings and drag him overboard.

" I mean untie the tow-line. We'll be smashed if you don't! I can't leave this tiller. Don't try to stand up; hold on to the boom and creep forward. Steady now, or you'll be overboard!"

Mr. Podington stumbled to the bow of the boat, his efforts greatly impeded by the big cork life-preserver tied under his arms; the motion of the boat was so violent and erratic that he was obliged to hold on to the mast with one arm and to try to loosen the knot with the other; but there was a great strain on the rope, and he could do nothing with one hand.

"Cut it! Cut it!" cried Mr. Buller.

"I haven't a knife," replied Podington.

Mr. Buller was terribly frightened; his boat was rushing through the water as never vessel of her class had sped since sail-boats were invented, bumping against the bank as if she were a billiard-ball rebounding from the edge of a table. He forgot he was in a boat; he only knew that for the first time in his life he was in a runaway. He let go the tiller. It was of no use to him.

"William," he cried, "let us jump out the next time we are near enough to shore!"

"Don't do that! Don't do that!" replied Podington. "Don't jump out in a runaway; that is the way to get hurt. Stick to your seat, my boy; he can't keep this up much longer. He'll lose his wind!"

ON'T TRY TO STAND UP; HOLD ON TO THE BOOM AND CREEP FORWAR
STEADY NOW, OR YOU'LL BE OVERBOARD."

Mr. Podington was greatly excited, but he was not frightened, as Buller was. He had been in a runaway before, and he could not help thinking how much better a wagon was than a boat in such a case.

"If he were hitched up shorter, and I had a snaffle-bit and a stout pair of reins," thought he, "I could soon bring him up."

But Mr. Buller was rapidly losing his wits. The horse seemed to be going faster than ever, the boat bumped harder against the bank, and at one time he thought they would turn over.

Suddenly a thought struck him.

"William," he shouted, "tip that anchor over the side! Throw it in, any way!"

Mr. Podington looked about him, and, almost under his feet, saw the anchor. He did not instantly comprehend why Buller wanted it thrown overboard, but this was not a time to ask questions. The difficulties imposed by the life-preserver, and the necessity of holding on with one hand, interfered very much with his getting at the anchor and throwing it over the side; but at last he succeeded, and just as the boat threw up her bow as if she were about to jump on shore, the anchor went out and its

line shot after it. There was an irregular
trembling of the boat as the anchor struggled
along the bottom of the canal; then there was
a great shock; the boat ran into the bank and
stopped; the tow-line was tightened like a
guitar-string, and the horse, jerked back with
great violence, tumbled in a heap upon the
ground.

Instantly Mr. Podington was on the shore
and running at the top of his speed toward the
horse. The astounded animal had scarcely
begun to struggle to his feet when Podington
rushed upon him, pressed his head back to the
ground, and sat upon it.

" Hurrah! " he cried, waving his hat above
his head. " Get out, Buller; he is all right
now! "

Presently Mr. Buller approached, very
much shaken up.

" All right? " he said. " I don't call a horse
flat in a road with a man on his head all right;
but hold him down till we get him loose from
my boat. That is the thing to do. William,
cast him loose from the boat before you let
him up! What will he do when he gets up? "

" Oh, he'll be quiet enough when he gets
up," said Podington. " If you've got a knife

you can cut his traces—I mean that rope
—but no, you needn't. Here comes the boy.
We'll settle this business in very short order
now."

When the horse was on his feet, and all
connection between the animal and the boat
had been severed, Mr. Podington looked at
his friend.

"Thomas," said he, "you seem to have had
a hard time of it. You have lost your hat and
you look as if you had been in a wrestling
match."

"I have," replied the other; "I wrestled
with that tiller and I wonder it didn't throw
me out."

Now approached the boy. "Shall I hitch
him on again, sir?" said he. "He's quiet
enough now."

"No," cried Mr. Buller. "I want no more
sailing after a horse, and, besides, we can't
go on the lake with that boat; she has been
battered about so much that she must have
opened a dozen seams. The best thing we can
do is to walk home."

Mr. Podington agreed with his friend that
walking home was the best thing they could
do. The boat was examined and found to be

leaking, but not very badly, and when her mast had been unshipped and everything had been made tight and right on board, she was pulled out of the way of tow-lines and boats, and made fast until she could be sent for from the town.

Mr. Buller and Mr. Podington walked back toward the town. They had not gone very far when they met a party of boys, who, upon seeing them, burst into unseemly laughter.

"Mister," cried one of them, "you needn't be afraid of tumbling into the canal. Why don't you take off your life-preserver and let that other man put it on his head?"

The two friends looked at each other and could not help joining in the laughter of the boys.

"By George! I forgot all about this," said Podington, as he unfastened the cork jacket. "It does look a little super-timid to wear a life-preserver just because one happens to be walking by the side of a canal."

Mr. Buller tied a handkerchief on his head, and Mr. Podington rolled up his life-preserver and carried it under his arm. Thus they reached the town, where Buller bought a hat, Podington dispensed with his bundle, and arrangements were made to bring back the boat.

" Runaway in a sail-boat! " exclaimed one of the canal boatmen when he had heard about the accident. " Upon my word! That beats anything that could happen to a man! "

" No, it doesn't," replied Mr. Buller, quietly. " I have gone to the bottom in a foundered road-wagon."

The man looked at him fixedly.

" Was you ever stuck in the mud in a balloon? " he asked.

" Not yet," replied Mr. Buller.

It required ten days to put Mr. Buller's sail-boat into proper condition, and for ten days Mr. Podington stayed with his friend, and enjoyed his visit very much. They strolled on the beach, they took long walks in the back country, they fished from the end of a pier, they smoked, they talked, and were happy and contented.

" Thomas," said Mr. Podington, on the last evening of his stay, " I have enjoyed myself very much since I have been down here, and now, Thomas, if I were to come down again next summer, would you mind—would you mind, not——"

" I would not mind it a bit," replied Buller, promptly. " I'll never so much as mention it;

so you can come along without a thought of it.
And since you have alluded to the subject,
William," he continued, " I'd like very much
to come and see you again; you know my
visit was a very short one this year. That is a
beautiful country you live in. Such a variety
of scenery, such an opportunity for walks and
rambles! But, William, if you only could
make up your mind not to——"

" Oh, that is all right! " exclaimed Podington. " I do not need to make up my mind.
You come to my house and you shall never
so much as hear of it. Here's my hand upon it! "

" And here's mine! " said Mr. Buller.

Whereupon they shook hands over a new
compact.

THE ROMANCE OF A MULE-CAR

THE ROMANCE OF A MULE-CAR

IT was early summer in the old French quarter of New Orleans, and they walked side by side along the narrow street of Toulouse toward that little harbor shut up and secreted in the very heart of the old town, and known as the Basin.

He was not a native of the Crescent City, although it was his purpose to make it his home, and he had never seen the Basin. She was a Creole of the Creoles, and her twenty-two spring-times had all been passed on the shores of the great river. Of herself she never would have thought of making a visit to the old Basin; but as he wished to see it, she was glad to see it with him. There were so many other places in this beautiful city which he had seen but seldom or not at all, and which were far more attractive than this little piece of town-inclosed water, that it might have seemed strange to her, had she not known him so well, that he had asked her to walk with him along this almost deserted street to the quiet harbor.

They had met by accident that afternoon, and it had been a long time since he had had such an opportunity of having her for an hour or two all to himself. He considered this opportunity such a rare piece of good fortune that his strongest present wish was to banish every fellow-being from the vicinity of himself and of her. The life and gayety of the town were, at that moment, distasteful to him. The crowded streets of the shops, the beautiful promenades, the smooth Shell Road, the shores of the glittering Pontchartrain, lively with bright eyes, bright colors, and merry voices, were all places to avoid. In the old street of Toulouse there was not a living being but himself and her.

But the distance from Rampart Street to the Basin was very short, and almost before he knew it they stood by the side of the little harbor, which reaches forth to the outer world of water by means of a long and slender canal stretching itself away, almost unseen, among the houses.

Here were some of those quaint vessels

which dreamily float down from the inland waters of the State, and, having reached the widened surface of the Basin, drop into a quiet nap by the side of the old gray piers. With their cargoes piled high up on their sterns, and the shadows of their masts stretching far, far down into the tranquil water, as if they were endeavoring to reach a bottom of mysterious and unknown depth, they lay, with the houses and the streets around and about them, as quietly as if they had been resting on the surface of a lagoon far away in the depths of the forest.

But the Basin was not entirely devoid of human life. A man in a straw hat sat in a shaded spot on one of the vessels, smoking a cigarette, and apparently waiting for some one who had been sent for. In the middle of the street, on the other side of the dock, were two men talking, one of whom was probably the messenger who had been sent for the person who was expected. There was a woman's head at the window of one of the houses which overlooked the water; and from an open doorway came a little child toddling in the direction of the Basin.

This was not the place he had expected it

to be. From what he had heard of it, he had imagined it a lonely spot with trees upon the water's edge, and in the air that perfume of roses which had helped to make the city dear to him. But there were people here—people with eyes and leisure—and in the air were many odors, but none of roses. There were scents of tar, of sugar, and of boards warmed by the sun, but none of these was in tune with his emotions.

They stood silent, and looked down upon the water. His soul was on fire to speak; but how could he stand here and say what he had to say? That man upon the vessel had already looked at them; and suppose, just as he was in the middle of what he had to say, that toddling child should fall into the water!

She saw that he was ill at ease, and that he did not care for basins.

" You have never seen the old St. Louis Cemetery," said she. " It is just over there; that is the wall of it. Shall we go and see it? "

But his mind was not attuned to cemeteries; he had never felt himself so much alive; his soul was like a panther drawn together for a spring.

" It is like the olden time, that cemetery,"

she said. " It is so still, so lonely; there seems
to be nothing there but——"

" Let us go," he said, eagerly.

They turned their backs upon the Basin,
and, crossing the street, approached the gateway in the brick wall which surrounds the
quaint and venerable resting-place of so many
of the ancient inhabitants of the Creole quarter.

The gate was open, and they saw no one in
the little lodge. They passed in, and walked
among the tombs, which reared themselves on
every side as if they might have been habita-
tions for living people who had shrunken small,
requiring but little room. He had never seen
such tombs, all built above ground on account
of the watery nature of the soil; and as they
walked along a narrow avenue bordered on
each side by these houses of the dead, many
gray with age, and some of them half covered
with clinging vines, she pointed out to him
how nearly all of the names inscribed upon
them were French or Spanish, and how far,
far back were some of the dates beneath them.
He had the tastes of an antiquarian, and the
quaintnesses of history were a joy to him. The
whole scene appeared as foreign to him as

though he had been in another land, and all his sympathies stood ready to be called forth. But they heard no call; his soul was still full of a desire to speak of something which had nothing to do with the past, nothing to do with tombs, gray stones, or clinging vines.

" Let us go this way," said he, turning into a narrower path.

At this moment the form of one of the inhabitants of the tombs seemed to rise up before them. It was very tall and very narrow, and the upper part of it was the head of a very old negro, bony, and adorned with patches of gray hair. Its osseous frame appeared to be covered by loose, hanging clothes instead of flesh. It took off its little cap, and saluted them in Negro-French. It was the guardian of the cemetery.

The young man was astonished and disgusted. If he could have done it, he would have hustled this intruding apparition into an empty tomb. But his companion smiled, and greeted the bony sexton in his own queer dialect.

This ancient keeper of the ancient tombs was as courteous as if he had been one of the stately personages now resting in his domain.

He would show them the cemetery; he would take them everywhere; they should see all. He knew it all, he had lived here so long; with his own hands he had put so many of them away.

The two young people followed him. In the soul of one of them there was bitter impatience.

" Must that creature go with us? " he whispered to his companion. " Is it necessary? Can I not give him some money and send him away? "

" Oh, no," said she, softly; " that would not be right; we cannot do that. This is his kingdom; he is very proud to show it."

They walked on, his face clouded.

" But the place is small," he said to himself, " and there must soon be an end to these avenues. Then he must leave us, and we can rest."

No young mistress of a newly furnished house could have exhibited her possessions with more satisfaction and delight than did this undulating structure of bones and clothes show forth the peculiar features of his mortuary establishment. Many of the tombs were made up of rows of narrow tunnels, each wide enough to receive a coffin, one row above another, the whole as high as a tall man could reach. These were family vaults; but the old sexton explained that, although they had so many apartments, the families often became so large, as time went on, that the accommodations were not sufficient.

When one of the tombs happened to be full, he explained, and there was another applicant for admission, the oldest tunnel was opened, and if any part of the coffin was left, it was taken out, and the " remenz " (by which the old sexton meant the bony residuum of the occupant) were pushed to one side, and the new coffin thrust in and sealed up. Then the ancient coffin was burned, and the new and the old inhabitant of the tunnel dwelt together in peace.

She listened with gentle attention, although she had heard it all before; but, standing by her side, he fumed. How utterly irrelevant were these dreadful details to the thoughts which filled his brain!

They passed a tomb smaller than some of the others, and so old that she stopped to look at it. The stone slab on which was the inscription was so covered with moss and shaded by vines that the words could scarcely be read; but she stooped, and he stooped with her, and they saw that this was the last resting-place of a noble Spanish gentleman whose virtues and lineage had never been obscured except by the lichens and ferns which spread themselves about the lower part of his tomb.

The sexton was happy to see them interested in this tomb; it was his favorite sepulchre. He spoke to them in broken Creole-French, in broken English, and in Negro-French—the very dust and débris of the different languages. The young man could understand scarcely a word the old negro said, but she picked out his meaning from the shattered lingual fragments.

He had been a great man, this ancient Spanish gentleman, the sexton said. Once everybody in this town looked up to him. Grand family he had. All people looked up at them too. Now family all gone; nobody come here to take care of tomb. Tomb would have disappeared, as the family had gone, had not he himself looked to it that the storms and the vines did not destroy it and cover it up out of sight. A very noble man he had been, this Spanish gentleman. Then, suddenly turning to the two young people, the old man inquired if they would like to see " him," and, without waiting for an answer, he stepped to the back of the tomb.

" Come," said she to her companion. " The gentleman receives; we must not be impolite."

Unwillingly he followed her.

The top of this tomb was low and of dome-like form, and at the back of it many of the bricks were loose. Looking about to see that there were no intruders near, for the receptions of the Spanish gentleman were very select, the old man removed a number of the loose bricks. Pointing to the large orifice thus made, he invited his visitors to look in and see " him." The vault was rather spacious, and on the dry and dusty floor the Spanish gentleman was reposing in a detached condition. The sexton thrust in his long arm, scarcely less bony than those of the hidalgo, and took out a skull, which he handed to the lady. After this he presented the young man with a thigh-bone, which, however, was declined. The day was becoming a hollow tomb to this lover; its floor was covered with dismal bones instead of the life and love which he had hoped for on this bright and sunny afternoon in early summer. He was morose.

"The Spanish gentleman must have had two heads," he said to his companion. "See; far back there is another skull!"

"Hush," said she; "we must not notice that; we must be polite at this reception."

The old man put the skull back into the tomb, replaced the bricks, and they passed on.

In one corner of the cemetery they came upon a charming little inclosure, a true garden of greenery, which adjoined a small chapel. There were a fence and a gate, and there was a suggestive shadowness in the rear of the quiet chapel which seemed to strike a note of perfect accord with the young man's emotions.

"Ah," said he, "let us go in here; it will be pleasant to rest in the shade after so much walking. Will you tell the sexton that we do not care to see any more tombs just now?"

She did not answer, but the old man spoke quickly. He had something to say. His voice was raised; he became excited. He declared that it was true what he was going to tell them; hardly could they believe it, but it was true. One day two young people came to the cemetery, and they went into the garden of the chapel, and they sat down in the shade and made love. He saw them, and he told them that they must not make love in the garden of the chapel; but they would not listen to him —they would not regard him at all; they sat and made love; and when he insisted that this was not the place to make love, they still made love. Then he went for the police, and when he came back with the officer, the love-making was over, and they had gone; but the priest locked that garden gate, and no visitors went in any more. Was it not dreadful, he said, all his bones quivering with earnestness, that Christian people should do that? The young man turned disgusted to her.

"I cannot bear any more tombs or skeletons, alive or dead. Let us go out into the world of life."

"Yes," said she, "the hours slip on; it is time that I go to my house."

The old sexton took the money that was offered him—far more than he had expected —but he was not satisfied; there was so much of the cemetery which they had not seen. But they would come again, he said, as he raised his little cap; then he would show them the rest.

"If it is not to be," the young man said

in his heart, " then will I gladly come again, and stay; but otherwise never."

Now they walked together in the broad and beautiful street of the Ramparts, and they moved slowly in the direction of Canal Street, that great central artery of movement and life. It should have been a joy to walk with her, but he was disappointed. There were people on the sidewalks, there were people on the piazzas, electric-cars passed them; and she talked to him about the houses, some of which had little histories; but houses, histories, electric-cars, and the people they met and the people who looked down upon them, were all as the taste of bitter herbs in his mouth. This was the first time he had been so completely alone with her, and the afternoon was passing. If he had had his day to live over again, he would have stopped short in the old street of Toulouse, and would there have said what he had to say. There had been absolutely nobody in the street of Toulouse.

They reached Canal Street, and they stood together, waiting until a car should come which would take her to her home. With whirring and roaring the cars passed this way and that, but the one she waited for did not come. He would have been glad to stand there waiting for the rest of the day. He could not speak as he would speak, but he was near her.

Presently there was heard the gentle tinkling of a bell. She almost clapped her hands.

"It is a mule-car!" she said. "I will go in a mule-car. It will not be long before the mule-car shall disappear. Look at it as it comes; see how that it is funny!"

Slowly the mule-car jingled toward them, and as it came it was truly funny. Among the last of its kind which once circulated placidly all over the old city, with its mule trotting deliberately in front of it, and its shabby sides suggestive of no memories of fresh paint, it formed a striking contrast to the swiftly rolling electric-cars, shining in bright colors, and gay with signs and lettering.

He stopped the car, and helped her in. As he seated himself by her side she raised her eyebrows a very little, as if she would say to herself that although it was not absolutely necessary for him to come with her—for it was out of his way—yet that was his affair, and she would no more interfere with him than she had interfered with the Spanish gentleman who had received that afternoon.

There were not many people in the mule-
car, for most persons preferred swifter methods
of transportation; but it carried some passengers.   All these persons—there were four of
them—sat on the opposite side of the car;
none of them had a newspaper to read, and
they seemed to have nothing upon their minds
but the two young people who were seated
quietly side by side not very far from one of
the front windows.   It must have been a pleasure to look at them, for in countenance and rai-
ment they were prepossessing in a high degree; but there are pleasures which should be
pursued with moderation—at least, the young
man thought so.   He knew that if he said to
her anything which was not commonplace
there would be a gleam of intelligence in the
faces opposite.

Slowly the mule-car trundled along the
shaded avenue into which it had turned, and
then, at a cross street, it stopped, and, wonder
of wonders! two of the passengers got out.   It
was hard to believe that such persons would be
willing to pay their money for so short a ride,
and yet perhaps they had come up all the way
from the river-front.

Now the bell on the mule tinkled again, and

again the car rolled on.   The passenger who
was nearest the door was an elderly woman,
very stout, with a dark and lowering visage.
The other was a man, thin and nervous, who
frequently looked out of the front window
near which he sat.   He had been the least ob-
jectionable of the four original passengers, for
the reason that he had sometimes turned his
eyes away from the couple on the other side
of the car.

It was not long before the car began to go
slower and slower, and then it stopped.   The
man in the front corner turned quickly, and
stared out of the window.

" Ha! " he exclaimed, " it is a ship! " and
with that he rose, picked up a paper package
by his side, and left the car.

The other occupants all looked out of the
windows, and they saw why the car had
stopped.   It had reached the little canal which
stretches along between the houses from the
Basin to the bayou of St. John, and the draw-
bridge was open to allow the passage of one
of the queer, stern-freighted vessels pursuing
its sluggish way toward the little harbor.   Its
bowsprit had barely reached the draw, but it
was moving.

The mule, the driver, and the car now settled themselves into a condition of repose. Repose was pleasant on such a warm and breeze-
less summer afternoon, and the driver, his back
resting against the front of the car, dropped
into a doze. These incidents of enforced in-
activity were familiar to him, and he knew
how to take advantage of them. But the mule,
although glad to rest upon his four motionless
legs, had no desire to sleep. He gazed upon
the slowly advancing vessel, and then, turning
his head from side to side, he glanced first
into one and then into the other of the front
windows of the car. Now he looked again at
the vessel; he cast his eyes upon the draw-
bridge, which seemed glad to rest for a time
in a new position; then he stood reflective,
but not for long. The occupants of the car
seemed to interest him, and again he turned
his gaze upon them.

The faces of the two young people had un-
dergone a slight change since the mule had
first regarded them. They were evidently under the influence of emotions which were growing upon them. She was very quiet, gazing
straight before her; but in her cheeks there
were some slight indications of the pallor of

expectancy. It was different with him: he was clearly agitated. His eyes moved quickly and anxiously from the vessel in the canal to the stout woman near the door of the car. He said but little, and one might have supposed that his heart was beating more rapidly than usual.

The woman with the basket was very much annoyed, and did not take any pains to conceal it. Even the mule could see that she was growling inwardly, and that now and then she gave vent to an exclamation of impatience; but she showed no signs of intending to get out. Even had she lived but one short block on the other side of the canal, she was a woman who wanted the full value of the five cents she had paid for her passage to her home. She could now cross the canal on another bridge if she chose. If she were in such a hurry, why did she not get out and walk the rest of the way? Her basket was a little one.

But although her face grew darker, and her muttered exclamations became more frequent, she did not move. To the eyes of the young man, she looked as if she had been pressed upon the seat in a partially melted condition, and had hardened there. His heart was heavy

as he turned his eyes away from her. How
could he have expected that such an opportunity should *almost* come to him! No one
would get into a car that was standing still by
an open draw. The driver was asleep. If he
could have hired a carriage to take that impa-
tient, fretting woman to the bosom of her
family—aye, if he could have bought a carriage to take her home, he would not have
hesitated at this supreme moment.

Few words passed between the two young
people. He was very restless. He looked out
of the open door, fearing, he could not have
told himself why, that another mule-car might
soon come along. Then he looked out front.
The vessel was nearly through the draw. For
himself he wished that it had stuck fast, that
it had gone aground, that it could move no
more for hours; then that she-demon must get
out and walk. The mule again looked back
into the car. He saw the agitation of the
young man; he saw the steady gaze and the
now fluctuating pallor of his companion; he
saw also the indignant irritation of the stolid
woman with the basket. He turned away his
head, and gazed reflectively before him.

The vessel moved entirely out of the draw;

the bridge came slowly and noiselessly back into its position; the man at the draw went away. Everything was quiet and still; an additional hush seemed to have come upon the scene. The mule gazed straight before him at the bridge now ready for his advance, but he moved not even enough to give the slightest tinkle to his bell; the driver slept.

The woman with the basket had been looking out at the back. Perhaps she thought that if another car came something might happen to hurry matters; but now she turned, and beheld the vessel clearly past the draw, and moving on to conceal itself between the houses. Why did not the car go on? She did not see that the bridge had come into its place. A thought flashed upon her.

"They wait for another ship!" she exclaimed. "This is terrible! It is that life has not enough of length for this." And with a sudden snap of her teeth, she rose and got out.

The motion given to the car by the descent of the heavy woman awoke the driver, who suddenly opened his eyes, stood up straight, and seeing that the way was clear before him, started his mule. This animal, slowly turning his head backward to look at the stout woman,

who was indignantly making her way toward
the sidewalk, went off at a great rate, as though
he were impressed with the idea that he must
make up lost time; then, when it was impossible for the woman to overtake the car, he
slackened his speed. As he did so he turned
his head, he gazed into the front window of
the car, he saw the young people side by side
and alone; then, with a gentle wave of his long
ears, as though he would say, " It is all arranged, my children," he discreetly turned
away his head, and trotted on.

The pallor on the face of the beautiful Creole changed to a flush. If she had obeyed the
dictates of her heart she would have clapped
her hands, exclaiming, " What a beautiful
mule! " But she knew how to control the dictates of her heart, and said nothing. He
moved quickly in his seat, like a man who
would make a bound into paradise as the gates
were closing; and as she, at the same moment,
turned her head, he looked into her eyes.
There was a light in those eyes—a tremulous
light which shone inward, so that he looked
back and back and back into the very inner-
most recesses of her soul. There he saw what
he wanted to see! He said no word, but he

clasped her right hand in both of his own. She did not withdraw it; her face was still turned toward him.

Gently the mule moved his head; with a backward glance of one eye he saw everything. Then again he looked in front of him, and lowering his ears, he let them drop between his eyes and the front windows of the car, so that it would be impossible for him, even by accident, to see what was going on within. If the young man perceived this considerate act, he did not appreciate the fact that he saw it, but there came upon him the feeling that for a moment he was free to forget everything in the world but himself and her, and folding her in his arms, he gave her the first warm kiss of love. Yes; thus it was, in broad day-light, and in a mule-car, these two plighted their troth!

Now the car rolled on, but it seemed no more to move on iron rails. It might have glided over soft masses of fleecy clouds, so gentle, so joyous was its motion. The tinkling of the bell on the mule changed into sweet strains of music from the harps of angels; the waters of the little branch canal, which ran along the middle of the wide avenue, sent up, in all their original fragrance, the odors of every flower or fruit that had ever fallen upon their tranquil surface, and the leaves of the tall live-oaks overhead changed their dull summer green, as if they had been suddenly transmuted, by a wind from some magic sky, into delicate sheets of sparkling emerald. For him there were no people in this great world except themselves. But she, as they sat there with their hands still clasped, threw over those hands a corner of her light summer wrap. Even in this sudden heaven she did not forget the world.

The mule looked back again. He saw both their faces, and he raised his ears to their normal position. Even to those ears his bell had never sounded so musical.

Suddenly, in the midst of all the fleecy clouds, the angel music, the delicate fragrance, the emerald green, and the low, impassioned speech, she started to her feet.

"We have reached the Esplanade," she said; "I must get out."

As they stood together upon the sidewalk, the mule gave them one last look, and then moved on upon his tinkling way.

"No," said she; "you must not walk to my

house with me. It is not right that I should promenade with one so happy."

With one long look, more effulgent than the overhanging sun, he left her. Like a swift stag breathing the strong wind of the hills, he ran after the mule-car, quickly caught up with it, and sprang inside. She was gone, but he would sit where she had been sitting; so long as he might, he would ride on in that heavenly car. But the young man could not sit still; he went out on the platform, and talked to the driver.

" Yes," said the man, " it will not be long that I shall drive this car. It will soon be taken off. The people here now have no use for mule-cars."

He did not know why it was, but, for some reason which he did not try to comprehend, the heart of the young man warmed toward that mule. He wished that it had a more comely tail.

When he and she were married they went to live in a little house far out upon a wide and flowery avenue. This cottage stood but one story high, but it spread itself here and there upon a grassy lawn, and lilies and roses and all manner of fragrant flowers and sweet-smelling bushes crowded about it, as though they would look into its windows, and so imbue themselves with fresh fragrance and fresh beauty. Love sat upon the little door-step to say " not at home " to every inharmonious visitor; and if there were but one blue patch in the sky, it hung tenderly above that roof. Rearward of the house there nestled a little yard of green, and above its odoriferous shrubbery there often raised themselves a pair of long, soft ears; these belonged to the mule of the mule-car. " Since they have use for him no more," she had said—it was not necessary now for her to control the dictates of her heart— " he must come to us; he must be our own."

Even though in the mule-car she had sat gazing straight before her, she had seen far more than her companion could see. She could appreciate, she could understand; and when, sitting together on their piazza in the quiet moonlight, she would hear the tinkle of a bell from behind the house, she would take him by the hand, and they would both remember how the angels once played their harps under the live-oak of Claiborne Avenue.

THE GOVERNOR-GENERAL

THE GOVERNOR-GENERAL

IT was the most beautiful time of the year in the island of Mañana; the waters of the encircling Pacific were warm, but the breezes which came from the neighboring islet of Pruga were cool and odorous with the fragranee from many an aromatic tree and shrub. There were no inhabitants on the islet of Pruga, for its coral reefs did not offer inducements to visiting craft, and it seemed to exist solely for the purpose of furnishing fragrance to the island of Mañana, where the winds blew from the northwest.

The Governor-General of the colony, Señor Gonzales Proventura y Torado, sat upon the front veranda of his official residence, on the plaza of Ruta, the capital city of the colony. The Governor was smoking sadly; the fumes from his rapid succession of cigarettes mingled with the odors floating over the sea from Pruga, but his senses were not gratified, nor was his soul comforted. Before him, on a little wooden perch, there stood a parrot, brilliant in yellow and red. It was motionless; it was dead; it was stuffed. Five weeks before that day he had shot it, and it had just been brought home by a native taxidermist. It was the last parrot he had shot, and his soul grew heavier as he gazed upon it.

Señor Proventura was a collector of parrots. In earlier days, in other spheres of colonial duties, he had been a collector of monkeys, but now he devoted his powers of marksmanship entirely to the bagging of the brilliantly colored parrots which were found in the island over which he exercised colonial authority. He was not only a sportsman, he was a man of scientific proclivities, and he had invented a new chromatic scale in which all the desired combinations of color were furnished by the plumage of parrots. Many of these birds were arranged in order in a corridor of his house, but the scale was not yet complete and more parrots were needed. It had been five weeks since he had shot one, and the soul of the Governor-General was downcast.

The morning air rested lightly on the rippling waters of the harbor of Ruta; a barefooted native brought fresh cigarettes to the Governor-General, and as he placed them on a small table he called the attention of his Excellency to something in the distance. The Governor-General looked up and beheld a man-of-war coming in from the sea.

"Bring me my glass!" cried Señor Proventura, rising hastily. "But stop. What is the flag?"

"It is the ensign of Cabotia, your Excelleney," answered the servant.

The Captain of the man-of-war raised his glass to his eyes and scanned the bay of Ruta. There was but one vessel moving upon its waters. This was a ferry-boat, small and of antique fashion. A man at the end of a long wooden tiller steered the boat, and the passengers, returning from their morning duties in the town to their homes on the other side of the harbor, were standing in the bow to catch the breeze.

"Fire a blank shot to bring her to," ordered the Captain.

The gunner was ready and a cannon roared. The disintegrated wadding of the charge, in the shape of a hundred thousand little pieces of cartridge-paper, fell in a shower upon the passengers of the ferry-boat, who were incensed with anger. " Those wretched sailors on that Cabotian ship are crazy with drink! " they cried. " They do not even know how to fire a salute. We shall complain to the Governor-General." The man at the tiller was very indignant and swore, but he kept on his course, for his passengers must reach their homes; but he would complain when he made his return trip.

" That did not bring her to," said the Captain of the man-of-war. " Fire a solid shot across her bow."

Again roared the cannon and an iron shot flew over the harbor. It whistled by the people of the ferry-boat, and the man at the tiller, turning pale with fright, ran half across the deck in his anxiety to turn his vessel about quickly and get her back to town. Such reckless firing of salutes he had never heard of.

The iron ball went on; it passed the head of the harbor; it flew over the marshes where the cryptogams grew in wild profusion; its little black shadow crossed palm-groves and patches of cultivated ground. An old woman was returning to her home, carrying a bread-

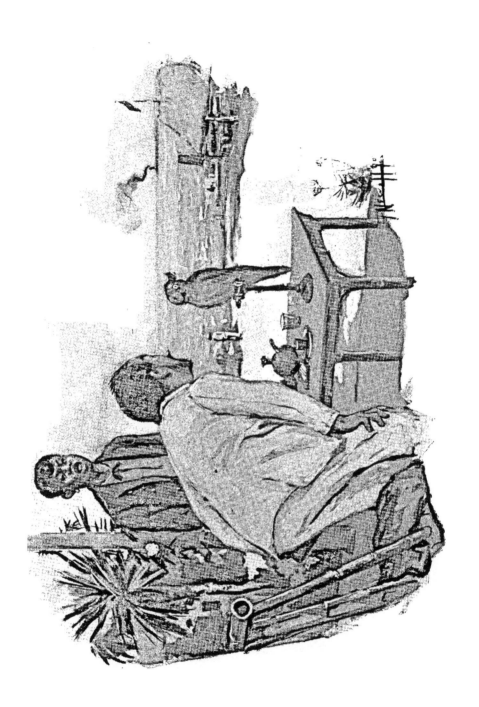

fruit for her noonday meal, but just before she reached her little hut, thatched with palmetto leaves, the cannon-ball, now descending toward the earth, struck the main cross-beam, above the door, and the cottage disappeared. It was like magic; it had been there—it was gone! The old woman fell upon her trembling knees. If she had wished to gather together the remnants of her home she would have needed a dustpan and brush.

"It is good," said the Governor-General; "they are firing salutes. Summon the Adjutaut-General and the Alcalde."

"Pardon, your Excellency," said the servant, "they are fishing on the west coast."

"Very well, then," cried the Governor-General, "order my boat's crew to be ready on the instant. I must go out alone to our visitors." And so saying he rushed into the house to put on his uniform.

His wife assisted him in arraying himself in his official costume. She was delighted at the news, for she was fond of social enjoyment and had two daughters likewise inclined, and officers from foreign ships, when they happened to touch at Ruta, always made things lively in the otherwise quiet town. It was even possible that there might be a ball. At that moment there was a ball. It struck the rocks at the base of El Morro, the antique fortress at the entrance of the harbor.

"Hurry, my dear!" cried the Governor-General. "They are still firing their salutes and I must get to them as quickly as possible. Give me my state hat."

His wife handed him the heavily plumed cocked-hat. He clapped it on and hurried to the water's edge, where he found his boat waiting him. The crew had wakened from their morning siesta at the first sound of the cannon. Everybody was excited; the town had been saluted and the fort had not returned the courtesy.

Just as the boat was about to push off, a slim native boy, wearing but a single white garment, which had been freshly washed, came flying toward the little pier.

"Your Excellency!" he shouted. "Señora Proventura has sent you your night-cap. She says your big hat makes your head hot, and when you take it off you must put something else on."

The Governor impatiently snatched the

nightcap and stuffed it into his pocket. " Give way! " he cried.

The slim boy had stepped upon the stern of the boat behind the Governor, to hand him the nightcap, and he was so much excited that he forgot to step off again; so he remained standing behind the Governor, who did not notice him.

The crew pulled hard. They were excited, for it was very interesting to visit a foreign man-of-war. The Captain of the protected cruiser from Cabotia stood on the quarter-deck, surrounded by his officers.

" They are sending us a flag of truce," he said, as he saw the one garment of the slim boy fluttering in the wind. " Order the firing to cease."

The Governor-General mounted to the quarter-deck, gracious, but dignified. He spoke English very well; he shook hands with the officers and welcomed them to Mañana.

" It grieves me greatly, your Excellency," he said to the Captain, " that we have not been able to return your salute, but you must not accuse us of discourtesy. We are absolutely out of powder. In fact, I have not been able, on the whole island, to scrape together enough to load my fowling-piece, and it is now five weeks since I have shot a parrot. I am a sportsman and I feel the deprivation keenly."

Some of the officers looked at each other and smiled, and the Captain thus addressed the Governor-General:

" Sir, you have introduced yourself as the chief official of this island, and you apologize for not returning our salute. We did not salute. Cabotia is at war with your country. I fired a solid shot across the bow of the only moving vessel in your harbor, and I have bombarded your defences."

The Governor-General stepped back in amazement. " At war with my motherland! " he exclaimed. " I have never heard of it! It is incredible! "

" I do not wonder that you have never heard of it," said the Captain, " for it is a very recent affair and it is not likely that the news could reach you sooner. But you know it now. We are at war with your mother-land, and I have sailed into your harbor to take this island and raise over it the flag of Cabotia. The best thing you can do is to capitulate, without loss of time."

Señor Gonzales Proventura y Torado drew

himself up and folded his arms. "Capitulate!" he exclaimed; "capitulate without striking a blow for the honor of my country, for the honor of my flag, for my own honor! Never!"

It was now the Captain's turn to be surprised. "Then what are you going to do?" he asked. "You decline to capitulate. What then?"

"I shall fight," returned the Governor-General. "So long as my duty calls upon me to do so I shall defend my flag; I shall defend my city; I shall defend my honor."

"But you can't fight," said the Captain. "If you haven't even powder enough to fire a salute or shoot a parrot, how are you going to defend yourself against my guns?"

The Governor-General bowed, and slightly raised his great cocked hat. "Your Excellency," said he, "you are a noble officer of a great country; I am sure you are a gentleman. If a gentleman with his drawn sword in his hand meets an enemy unarmed, he does not plunge the blade into his undefended adversary. He lowers the point of his sword, and requests his enemy to arm himself and come on. If he happens to be provided with an ex-

tra sword he presents it to his foe, so that no
time may be lost. Your Excellency is a gentleman; you will not deny me the right to defend my flag, my city, and my honor; you
will not take advantage of my defenceless position. You will lend me some powder."

The Captain turned to his officers. "These
people will not capitulate, and it will be a
mean thing to fire on them when they have
no powder. I don't suppose they could use
our modern charges in their old-fashioned
guns, but you can lower a boat and send them
that barrel of loose powder in the magazine."

The eyes of the Governor-General were suf-
fused with tears of gratitude. A barrel of
powder! It sounded like untold wealth! He
removed his cocked hat entirely from his head
and shook hands with the Captain and all of
his officers.

"Gentlemen," said he, "I thank you from
my heart; I thank you for myself; I thank
you for my mother-land. I will go to my
fort. I will put myself at the head of my
garrison. I will defend my city, my honor,
and my flag."

"All right," said the Captain, "I will give
you an hour to get ready; but let me tell you

this, when you think it is time to capitulate haul down your colors and send a real flag of truce to me. If that darkey had sat down while you were coming here we would not have thought you were asking for a truce, and we might have fired on you."

The noise of the cannon had aroused everybody; not a man in the garrison was asleep, and when the Governor-General ordered the drums to beat to quarters the soldiers came running from every direction. There were not many of them, but they were wildly enthusiastic when they heard that they had been furnished with powder and were to fight. As rapidly as possible everything was made ready for the battle. The barrel of powder was placed in a central position in the fort and the Governor-General stood by it, issuing his orders.

There were several mounted cannon in the fort, but the gunners were not able to find many balls, and those they did collect were small, about the size of a croquet ball. This made it impossible to use the two large guns of the castle.

"Never mind!" cried the Governor-General. " The small guns require less powder and we can fire more frequently. Every man to his post! The hour of truce has nearly expired."

Fiery martial commotion filled the fort. The garrison, whose gunnery practice had hitherto been confined to harmless salutes, were mad with delight at the idea that they were about to fire solid shot upon a real enemy, and when the first gun from the ship announced the termination of the truce, it was almost immediately answered by three shots from the fort.

Now loudly roared the cannon, on water and on land, and the people of the town ran up and down, wildly asking each other what was likely to happen next.

The heavy shot and shell from the man-of-war tore away great masses of the rock on which the castle stood, but none of them penetrated into the interior of the fortification, and the guns of the Mañanian stronghold were served with an alacrity and ardor which were surprising in gunners who were in the habit of spending their days in the most torpid kind of garrison duty. The cannon were all muzzle-loaders, and as soon as one was discharged half a dozen gunners were ready to thrust into her muzzle a fresh charge of powder and another ball. These small projectiles flew out over the water as if some one had been shaking an apple-tree over the harbor. Sometimes one of them would hit the side of the protected cruiser, and in these cases the Second Officer of the vessel, who was a wit, always facetiously remarked, " Come in! "

Balls and shells flew backward and forward and bits of rock went tumbling and splashing down into the water; clouds of smoke hung over the castle and over the man-of-war, and the townspeople grew more and more anxious, for they could perceive no signs of victory or defeat, on their own side or on that of the enemy.

But the Governor-General was more anxious than anybody else. He was standing by the barrel of powder, and it made his heart sink to see how rapidly its contents were diminishing. There was scarcely a quarter of the powder left. A quarter of a barrel of powder! With that he could go out with his gun for days and weeks, and even months; with that he could secure all the parrots he needed for the completion of the model of his great chromatic scale; with that amount of powder, life would indeed be worth living! And these men were scooping it up and ramming it into the cannon as if the precious grains were of no more value than the dust of the earth. He stooped forward and looked at the cannon-balls which had been gathered together. There were not many of them left, but in the eyes of the Govcruor-General there were entirely too many.

Just as a cannon was fired and as the gunners turned away their faces and shut their eyes, the Governor-General kicked three of the balls into a small gutter which opened outside the walls, and they dropped down the cliff. He would have been glad to pick up the rest of them and put them in his pockets, if it had been possible.

But he did not have to worry long. In a few minutes the last little ball was shot out from the fort and fell into the water with a splash close to the side of the man-of-war.

" They are trying to knock off our keel," said the facetious Second Officer.

Now the heart of the Governor-General rose and his eyes sparkled. " My brave men," he shouted, " we have done our duty, we have fought for the honor of our flag, and for the honor of our mother-land, but we are out of ammunition. We have no more balls and we must submit to the inevitable; we must capitulate." And as he said these words he cast his eye into the barrel of powder, of which at least one-fifth remained.

The garrison gathered around him and shouted in indignation. "We will never give up the fight," they cried, "while there is a drop of blood in our veins!"

"Blood will not do!" shouted the Governor-General in return. "Balls are what we want, not blood."

"And balls we must have!" cried some of the men. "If there are no more little ones left, perhaps we can find some that will fit the larger cannon."

The Governor-General trembled; it would be a dreadful thing if they should really find some larger balls.

"Be careful what you do!" he shouted. "One of the big cannon has a great crack in it. The light shines into the inside of it."

"The other one is good," replied one of the men; "let us find some balls for it."

In a very short time some of the men came running back, carrying balls which they found lying about the fort, but they were all two or three sizes too large.

"I knew it!" cried the Governor-General. "I understand the conditions of our munitions of war. We can fire no more of our guns. It is absolutely necessary that we capitulate immediately, otherwise the enemy will begin to shell the town. Think of our wives, our children," and in his heart the Governor-General added, "our stuffed birds."

The men turned sullenly away and began to roll cigarettes; of course they could not fight without balls to fit their cannon. But there was a young fellow, named Bartolomo Larrisda, who would not give the fight up so easily.

"I believe I can find balls to fit that gun!" he cried. "There must be some, somewhere!" and away he ran.

The Governor-General frowned and called to the young man to come back, but the latter did not hear him.

"Fool!" ejaculated Señor Proventura, "he will ruin everything," and as he spoke he fiercely thrust his hands into his pockets. In one of them he felt the nightcap. "Ha!" he said to himself, "this will do," and looking about to see that he was not observed, he thrust his nightcap into the muzzle of the one good gun, and with a rammer he pushed it home. " Now then," said he to himself, " he cannot fire off that cannon, even if he finds a ball to fit."

Having said this, he hurried out of the fort and down to the place where he had left his boat. He took with him a small table-cloth which he had snatched from one of the living-rooms of the fort, and this, tied to a pole, was waved high in the air, whereupon the cannon-ading from the man-of-war, which had become infrequent since it was not returned by the fort, now ceased altogether.

The boat of the Governor-General was rowed rapidly to the man-of-war, and he soon stood upon the quarter-deck. Advancing to the Captain, he drew his sword from his scab-bard and held it in front of him, hilt first, and said:

" Your Excellency, I surrender. We are out of——" he was about to say " cannon-balls," but he thought it wiser to make an amendment and said, " ammunition. We can fire no more. Our honor is satisfied. That is the great thing. El Morro capitulates. The town of Ruta capitulates. The island of Mañana, with the neighboring islets, all capitulate. Accept my sword."

The Captain waved back the proffered weapon. "You can keep that," he said, "but I will take the rest. I will go ashore to hoist the Cabotian flag above your fort. What is the size of your garrison?"

This question puzzled the Governor-General. It had been some time since he had heard roll-call, or given any thought to the subject, but it was necessary to make an answer which would not belittle his position as first official of the colony, and therefore he said:

"One hundred and forty-five men, your Excellency."

"What!" cried the Captain, "I did not suppose that you had as many men as that. Mr. Mannering," he continued, addressing the First Officer, "did you hear that? One hundred and forty-five soldiers in the garrison. What could we do with so many prisoners?"

"I don't know, sir," was the reply. "We could not accommodate them upon this ship."

The Governor-General listened in wonder. "Does your Excellency mean," said he, "that

you are going to carry away our soldiers as
prisoners!"

"I have planned to take you all, the officials
of the town and your officers and soldiers, as
prisoners of war and to carry you away with
me, leaving behind some one commissioned
by me as temporary Governor-General, acting
under the authority of the Cabotian Government. But your number embarrasses me. I
did not suppose you had so many men."

To be carried away! The Governor-General turned pale. He had never thought of
anything of that sort. It was bad enough to
be obliged to change flags, but if he were
forced to leave his home, his family, the fifth
of a barrel of gunpowder, and all the stuffed
parrots in the corridor, as well as those still
flying freely in the woods, it would be terrible
indeed. But he did not lose hope.

"Your Excellency," he said, "we have
truly a large garrison in the castle, and besides,
there is the garrison of the inland battery,
above the town."

"More men!" cried the Captain. "And
how many officers and men are in that garrison, I should like to know?"

"I should say," replied the Governor-General, " that, excluding the sick in the hospitals, there must be sixty men and officers, all told, in the garrison of the inland battery."

The Captain clapped his forehead. " Two hundred and five men!" said he. " Mr. Mannering, how are we to accommodate them?"

Bartolomo Larrisda was a young man of energetic loyalty; he did not know that the Governor-General had rowed away under a flag of truce; he knew nothing except that somewhere there must be some balls that would fit that large gun, and with which the fight for the honor of his flag and his mother-land might be continued. At last he found a ball which looked to be the right size. Only one, but with it he ran to the gun. One shot, well directed, might explode the enemy's magazine.

Bartolomo tried the ball and to his delight he found that it would go into the muzzle of the cannon. In fact, it was a trifle too small, and as he was about to remove it from the muzzle, preparatory to putting in a charge of powder, the smooth ball slipped from his nervous fingers and rolled down into the cannon, which was somewhat elevated, and did not stop until it rested safely against the nightcap of the Governor-General, at the very bottom of the bore.

Bartolomo was horrified; with a great deal of trouble he lowered the muzzle of the cannon, but the ball would not roll out, for it was jammed by the nightcap. The young man tore his hair and beat the cannon with the rammer, but the concussion did not loosen the ball. For a moment he stood in despair and then he gave a spring toward the barrel of powder, which he picked up and placed close to the gun.

"Ha!" he exclaimed, "I may load it yet. I will pour powder into the touch-hole until there is enough behind the ball to enable me to make this last shot for the honor of my flag and my mother-land."

Frantically he poured the powder into the touch-hole, ramming it in with a piece of wire, wriggling the wire so as to make more room inside, and pouring in more and more powder, until finally he believed he had enough to make his last great shot, by which, perchance, he might explode the magazine of the insolent enemy.

Dashing into an adjoining casemate he snatched a live cigarette from the mouth of a comrade and in two seconds had touched off the cannon.

" It is true, sir," said the First Officer of the man-of-war to his Captain, " there is no room here for two hundred and five men. We might as well try to ship another crew."

At this moment there was the report of a cannon. It came from the fort. It was not a very loud report, but everybody jumped, and all eyes were directed toward El Morro. A cannon-ball was seen coming through the air. It came so slowly that it was perfectly easy to observe it. It moved in a great arc over the harbor and then began slowly to descend. It came directly toward the quarter-deck of the man-of-war.

" Look out! " cried the captain of the watch. Everybody looked out, and when the ball approached the deck they all stepped back out of its way. It struck not three feet from where the Governor-General had been standing.

The Captain's face was as red as fire. " What is the meaning of this? " he shouted. " What vile treachery have you been hatching? You fly a flag of truce; you surrender; and then your fort fires upon us! "

The Governor-General did not immediately answer; his eyes were fixed upon the cannon-ball which lay in the middle of the deck. He advanced toward it and raised it in his hand.

"Your Excellency," said he, to the Captain, "do not condemn me; do not be indignant. There is no harm done, there was none intended. You see this nightcap which partially envelops the ball? It is my nightcap, which I always should put on when I remove my hat of state. This great hat makes my head hot, and when I take it off I am in danger of catching cold if I do not put on something else. My wife urged me to take this cap with me to-day, and as I forgot it she has thoughtfully sent it after me in this fashion. There was no other way. Your Excellency, she has ordered one of the gunners to forward it with a very light charge of powder."

"A dangerous conjugal attention," said the Captain, his face recovering its natural brown. "It was a pretty good shot, though, I must say. It came nearer to you than to anybody else, and even if you had not moved, it would not have hit you."

"Aye, your Excellency," said the Governor-General, putting on the nightcap, for it was impossible for him to seem to slight the affectionate attention of Señora Proventura, "my wife is a most considerate woman. She never forgets my health, and she doubtless selected the most careful gunner to send me this nightcap."

At this moment luncheon was announced, and as everybody was hungry the conference was suspended, and the Governor-General was invited to step below and join the Captain's mess.   The invitation was most gladly accepted, and the Governor's boat was sent back to inform his lady that he would take his midday meal on the man-of-war.

The Governor-General made a very fine meal.   He drank good wine, and the cigar which he afterward smoked, sitting in a comfortable chair on the deck with the Captain and some of the other officers, was of remarkable fragrance.   Tobacco grew on Mañana, but the island produced nothing like this.

" It comes from some of our other colonies," thought the Governor-General, " but it is only through the foreigners that we have it here."

" Now then," said the Captain, puffing a cloud of smoke toward the flag of his country, which was gently waving in the breeze from Pruga, " we might as well arrange the terms of surrender.   I have taken two hundred and five prisoners, besides yourself and the officers of the town.   Now we must decide what to do with you.　You must be taken away, in some manner or other."

"Of course," said the Second Officer, "if we take prisoners and don't take them, of course we haven't taken them."

"Very good," remarked the Captain, and they all laughed.　"That brings us to the next point," he continued—"how are we going to take them?　One thing is certain—I shall not stuff them into this ship."

"May I ask, your Excellency," interrupted the Governor-General, "to what place you propose to take your prisoners, when you do take them?"

"I don't know about that," answered the Captain; "the main thing is to get you all away from here.　When a place is captured, its garrison and municipal officers must be removed.　That is one of the principles of war, and we can't get around it.　If there were a merchant vessel in this port I would put you all into it and send you somewhere, probably to your own country, for I am sure you would not be wanted in mine; but the main point, as I have said, is to get you away from here."

"Yes, your Excellency," said the Governor-General, "I understand perfectly.　But there is no ship in port, and no vessel larger than our ferry-boat, and that is a very little one."

" It seems to me, Mr. Mannering," said the Captain, addressing his First Officer, " that the only thing we can do is to leave these prisoners here for the present and to send a transport for them as soon as possible. They can then be taken to their own country and we shall have no further trouble with them is plain."

" Yes," said the First Officer, " I see nothing else to do but that."

" Your Excellency," the Governor now asked, " how long do you suppose it will be before we could expect a ship which would carry us away? "

The Captain shook his head and looked at Mr. Mannering. The latter began to count on his fingers.

" Three weeks to port," he said, " a week to telegraph and make arrangements, five weeks for the transport to reach this island, two weeks for unavoidable delays. That makes, let me see, eleven weeks."

The Governor-General sat for a few moments and thought. " And what shall be done with your prisoners in the mean time, your Excellency?" he asked. "Of course they must be fed."

"Without doubt," said the Captain; "that is understood. They are prisoners of my country, my country will take care of them. I will leave rations for them until they are sent for. And, by the way, I must appoint some one to take charge here. Is there a naturalized Cabotian on the island?"

The Governor-General shook his head. "No, your Excellency," said he, "there is not one. In fact, there are but very few of us who can even speak your language. But if I might be allowed to offer a suggestion——"

"Certainly," interrupted the Captain; "I shall be glad to hear it."

"Well, then, your Excellency," said the Governor, "if it will help you out of your difficulty I am perfectly willing to be naturalized. I speak your language, and now that this island belongs to your country, and as it is necessary to find some one to take temporary charge of affairs, I am ready to do whatever is needed to make me a naturalized Cabotian."

"That's not a bad idea," said the Captain to Mr. Mannering. "He can keep the people in order better than anybody else and there will be no rupture, no strain. I am in favor of his plan."

"Yes," said the First Officer, "I think that would work very well, but I don't know that we have the authority to naturalize him. I suppose, however, we might make him a brevet-citizen, just for a time, you know."

"Very good," said the Captain, rising, "we will settle it that way. He can retain his officers, and things will go on smoothly and comfortably. And now, Mr. Governor, I am going to take a little nap. About five o'clock, when the day is cooler, I'll go over to the fort to receive the surrender of your prisoners, and I will also go to the town to raise the flag of Cabotia upon your principal building, whatever it may be. Until then, I will bid you a very good-afternoon."

The Governor-General rose, took off his nightcap, put on his plumed hat of state, shook hands all around and departed in his boat, which had returned for him.

He had no time to lose. He had surrendered two garrisons of two hundred and five men, and where was he to find those men? He was rowed first to the fort. The garrison was hastily gathered together and counted. Ineluding those who had gone to town for their luncheon and had not yet returned, and even reckoning the laborers who worked in the castle garden, the waiters, and a man who had a license to sell candy and cake to the soldiers, there were exactly seventy-three men belonging to the fort. But the Governor was not daunted; he called his Lieutenant.

"Señor Hernandez," said he, "I want, instantly, seventy-two men. I have surrendered one hundred and forty-five members of this garrison, and we are seventy-two short. Go bring them in quickly. Take a file of soldiers with bayonets. Anybody will do to help make up the garrison. We must have them quickly. The Cabotian Captain will be here by five o'clock. Take shopkeepers, carpenters, cooks, any one you please. If they have shirts and trousers, that's enough. There are a lot of old military caps in the fort; clap one on every man jack of them. All our soldiers cannot be expected to wear their uniforms in this hot weather. As for arms, divide them up as well as you can. If there are not enough to go around, give one fellow a sword and another a scabbard, and if you can't do any better, serve out the curiosities in the museum, stone hatchets and all. They can't expect that we have only modern arms in this island. Now I must hurry away and see the Alcalde and the Adjutant-General. And mind you, Hernandez, this garrison must number one hundred and forty-five by five o'clock."

When the Governor-General reported the terms of surrender of the town and the forces, the citizens were much agitated of course, but the Governor-General's words, as he addressed them in the Plaza, were very encouraging.

"My people!" he shouted, "there is nothing to fear. Very little will be changed. To-morrow, everything will go on as well as it did yesterday, if not better."

Continuing, he said: "This afternoon the Cabotian flag will be raised in this town and on the castle, and in return for this privilege the Cabotians will land a large amount of stores, not only canned goods of many varieties, but flour, coffee, sugar, salt meat, potatoes, and many other things. The man-of-war will then depart, and if she should be overtaken by a typhoon before she reaches her destination there will be no report of the capture of this town. My friends, be calm; we have our honor and the stores I have mentioned."

At five o'clock the Captain of the man-of-war, accompanied by a party of officers, was rowed to El Morro. At the landing-place they were met by the Governor-General, who accompanied them up to the fort. There they found the garrison drawn up in two long lines to receive them, those wearing uniforms and with the best arms in the front rank. The Governor glanced along the lines.

"Heavens!" he whispered to the officer in command, "three of those in the second line are women."

"It could not be helped, your Excellency," said the officer; "three men got away and we had to clap in these women who were bringing yams to the fort. We put military caps on them, you see, and they each have a ramrod."

The garrison was counted and the number of prisoners found to be correct. But the three women were noticed.

"Hello!" cried the Cabotian Captain. "What is the meaning of this?"

"Your Excellency," said the Governor-General with a bow, "those are vivandières; very necessary for the refreshment of the troops in this hot climate."

The Captain nodded. "All right," said he.

" Hoist our flag over the fort, and then we will proceed to the town."

When the Captain and his party, with the Governor-General, were rowed to the town, they were joined by a file of marines from the ship, and all proceeded to the town hall. There the Cabotian flag was raised, a salute was fired, and the Captain, in the name of Cabotia, took possession of the town, the island and the neighboring islets.

" Now then," said he, when the ceremonies had been concluded, " how about that inland battery you spoke of. Where is it? "

These words sent dismay to the heart of the Governor-General. He had been thinking about that battery and hoping that no present reference would be made to it. He had not visited it for a long time and knew very little about it except that it did not contain anything like a garrison of sixty men.

" Your Excellency," said he, " it is a long way up to that battery and I would suggest the postponing of the reception of its surrender until to-morrow morning. I hope that you and your officers will now accept the poor hospitality of my official residence, and I crave the honor of presenting you to my wife and daughters."

There was a gay time in the town that evening. There was a dinner and a dance at the Governor-General's house, and the example thus set by the official head of the colony was cheerfully followed by many of the citizens.

In the course of the evening the Governor-General withdrew himself from his company, and wrote a note to the officer in command of the castle and sent it by a fleet-footed messenger. It was to this effect:

" At daybreak to-morrow march sixty of your best-equipped men to the dell behind the inland battery. There they will await my orders.   PROVENTURA Y TORADO."

Early the next morning the Governor-General walked up the hill and there he found the sixty men from the fort, smoking cigarettes at the place appointed. Leaving them, he repaired to the battery, where he was received with all due military etiquette by the officer in command. Major Cascaro, a true soldier of his mother-land, was a medium-sized man, very lean, very erect, very punctilious. He had a long nose with nostrils like wings, and under this nose was a mustache of such size and density that it looked as if it had been punched into place, a little at a time, until a great mass of it had been securely adjusted.

" Major," said the Governor-General, " you must prepare, as rapidly as possible, to surrender this fortification with its garrison. Officers from the Cabotian man-of-war may arrive here at any moment."

The Major stared fixedly at the Governor-General. " Your Excellency," said he, " what have I to do with the officers of the Cabotian man-of-war? "

" You have to surrender to them," said the Governor-General, " and the quicker you prepare for it, the better."

The Major drew out the ends of his mustache and folded his arms.

" Your Excellency," said he, " I was appointed to command this fortification and thereby prevent the wild natives from intruding upon the town. It is true that all these natives have disappeared, but that makes no difference. The command has been entrusted to me by the crown of my mother-land. I shall hold it until that crown shall request me to give it up. I have heard the firings and the cannonadings and I have seen the flag-raisings, but all that is nothing to me. I have nothing to do with the forces of Cabotia, and I will not surrender to them."

" Well, then," impatiently cried the Governor-General, " surrender to me. It does not make any difference to whom you surrender."

" Your Excellency," said the Major, " I do not surrender to an enemy, still more firmly do I decline to surrender to a friend."

" Look here, Major," said the Governor-General, more impatiently, " we are spending too much time in talk. How many men have you in this battery? "

" Twelve," said the Major, " besides myself."

" Any officers under you? "

" Not at present," said the Major. " There were some assigned to this post, but I fill their positions myself."

" And draw their salaries? " asked the Governor-General.

" Of course," said the Major, " as I take their places."

" Now listen to me," said the Governor-General; " the whole colony has capitulated, including this battery with a garrison of sixty men. I have prepared for all emergencies. I have sixty soldiers from the castle, waiting down here in the dell. If you choose you may have forty-eight of those men to add to your garrison and may surrender them as a whole. If you do not choose, I will pack your fellows off into the woods and surrender the fortification myself, with the men from the castle. There must be sixty men surrendered from this spot in less than half an hour. I see now a boat putting off from the ship."

The Major looked at the Governor-General. " Your Excellency," said he, " what are the terms of surrender? "

" Rations for all prisoners of war until a ship can be sent to take them to their native land."

" Pay for the officers during that time? " the Major asked.

" Certainly, that is understood, of course."

" What is the usual rank of officers commanding a fortress of Cabotia? " asked the Major.

" A colonel, I should say," was the answer; " surely no lower than that."

" With the usual officers under him? "

" Of course," said the Governor-General; " that goes without saying."

"Your Excellency," said Major Cascaro, "I will surrender. Will you kindly send me your forty-eight men."

That morning, when the Captain of the man-of-war went on deck he stretched himself and yawned.

"We were up pretty late last night, Mr. Mannering," he said, "and I must say I don't want to go to receive the surrender of that little battery. Send the officers who were in charge of the vessel yesterday. It is fair that they also should have a little skip on shore."

The remainder of that day was spent in landing stores. As far as it was possible, clothing was humanely issued to the prisoners. The Governor-General spent most of his time on the deck of the man-of-war, for it was necessary for him to have frequent conferences with the Captain.

Among the things which might have been overlooked, had it not been for his thoughtful suggestion, was the necessity of leaving money for the pay of the officials who were to have charge of the prisoners and the captured town. There were other things which were not forgotten by the prudent Governor-General. Among so many prisoners, medicine would probably be necessary, and he hinted that it would not be wise to leave an entire colony without any powder suitable for fowling-pieces and ordinary domestic defence. If there happened to be any powder left from the former generous gift, it was really best suited for artillery and barely enough for the firing of a salute when the transport should arrive to take the garrison home.

All these suggestions were favorably received by the Captain, and he was so willing to be just as well as generous that when the Governor-General mentioned the case of an elderly female whose family residence had been destroyed by the bombardment on the previous day, and who was now obliged to live in the open air, the Captain ordered the paymaster to put into the hands of the Governor-General sufficient coin to enable this unfortunate sufferer to erect a moderate-sized dwelling, with kitchen and other desirable out-buildings.

Late in the afternoon the man-of-war weighed anchor and steamed out of the harbor, and, as she passed over the bar, the man at the lead noticed that she drew considerably less water than when she went in.

It was many months after the occurrences above narrated that the Governor-General of Mañana stood on the edge of a forest in the southern part of the island. It was a lovely day, but though the waters of the encircling Pacific were warm, the breezes which came over from the neighboring islet of Aribo were cool and odorous with the fragrance from many an aromatic tree and shrub. There were no inhabitants on the islet of Aribo and it seemed to exist solely for the purpose of furnishing fragrance to the island of Mañana when the winds blew from the southeast.

The soul of the Governor-General was sad; he had just fired his last charge of powder at a parrot and missed it, and his chromatic scale, although nearly finished, still needed two or three birds.

The rations left by the Cabotian Captain had long since been consumed. The money for the officials' salaries had all been paid out, no transport had entered the harbor of Ruta, and the people of the little colony believed that they had been forgotten.

The Governor-General felt assured that peace between his mother-land and Cabotia must have been completed, for no nation could

stand up long before the valor of the people
of his blood, but he feared that in the confu-
sion and bustle of the necessary negotiations,
his colony had been totally overlooked both
by the victors and the vanquished.

He seated himself on a little rock and gazed
out over the sea. His days of prosperity were
past; like Alexander, he sighed; there were
no other worlds to conquer him!

OLD APPLEJOY'S GHOST

OLD APPLEJOY'S GHOST

THE large and commodious apartments in the upper part of the old Applejoy mansion were occupied exclusively, at the time of our story, by the ghost of the grandfather of the present owner of the estate.

For many, many years old Applejoy's ghost had been in the habit of wandering freely about the grand old house and the fine estate of which he had once been the lord and master, but early in that spring a change had come over the household of his grandson, John Applejoy, an elderly man and a bachelor, a lover of books, and—for the later portion of his life —almost a recluse. A young girl, his niece Bertha, had come to live with him, and make part of his very small family, and it was since the arrival of this newcomer that old Applejoy's ghost had confined himself almost exclusively to the upper portions of the house.

This secluded existence, so different from

his ordinary habits, was adopted entirely on account of the kindness of his heart. During the lives of two generations of his descendants he knew that he had frequently been seen by members of the family and others, but this did not disturb him, for in life he had been a man who had liked to assert his position, and the disposition to do so had not left him now. His grandson John had seen him, and two or three times had spoken with him, but as old Applejoy's ghost had heard his sceptical descendant declare that these ghostly interviews were only dreams or hallucinations, he cared very little whether John saw him or not. As to other people, it might be a very good thing if they believed that the house was haunted. People with uneasy consciences would not care to live in such a place.

But when this fresh young girl came upon the scene the case was entirely different. She might be timorous and she might not, but old Applejoy's ghost did not want to take any risks. There was nothing the matter with her conscience, he was quite sure, but she was not twenty yet, her character was not formed, and if anything should happen which would lead her to suspect that the house was haunted she

might not be willing to live there, and if that
should come to pass it would be a great shock
to the ghost.

For a long time the venerable mansion had
been a quiet, darkened, melancholy house. A
few rooms only were opened and occupied, for
John Applejoy and his housekeeper, Mrs. Dipperton, who for years had composed the family, needed but little space in which to pass
the monotonous days of their lives. Bertha
sang, she played on the old piano; she danced
by herself on the broad piazza; she wandered
through the gardens and brought flowers into
the house, and, sometimes, it almost might
have been imagined that the days which were
gone had come back again.

One winter evening, when the light of the
full moon entered softly through every un-
shaded window of the house, old Applejoy's
ghost sat in a stiff, high-backed chair, which
on account of an accident to one of its legs
had been banished to the garret. It was not
at all necessary either for rest or comfort that
this kind old ghost should seat himself in a
chair, for he would have been quite as much
at his ease upon a clothes-line, but in other
days he had been in the habit of sitting in

chairs, and it pleased him to do so now. Throwing one shadowy leg over the other, he clasped the long fingers of his hazy hand, and gazed thoughtfully out into the moonlight.

"Winter has come," he said to himself. "All is hard and cold, and soon it will be Christmas. Yes, in two days it will be Christmas!"

For a few minutes he sat reflecting, and then he suddenly started to his feet.

"Can it be!" he exclaimed. "Can it possibly be that that close-fisted old John, that degenerate son of my noble George, does not intend to celebrate Christmas! It has been years since he has done so, but now that Bertha is in the house, since it is her home, will he dare to pass over Christmas as though it were but a common day? It is almost incredible that such a thing could happen, but so far there have been no signs of any preparations. I have seen nothing, heard nothing, smelt nothing, but this moment will I go and investigate the state of affairs."

Clapping his misty old cocked hat on his head, and tucking under his arm the shade of his faithful cane, he descended to the lower part of the house. Glancing into the great

parlors dimly lighted by the streaks of moonlight which came between the cracks of the
shutters, he saw that all the furniture was
shrouded in ancient linen covers, and that the
pictures were veiled with gauzy hangings.

"Humph!" ejaculated old Applejoy's
ghost, "he expects no company here!" and
forthwith he passed through the dining-room
—where in the middle of the wide floor was a
little round table large enough for three—and
entered the kitchen and pantry. There were
no signs in the one that anything extraordinary in the way of cooking had been done, or
was contemplated, and when he gazed upon
the pantry shelves, lighted well enough from
without for his keen gaze, he groaned. "Two
days before Christmas," he said to himself,
"and a pantry furnished thus! How widely
different from the olden time when I gave
orders for the holidays! Let me see what the
old curmudgeon has provided for Christmas?"

So saying, old Applejoy's ghost went
around the spacious pantry, looking upon
shelves and tables, and peering through the
doors of a closed closet. "Emptiness! Emptiness! Emptiness!" he ejaculated. "A cold
leg of mutton with, I should say, three slices

cut out of it; a ham half gone, and the rest of it hardened by exposure to the air; a piece of steak left over from yesterday, or nobody knows when, to be made into hash, no doubt! Cold boiled potatoes—it makes me shiver to look at them!—to be cut up and fried! Pies? there ought to be rows and rows of them, and there is not one! Cake? Upon my word, there is no sign of any! and Christmas two days off!

"What is this? Is it possible? A fowl! Yes, it is a chicken not full grown, enough for three, no doubt, and the servants can pick the bones. Oh, John, John! how have you fallen! A small-sized fowl for Christmas day!

"And what more now! Cider? No trace of it! Here is vinegar—that suits John, no doubt," and then forgetting the present condition of his organism, he said to himself, " It makes my very blood run cold to look upon a pantry furnished out like this! I must think about it! I must think about it! " And with bowed head he passed out into the great hall.

If it were possible to do anything to prevent the desecration of his old home during the sojourn therein of the young and joyous Bertha, the ghost of old Applejoy was determined to do it, but in order to do anything he must put himself into communication with some living being, and who that being should be he did not know. Still rapt in reverie he passed up the stairs and into the great chamber where his grandson slept. There lay the old man, his hard features tinged by the moonlight, his eyelids as tightly closed as if there had been money underneath them. The ghost of old Applejoy stood by his bedside.

"I can make him wake up and look at me," he thought, "for very few persons can remain asleep when anyone is standing gazing down upon them—even if the gazer be a ghost—and I might induce him to speak to me so that I might open my mind to him and tell him what I think of him, but what impression could I expect my words to make upon the soul of a one-chicken man like John? I am afraid his heart is harder than that dried-up ham. Moreover, if I should be able to speak to him and tell him his duty, he would persuade himself that he had been dreaming, and my words would be of no avail. I am afraid it would be lost time to try to do anything with John!"

Old Applejoy's ghost turned away from the
bedside of his sordid descendant, crossed the
hall, and passed into the room of Mrs. Dipperton, the elderly housekeeper. There she lay
fast asleep, her round face glimmering like a
transparent bag filled with milk, and from her
slightly parted lips there came at regular inter-
vals a feeble little snore, as if even in her
hours of repose she was afraid of disturbing
somebody.

The kind-hearted ghost shook his head as he
looked down upon her. " It would be of no
use," he said, " she hasn't any backbone, and
she would never be able to induce old John to
turn one inch aside from his parsimonious path.
More than that, if she were to see me she
would probably scream and go into a spasm
—die, for all I know—and that would be a
pretty preparation for Christmas! "

Out he went, and into the dreams of the
good woman there came no suspicion that the
ghost had been standing by her considering
her character with a pitying contempt.

Now the kind ghost, getting more and more
anxious in his mind, passed to the front of the
house and entered the chamber occupied by
young Bertha. Once inside the door, he

stopped reverently and removed his cocked hat. The head of the little bed was near the uncurtained window, and the bright light of the moon shone upon a face more beautiful in slumber than in the sunny hours of day.

She was not under the influence of the sound, hard sleep which lay upon the master of the house and the mild Mrs. Dipperton. She slept lightly, her delicate lids, through which might almost be seen the deep blue of her eyes, trembled now and then as if they would open, and sometimes her lips moved, as if she would whisper something about her dreams.

Old Applejoy's ghost drew nearer to the maiden, and bent slightly over her. He knew very well that it was mean to be eavesdropping like this, but it was really necessary that he should know this young girl better than he did. If he could hear a few words from that little mouth he might find out what she thought about, where her mind wandered, what she would like him to do for her.

At last, faintly whispered, scarcely more audible than her breathing, he heard one word, and that was " Tom! "

" Oh," said old Applejoy's ghost, as he

stepped back from the bedside, "she wants Tom! I like that! I do not know anything about Tom, but she ought to want him. It is natural, it is true, it is human, and it is long since there has been anything natural, true, or human in this house! But I wish she would say something else. She can't have Tom for Christmas—at least, not Tom alone. There is a great deal else necessary before this can be made a place suitable for Tom! "

Again he drew near to Bertha and listened, but instead of speaking, suddenly the maiden opened wide her eyes. The ghost of old Applejoy drew back, and made a low, respectful bow. The maiden did not move, but her lovely eyes opened wider and wider, and she fixed them upon the apparition, who trembled as he stood, for fear that she might scream, or faint, or in some way foil his generous purpose. If she did not first address him he could not speak to her.

"Am I asleep?" she murmured, and then, after slightly turning her head from side to side, as if to assure herself that she was in her own room and surrounded by familiar objects, she looked full into the face of old Applejoy's ghost, and boldly spoke to him. "Are you a spirit?" said she.

If a flush of joy could redden the countenance of a filmy shade, the face of old Applejoy's ghost would have glowed like a sunlit rose.

"Dear child," he exclaimed, "I am a spirit! I am the ghost of your Uncle's grandfather. His sister Maria, the youngest of the family, and much the most charming, I assure you, was your mother, and, of course, I was her grandfather, and just as much, of course, I am the ghost of your great grandfather, but I declare to you I never felt prouder at any moment of my existences, previous or present!"

"Then you must be the original Applejoy," said Bertha; "and I think it very wonderful that I am not afraid of you, but I am not. You look as if you would not hurt anybody in this world, especially me!"

"There you have it," he exclaimed, bringing his cane down upon the floor with a violence which had it been the cane it used to be would have wakened everybody in the house. "There you have it, my dear! I vow to you there is not a person in this world for whom I have such an affection as I feel for you. You remind me of my dear son George. You are the picture of Maria when she was about your age. Your coming to this house has given me the greatest pleasure; you have brought into it something of the old life. I wish I could tell you how happy I have been since the bright spring day that brought you here."

"I did not suppose I would make any-one happy by coming here," said Bertha. "Uncle John does not seem to care much about me, and I suppose I ought to be satisfied with Mrs. Dipperton if she does not object to me—but now the case is different. I did not know about you."

"No, indeed," exclaimed the good ghost, "you did not know about me, but I intend you to know about me. But now we must waste no more words—we must get down to business. I came here to-night with a special object."

"Business?" said Bertha, inquiringly.

"Yes," said the ghost, "it is business, and it is important, and it is about Christmas. Your uncle does not mean to have any Christmas in this house, but I intend, if I can possibly do so, to prevent him from disgracing himself, but I cannot do anything without somebody's help, and there is nobody to help me but you. Will you do it?"

Bertha could not refrain from a smile. " It would be funny to help a ghost to do any-thing," she said; " but if I can assist you I shall be very glad."

" I want you to go into the lower part of the house," said he. " I have something to show you that I am sure will interest you very much. I shall now go down into the hall, where I shall wait for you, and I should like you to dress yourself as warmly and comfort-ably as you can. It would be well to put a shawl around your head and shoulders. Have you some warm, soft slippers that will make no noise? "

" Oh, yes," said Bertha, her eyes twinkling with delight at the idea of this novel expedi-tion, " I shall be dressed and with you in no time."

" Do not hurry yourself," said the good ghost, as he left the room, " we have most of the night before us."

When the young girl had descended the great staircase almost as noiselessly as the ghost, who had preceded her, she found her venerable companion waiting for her.

" Do you see the lantern on the table," said he. " John uses it when he goes his round of the house at bedtime. There are matches hanging above it. Please light it. You may be sure I would not put you to this trouble if I were able to do it myself."

She dimly perceived the brass lantern, and when she had lighted it the ghost invited her to enter the study.

"Now," said he, as he led the way to the large desk with the cabinet above it, " will you be so good as to open that glass door? It is not locked."

Bertha hesitated a little, but she opened the door.

"Now, please put your hand into the front corner of that middle shelf. You cannot see anything, but you will feel a key hanging upon a little hook."

But Bertha did not obey. "This is my uncle's cabinet," she said, "and I have no right to meddle with his keys and things!"

Now the ghost of old Applejoy drew himself up to the six feet two inches which had been his stature in life; he slightly frowned, his expression was almost severe—but he controlled himself, and spoke calmly to the girl. "This was my cabinet," he said, " and I have never surrendered it to your uncle John!

With my own hands I screwed the little hook into that dark corner and hung the key upon it! Now I beg that you will take down that key. You have the authority of your great-grandfather."

Without a moment's hesitation Bertha put her hand into the dark corner of the shelf and took the key from the hook.

" Thank you very much," said the ghost of old Applejoy. " And now please unlock that little drawer—the one at the bottom."

Bertha unlocked and opened the drawer. " It is full of old keys! " she said.

" Yes," said the ghost, " and you will find that they are all tied together in a bunch. Those keys are what we came for! Now, my dear," said he, standing in front of her and looking down upon her very earnestly, but so kindly that she was not in the least afraid of him, " I want you to understand that what we are going to do is strictly correct and proper, without a trace of inquisitive meanness about it. This was once my house—everything in it I planned and arranged. I am now going to take you into the cellars of my old mansion. They are wonderful cellars; they were my pride and glory! I often used to take my vis-

itors to see them, and wide and commodious
stairs lead down to them. Are you afraid," he
said, " to descend with me into these subter-
ranean regions? "

" Not a bit of it! " exclaimed Bertha, almost too loud for prudence. " I have heard of
the cellars and wanted to see them, though
Mrs. Dipperton told me that my uncle never
allowed anyone to enter them; but I think it
will be the jolliest thing in the world to go
with my great-grandfather into the cellars
which he built himself, and of which he was
so proud! "

This speech so charmed the ghost of old Applejoy that he would instantly have kissed his
great-granddaughter had it not been that he
was afraid of giving her a cold.

" You are a girl to my liking! " he exclaimed, " and I wish with all my heart that
you had been living at the time. I was alive
and master of this house. We should have
had gay times together—you may believe
that! "

" I wish you were alive now, dear great-
grandpapa," said she, " and that would be
better than the other way! And now let us
go on—I am all impatience! "

They then descended into the cellars, which, until the present owner came into possession of the estate, had been famous throughout the neighborhood. " This way," said old Applejoy's ghost. " You will find the floor perfectly dry, and if we keep moving you will not be chilled.

" Do you see that row of old casks nearly covered with cobwebs and dust? Now, my dear, those casks contain some of the choicest spirits ever brought into this country, and most of them are more than half full! The finest rum from Jamaica, brandy from France, and gin from Holland—gin with such a flavor, my dear, that if you were to take out the bung the delightful aroma would fill the whole house! There is port there, too, and if it is not too old it must be the rarest wine in the country! And Madeira, a little glass of which, my dear, is a beverage worthy even of you!

" These things were not stowed away by me, but by my dear son George, who knew their value; but as for John—he drinks water and tea! He is a one-chicken man, and if he has allowed any of these rare spirits to become worthless, simply on account of age, he ought to be sent to the county prison!

"But we must move on! Do you see all these bottles—dingy looking enough, but filled with the choicest wines? Many of these are better than ever they were, although some of them may have spoiled. John would let everything spoil. He is a dog in the manger!

"Come into this little room. Now, then, hold up your lantern, and look all around you. Notice that row of glass jars on the shelf. They are filled with the finest mincemeat ever made by mortal man—or woman! It is the same kind of mincemeat I used to eat. George had it put up so that he might have the sort of pies at Christmas which I gave him when he was a boy. That mincemeat is just as good as ever it was! John is a dyspeptic; he wouldn't eat mince-pie! But he will eat fried potatoes, and they are ten times worse for him, if he did but know it!

"There are a lot more jars and cans, all sealed up tightly. I do not know what good things are in them, but I am sure their contents are just what will be wanted to fill out a Christmas table. If Mrs. Dipperton were to come down here and open those jars and bottles she would think she was in Heaven!

"But now, my dear, I want to show you

the grandest thing in these cellars, the dia-
mond of the collection! Behold that wooden
box! Inside of it is another box made of tin,
soldered up tightly, so that it is perfectly air-
tight. Inside of that tin box is a great plum-
cake! And now listen to me, Bertha! That
cake was put into that box by me. I intended
it to stay there for a long time, for plum-cake
gets better and better the longer it is kept, but
I did not suppose that the box would not be
opened for three generations! The people
who eat that cake, my dear Bertha, will be
blessed above all their fellow mortals! that
is to say, as far as cake-eating goes.

"And now I think you have seen enough to
understand thoroughly that these cellars are
the abode of many good things to eat and to
drink. It is their abode, but if John could
have his way it would be their sepulchre! I
was fond of good living, as you may well imagine, and so was my dear son George, but
John is a degenerate!"

"But why did you bring me here, great-
grandpapa?" said Bertha. "Do you want me
to come down here, and have my Christmas
dinner with you?" And as she said this she
unselfishly hoped that when the tin box should

be opened it might contain the ghost of a cake,
for it was quite plain that her great-grandfather had been an enthusiast in the matter of
plum-cake.

"No, indeed," said old Applejoy's ghost.
"Come up-stairs, and let us go into the study.
There are some coals left on the hearth, and
you will not be chilled while we talk."

When the great cellar-door had been locked,
the keys replaced in the drawer, the little key
hung upon its hook, and the cabinet closed,
Bertha sat down before the fireplace and
warmed her fingers over the few embers it contained, while the spirit of her great-grandfather stood by her and talked to her.

"Bertha," said he, "it is wicked not to celebrate Christmas—especially when one is able
to do so—in the most hospitable and generous
way. For years John has taken no notice of
Christmas, and it is full time that he should
reform, and it is your duty and my duty to
reform him if we can! You have seen what
he has in the cellars; there are turkeys in the
poultry-yard—for I know he has not sold
them all—and if there is anything wanting
for a grand Christmas celebration he has an
abundance of money with which to buy it.

There is not much time before Christmas Day, but there is time enough to do everything that has to be done, if you and I go to work and set other people to work."

"And how are we to do that?" asked Bertha.

"We haven't an easy task before us," said the ghost, "but I have been thinking a great deal about it, and I believe we can accomplish it. The straightforward thing to do is for me to appear to your uncle, tell him his duty, and urge him to perform it, but I know what will be the result. He would call the interview a dream, and attribute it to too much hash and fried potatoes, and the result would be that he would have a plainer table for awhile and half starve you and Mrs. Dipperton: But there is nothing dreamlike about you, my dear. If anyone hears you talking he will know he is awake."

"I think that is very true," said Bertha, smiling. "Do you want me to talk to uncle?"

"Yes," said old Applejoy's ghost, "I do want you to talk to him. I want you to go to him immediately after breakfast to-morrow morning, and tell him exactly what has happened this night. He cannot believe dreams are fried potatoes when you tell him about the little key in the corner of the shelf, the big keys in the drawer, the casks of spirits (and you can tell him what is in each one), the jars of mincemeat, and the wooden box nailed fast and tight with the tin box inside holding the cake. John knows all about that cake, for his father told him, and he knows all about me, too, although he tries not to believe in me, and when you have told him all you have seen, and when you give him my message, I think it will make him feel that you and I are awake, and that he would better keep awake, too, if he knows what's good for him."

"And what is the message?" asked Bertha.

"It is simply this," said old Applejoy's ghost. "When you have told him all the events of this night, and when he sees that they must have happened, for you could not have imagined them, I want you to tell him that it is my wish and desire, the wish and desire of his grandfather, to whom he owes everything he possesses, that there shall be worthy festivities in this house on Christmas Day and Night —I would say something about Christmas Eve, but I am afraid there is not time enough for that. Tell him to kill his turkeys, open his cellars, and spend his money. Tell him to send for at least a dozen good friends and relatives, for they will gladly give up their own Christmas dinner when they know that the great holiday is to be celebrated in this house. There is time enough, messengers and horses can be hired, and you can attend to the invitations. Mrs. Dipperton is a good manager when she has a chance, and I know she will do herself honor this time if John will give her the range.

"Now, my dear," said old Applejoy's ghost, drawing near to the young girl, " I want to ask you a question—a private, personal question. Who is Tom?"

At these words a sudden blush rushed into the cheeks of Bertha.

" Tom?" she said; " what Tom?"

" Now, don't beat about the bush with me," said old Applejoy's ghost; " I am sure you know a young man named Tom, and I want you to tell me who he is. My name was Tom, and for the sake of my past life I am very fond of Toms. But you must tell me about your Tom—is he a nice young fellow? Do you like him very much?"

"Yes," said Bertha, meaning the answer to cover both questions.

"And does he like you?"

"I think so," said Bertha.

"That means you are in love with each other!" exclaimed old Applejoy's ghost. "And now, my dear, tell me his name? Out with it! You can't help yourself."

"Mr. Burcham," said Bertha, her cheeks now a little pale, for it seemed to her a very bold thing for her to talk in this way even in the company of only a spirit.

"Son of Thomas Burcham of the Meadows? Grandson of old General Burcham?"

"Yes, sir," said Bertha.

The ghost of old Applejoy gazed down upon his great-granddaughter with pride and admiration.

"My dear Bertha," he exclaimed, "I congratulate you! I knew the old general well, and I have seen young Tom. He is a fine-looking fellow, and if you love him I know he is a good one. Now, I'll tell you what we will do, Bertha. We will have Tom here on Christmas."

"Oh, great-grandfather," exclaimed the girl, "I can't ask uncle to invite him."

" We will make it all right," said the beaming ghost. " We will have a bigger party than we thought we would. All the guests when they are invited will be asked to bring their families. When a big dinner is given at this house Thomas Burcham, Esq., must not be left out, and don't you see, Bertha, he is bound to bring Tom. And now you must not stay here a minute longer. Skip back to your bed, and immediately after breakfast come here to your uncle and tell him everything I have told you to tell him."

Bertha rose to obey, but she hesitated.

" Great-grandfather," she said, " if uncle does allow us to celebrate Christmas, will you be with us? "

" Yes, indeed, my dear," said he. " And you need not be afraid of my frightening anybody. When I choose I can be visible to some and invisible to others. I shall be everywhere and I shall hear everything, but I shall appear only to the loveliest woman who ever graced this mansion. And now be off to bed without another word."

" If she hadn't gone," said old Applejoy's ghost to himself, " I couldn't have helped giving her a good-night kiss."

The next morning, as Bertha told the story
of her night's adventures to her uncle, the face
of John Applejoy grew paler and paler. He
was a hard-headed man, but a superstitious one,
and when the story began he wondered if it
were a family failing to have dreams about
ghosts; but when he heard of the visit to the
cellars, and especially when Bertha told him of
his grandfather's plum-cake, the existence of
which he had believed was not known to anyone but himself, he felt it was impossible for
the girl to have dreamed these things. When
Bertha had finished he actually believed that
she had seen and talked with the ghost of her
great-grandfather. With all the power of his
will he opposed this belief, but it was too much
for him, and he surrendered. But he was a
proud man and would not admit to his niece
that he put any faith in the existence of ghosts.

" My dear," said he, rising and standing before the fire, his face still pale, but his expression under good control, " you have had
a very strange dream. Now, don't declare that
it wasn't a dream—people always do that—
but hear me out. Although there is nothing
of weight in what you have told me—for traditions about my cellars have been afloat in

the family—still your pretty little story sug-
gests something to me. This is Christmas-time
and I had almost overlooked it. You are
young and lively and accustomed to the celebration of holidays. Therefore, I have determined, my dear, to consider your dream
just as if it had been a real happening, and
we will have a grand Christmas dinner, and
invite our friends and their families. I know
there must be good things in the cellars, although I had almost forgotten them, and
they shall be brought up and spread out and
enjoyed. Now go and send Mrs. Dipperton
to me, and when we have finished our consultation, you and I will make out a list of
guests and send off the invitations."

When she had gone, John Applejoy sat
down in his big chair and looked fixedly into
the fire. He would not have dared to go to
bed that night if he had disregarded the message from his grandfather.

Never since the old house had begun to
stand upon its foundations had there been such
glorious Christmas-times within its walls. The
news that old Mr. Applejoy was sending out
invitations to a Christmas dinner spread like
wildfire through the neighborhood, and those

who were not invited were almost as much excited as those who were asked to be guests. The idea of inviting people by families was considered a grand one, worthy indeed of the times of old Mr. Tom Applejoy, the grandfather of the present owner, who had been the most hospitable man in the whole country.

For the first time in nearly a century all the leaves of the great dining-table were put into use, and chairs for the company were brought from every part of the house. All the pent-up domestic enthusiasm in the soul of Mrs. Dipperton, the existence of which no one had suspected, now burst out in one grand volcanic eruption, and the great table had as much as it could do to stand up under its burdens brought from cellar, barn, and surrounding country.

In the very middle of everything was the great and wonderful plum-cake which had been put away by the famous grandfather of the host.

But the cake was not cut. " My friends," said Mr. John Applejoy, " we may all look at this cake but we will not eat it! We will keep it just as it is until a marriage shall occur in this family. Then you are all invited to come and enjoy it! "

At the conclusion of this little speech old Applejoy's ghost patted his degenerate grandson upon the head. " You don't feel that, John," he said to himself, " but it is approbation, and this is the first time I have ever approved of you! You must know of the existence of young Tom! You may turn out to be a good fellow yet, and if you will drink some of that rare old Madeira every day, I am sure you will! "

Late in the evening there was a grand dance in the great hall, which opened with an old-fashioned minuet, and when the merry guests were forming on the floor, a young man named Tom came forward and asked the hand of Bertha.

" No," said she, " not this time. I am going to dance this first dance with—well, we will say by myself! "

At these words the most thoroughly gratified ghost in all space, stepped up to the side of the lovely girl, and with his cocked hat folded flat under his left arm, he made a low bow and held out his hand. With his neatly tied cue, his wide-skirted coat, his long waistcoat trimmed with lace, his tightly drawn stockings and his buckled shoes, there was not such a gallant figure in the whole company.

Bertha put out her hand and touched the shadowy fingers of her partner, and then, side by side, she and the ghost of her great-grandfather opened the ball. Together they made the coupée, the high step, and the balance. They advanced, they retired, they came together. With all the grace of fresh young beauty and ancient courtliness they danced the minuet.

" What a strange young girl," said some of the guests, "and what a queer fancy to go through that dance all by herself, but how beautifully she did it! "

" Very eccentric, my dear! " said Mr. John Applejoy, when the dance was over. " But you danced most charmingly. I could not help thinking as I looked at you that there was nobody in this room that was worthy to be your partner."

" You are wrong there, old fellow! " was the simultaneous mental ejaculation of young Tom Burcham and of old Applejoy's ghost.

STRUCK BY A BOOMERANG

STRUCK BY A BOOMERANG

I.

WHEN I opened my law office in the little country town of Camborough, I was just twenty-five years old. I made it a point to begin my legal career with my second quarter of a century. When my twenty-sixth birthday arrived, and no client had yet come to me, I felt a little low in spirits, although I knew very well there was no good reason that I should do so; but as hoping without reason is a mental occupation so common to the human race, I felt that I had as good a right as any other of my fellow-beings to indulge in it.

In the meantime, while waiting for clients, I studied, I sedulously attended the courts, and I fell in love. Whether or not this last-mentioned affair was connected in any way with hoping without reason, I could not say, but I still followed the example of the human race, and loved with the earnestness and steadfastness which I should have been glad to put into law business, if I had had the opportunity.

Natalie Kefford was the eldest daughter of Mr. Archibald Kefford, one of the leading citizens of Camborough. She was a beautiful woman, with a soul—so far as I could discover—in thorough harmony with my own. I had become acquainted with the family when I first came to the town as a law student, and thus I had learned to know them all well, and to love Natalie. She was not engaged to me, but I considered that I was engaged to her. It was a solemn compact made with myself.

Feeling as I did toward the Kefford family, it is not surprising that I should have derived an unmistakable satisfaction, I may say pleasure, in the news of the death of Nicholas Kefford, an uncle of Natalie's father. This old gentleman had been a farmer residing near the village of Satbury, about five miles from Camborough. His agricultural operations and his success in speculations of various kinds had given him a very fair property, and he was generally considered one of the rich men of the county. He was unmarried, and his only

natural heirs were Mr. Archibald Kefford and
his sister, Mrs. Crown, a widow with several
children, living near Baltimore.

As the old man had always been on very
friendly terms with his nephew and his niece,
it was natural to expect that the whole or a
part of his property would be divided between
them. Neither of them was rich, for although
Mr. Kefford's business—he was a real estate
agent—was fairly good, his family was growing more expensive each year. Mrs. Crown
possessed but a limited income, and she had
probably built high hopes upon her uncle's inevitable demise.

I did not blame myself for my gratification
at the news of the death of Nicholas Kefford.
If I had known Mrs. Crown I should not have
blamed her for any pleasure she might have
shown on account of the event, and although
Mr. Archibald Kefford, who had always lived
so near his uncle and had been on terms of
more intimacy with him, showed a genuine
sorrow when he died, I should have found no
fault with any quiet illumination of his inner
soul if I could have looked into those recesses.
To die for the benefit of others after a man
had lived long for his own benefit, may be

considered a most commendable close to a successful life.

But when Mr. Nicholas Kefford's will was opened, it was discovered that his property was not left to his nephew and his niece. The will, which was found in the old gentleman's desk, was dated about a year back, and in it the testator left all his property, without reservation, to charity; more than this, he left it to a single charity: "The Satbury Institution for the Cure of Nervous Diseases."

The announcement of the contents of the will occasioned surprise and indignation throughout Camborough and the vicinity. It was almost impossible to understand such depravity in one who, for so many years, had been considered an estimable citizen. Old Kefford apparently had never had any nerves himself, and why should he suddenly evince such an interest in the nerves of other people?

The institution to which this most amazing bequest had been made, consisted at that time of a large house standing in an open field. It contained a few officers and attendants, a very few patients, all from a distance, and was presided over, directed, and managed by Spencer Latimer, M.D., also from a distance. This gentleman had come from the salubrious region of Satbury about three years before, had bought some land of Nicholas Kefford, and had erected his institution. The Camborough people had never cared for Doctor Latimer; and although there were persons in the town who, to my certain knowledge, were afflicted with nervous disorders—such, for instance, as an unreasonable distrust for attorneys and barristers who might happen to be at the beginning of their careers—none of them ever patronized the institution, and although it was known that old Nicholas Kefford did show a certain interest in the establishment, it was supposed that he held mortgages upon said property, and was looking out for the moment when it would be advisable for him to foreclose. He was a sagacious speculator and exceedingly skilful in the art of calculating the probable period of a mortgage.

It was very easy to see, when this affair had been thoroughly discussed from various points of view, that the estate of Nicholas Kefford had, in reality been left, not to charity, more or less worthy, but to Spencer Latimer, M.D., for his sole benefit and uses. He, in fact, was the Institution. There seemed to be nobody to whom he was responsible, and why he should become the owner of this property and why Nicholas Kefford should have left it to him, were questions which nobody in Camborough troubled himself to answer, for nobody believed that the will was a true one.

Mr. Kefford and Mrs. Crown took legal advice, the will was disputed, and when it was submitted to the court it was not admitted to probate. These proceedings were resented and opposed by Doctor Latimer. They not only interfered with the interests of the Institution to which he had the honor to be attached, but they struck a cruel blow at his reputation. He asserted that old Mr. Kefford had long been his valued friend; that he, Latimer, would not have come to Satbury if Mr. Kefford had not advised it; that he could not have afforded to establish himself there had it not been for Mr. Kefford's assistance. He also declared that this bequest was not surprising to him, for it had been talked over between him and the old gentleman, who had assured him that his nephew and his niece were in comfortable circumstances, and that he desired to leave his hard-earned money to an institution where it would be of lasting benefit. The doctor was

confident that he could establish the validity
of the will, and he also engaged legal advisers.

In reference to the legal advice I have mentioned, I am obliged to say that none of it was
my own, and I must also admit that this omis-
sion to consider me in connection with the proceedings contemplated by Mr. Kefford and his
sister, touched, not pleasantly, my somewhat
sensitive feelings. It did seem to me that here
was a chance to assist a deserving young friend,
of which Mr. Kefford should have gladly
availed himself, especially when he knew, as he
could not fail to know, that it was not only for
myself that I desired to work and to succeed.
This case, too, was a very simple one, a mere
matter of a will probably forged or altered,
such as I have often read of in law books and
even in novels. It would have been in every
way a most suitable case for me to begin upon,
but I was not asked to give the slightest assistance, and Mr. Kefford put the case of himself
and Mrs. Crown into the hands of Messrs.
Shallcross & Dorman, a firm of lawyers, who
already had so much business they did not
know what to do with it.

Although sorely hurt, I determined that I
would not let any of the Kefford family know

it. Even to Natalie I made no complaint, and
to Mr. Kefford I talked of the affair as I would
of any matter in which it was not expected
that I should take anything but a friendly interest. The wound rankled, but I believe I
concealed it.

One strong objection to the validity of the
will was the fact that everything which had
been owned by the testator was given without
reserve to the Institution. It was reasonably
argued that even if old Mr. Kefford had desired to give the greater part of his property
to this charity, he would have made some bequests to his relatives. I had studied the will
very carefully, and in conversation with Mr.
Kefford I took occasion to give my ideas concerning this peculiar feature of it.

" I believe, sir," said I, " that this will is
a copy of a true will made by old Mr. Kefford,
and of which Doctor Latimer had gained possession. The property bequeathed is described
so clearly and in such detail that I do not
believe anyone but the old gentleman could
have drawn it or dictated it. It was probably
all left to yourself and your sister, and the only
alteration which Doctor Latimer dared to make
was the substitution of his name for those orig-

inally mentioned. If he could have done so, I believe he would have inserted other bequests so as to give the document an air of naturalness and credibility, but as he could not consult anyone of legal experience in the matter of altering a will, and as he was afraid to do it himself for fear of making a mistake which would have spoilt everything, he confined himself to the change of names. That is the way I look at it, sir."

Mr. Kefford replied that he thought it was not at all unlikely that I was correct in my suppositions, and I have reason to believe that he mentioned these suppositions to Shallcross & Dorman; but I did not mind this. If there was anything I could do for Natalie's family I would do it, asking only that they should do one thing for me—that is, if I should find that Natalie was willing it should be done.

In regard to the signature of the will there were diverse opinions, but the majority of those who examined it thought that if it were not the writing of Nicholas Kefford it looked very much like it. However, it could not be expected that a man of Doctor Latimer's shrewdness would undertake to fabricate a false will without being able to counterfeit a signature.

Of the witnesses to the will, one, John Ashmore, an elderly man employed on old Kefford's farm, had died soon after the date of the will, and no one had heard him say anything about witnessing such a document. The other witness, Reuben Farris, was a man who also had been employed by old Mr. Kefford. He was a carpenter, and had been engaged at various times in making repairs to barns and out-houses. He was of a wandering disposition and had left this part of the country some time in the last summer, but no one could be found who recollected exactly whether or not he had been on the Kefford farm at the date of the will. Of course it was very necessary to find Farris. If he could testify that he had witnessed the will it would be an advantageous thing for Doctor Latimer, and if he could testify that he had not witnessed such a will, it would be equally advantageous for the contestants.

Inquiries regarding the whereabouts of Reuben Farris were now set on foot. It was known that he had gone West, and that he had relatives in Missouri. In the meantime there turned up an old woman in Satbury who felt quite certain that Reuben Farris had put a hinge on her garden gate early in August, and she thought it was about the tenth of August of the preceding year. She based this belief upon the fact that while he was at work upon the gate he remarked that he had not yet seen tomatoes so nearly ripe as those in her little patch, and she was of the opinion that she had had ripe tomatoes very early in August. As she could swear to no part of her belief, having a poor memory for exact dates, no legal notice could be taken of her opinions, especially as one of her neighbors asserted that he had gathered ripe tomatoes on the second day in August, and therefore, if Mrs. Budlong had had good success with her tomatoes, Reuben Farris might have made his remarks concerning them considerably earlier than August the tenth.

But although the opinions of Mrs. Budlong and her neighbor did not possess a legal value, they made an impression in Camborough. So little was known about Farris, even in Satbury, that the incident of the gate-hinge was considered of importance, giving some reason to believe that the second witness had been in the vicinity of the Kefford farm on or about the tenth of August.

Reuben Farris was finally discovered to be living in St. Louis, and, having been offered his travelling expenses and something besides if he would come and give some desired testimony in regard to old Kefford's property, he readily consented, and set out without loss of time. It must be mentioned that Doctor Latimer insisted upon bearing part of the expenses of bringing Farris to Camborough. He declared that he desired more than anyone else that everything in relation to the will should be made clear and plain. This was somewhat disheartening to the Kefford interest. They would have preferred that the doctor should have the desire that Farris should not testify.

On the twenty-first day of August, about half-past nine in the evening, Reuben Farris arrived at Camborough. He had been told to report at the Mansion House, and the nearest way from the station to that hotel was through Decatur Street, a small street in the business part of the town and very little frequented at night. About quarter past ten two men hurrying through Decatur Street to make a short cut, because the night was dark and rainy, nearly stumbled upon a man lying upon the sidewalk, apparently dead. When assistance

had been called, and the man had been conveyed to the station-house, it was found that
he was Reuben Farris.

This occurrence created great excitement in
Camborough. Farris was not dead, but had
been stunned by a terrible blow on the head.
There had been a murderous assault upon him,
and such a crime was almost unknown in Camborough. It is true that Decatur Street was
lonely, that the night was dark and rainy, but
no one, even a woman, would have been afraid
to make a short cut through that street at any
hour. There was a hospital in Camborough,
and thither Farris was conveyed. Surgical examination revealed the fact that the man had
been struck almost on the exact top of the
head with some heavy object, and in such a
way as to make a circular fracture in his skull
nearly two inches in diameter, breaking both
plates of the skull and pressing the detached
piece of bone against the brain, thus causing
insensibility.

The terrible blow which had occasioned
this fracture had evidently been given for the
purpose of killing the man, and there could
be no idea of robbery connected with the case.
Farris's valise, which he had carried in his

hand, was found unopened by his side. He had money in his pocket and his silver watch was undisturbed. All the surgical talent of the town was gathered together at the hospital, and, although the wound was considered a most serious one, it was thought possible that the man's life might be saved.

For the greater part of the night this murderous business in Camborough was discussed, and early the next morning I went to the sheriff's office, where I found a number of the town officers and lawyers of the place. Of course they were all talking about the terrible assault on Farris. He was still alive and an operation had been performed, but the doctors were not at all certain of the result. The small police force of the town had been busy nearly all night, but they had nothing to report.

Upon one point everybody was agreed, and this was that the assault was very nearly related to the Kefford will case. Here was a man who had come to town for the purpose of testifying in that case. Someone had wished to prevent him from testifying, and had struck him down. This seemed plain enough, but beyond, all was dark and mystery. Of course it was natural to think of Doctor Latimer in connection with the matter. He was a party to the will case, and, moreover, people did not like him; but two citizens who had been sent out to the Institution soon after the crime had been discovered, ostensibly to give the news to the superintendent, but really to find out if he were there, had found him in bed and had greatly shocked him by the account of the assault upon Farris. They also discovered, by adroit remarks to the attendants, that the doctor had been at home all the evening.

When the doctor came to town, early the next morning, everybody could see that the unfortunate affair had had a great effect upon him. He did not hesitate to say that if Farris did not recover his case would be lost. Without the testimony of that witness it would be impossible to prove the validity of Nicholas Kefford's will. Everything in regard to himself, the true legatee of Nicholas Kefford, had depended upon Reuben Farris.

A great deal of detective work was now begun in the town by amateurs as well as lawyers. The wound in Farris's head was a very peculiar one. Probably it had been inflicted with some heavy instrument, such as a hammer, but it was found that it would not be easy, with even a very large hammer, to make such a fracture in the skull of a man. The indented portion of bone had been forced down so evenly, no part of its circular edge having descended deeper than any other part, that it was certain that the handle of the weapon which inflicted it must have been in nearly a horizontal position. Now, a man standing on the ground and striking the head of another man as tall as Reuben Farris could not hold a hammer in that position. Many experiments with hammers proved that such an instrument, wielded by a person of ordinary height, would strike the second person's skull with the edge of its lower surface nearest to the handle. To strike the top of a man's head with the bottom surface of the hammer-head held perfectly horizontal would be difficult, and would prevent the full force of the blow. It was evident, therefore, that the man who had struck Farris with a hammer must have stood higher than his victim.

This conclusion led to further investigation: was there anything in Decatur Street, near the place of the assault, on which the person who struck Farris could have stood at a sufficient height to make a horizontal blow? Such a place was soon found. Decatur Street at the place where the assault had occurred ran at the back of a large building three stories high, which contained offices of lawyers and business men. The back windows on the first floor of this building were about four feet from the ground. If one of these were open, it might be possible for a man with a hammer in his hand to reach out into the street and strike a horizontal blow upon the head of another man upon the sidewalk. Such a window directly overlooked the scene of the assault, and the two men who nearly stumbled over the body of Farris were now quite certain that when they made the terrible discovery this window was open, because one of them, in looking about to call for assistance, had shouted into it. Everything was dark inside, but he thought someone might hear him. This window was in the back office of Mr. Archibald Kefford.

When this stage of the investigation had been reached, it made me perfectly furious to see how people looked at each other and said nothing. But I did not say anything; I would remain silent forever rather than even hint at the diabolical idea which seemed to come into other people's minds.

I went that morning to Mr. Kefford's office, but he was not there. Then I went across the street to a carpenter's shop and borrowed a hammer, the largest one I could find. With this I repaired to Mr. Kefford's back room. The window was open, for the weather was warm. I leaned out with the hammer in my hand and I found that it would have been very difficult for me to reach, with the head of the hammer, the head of a man walking on the sidewalk. An iron railing about two feet from the wall of the building separated it from the sidewalk, and unless the man assaulted should stand up close to that railing, a person at the window could not reach him with a hammer. Farris had not been found close to the railing, he had been found in the middle of the sidewalk.

I summoned several persons and proved, by experiments which I made myself and which I urged them to make, that if any ruffian had made his way into Mr. Kefford's back office, he could not, even with the largest hammer, have struck a passer-by on the top of the head. I insisted that the notion that Farris had been struck from that window was so utterly preposterons and absurd that it ought to be immediately abandoned.

Before that night, however, I discovered that a good many people were saying that it was a very strange coincidence that the man .Farris should have been struck down under the very window of a person whose interests might have been very greatly advanced by the death of said Farris. The more people thought about it, the plainer it was to see that if the only surviving witness to the signature of the will should not be able to swear he saw Nicholas Kefford sign it, the will would be considered invalid, and the property would go to the natural heirs of the testator.

Some days passed on. Farris remained insensible, often delirious, and in a precarious condition. Natalie wondered at the effect this occurrence had had upon me. She believed that lawyers thought a great deal more about such things than did other people, and she was sorry for it. She did not think lawyers should allow their lives to be darkened by events which concerned only other people. She had not heard of the notions and the suppositions connected with the .window of her father's back office.

Mr. Kefford did not publicly insist, as Latimer had done, that the death of this witness

would have a disastrous effect upon his interests, for it would not be the impulse of a
humane man to make that feature of the affair
prominent. This reticence regarding the con-.
sequences of the affair was commented upon
by several persons who thought that silence in
such a case showed an effort to conceal a certain satisfaction in the disability of Farris to
give testimony. It is wonderful how people
whose minds are not naturally evil will, in
cases like this, pick at this little thing and that
little thing, thinking that by so doing they
will expose depravity in spots where it was not
supposed to exist.

On the morning after I had made my experiments with the hammer from the window
of Mr. Kefford's office, Mr. Shallcross was
walking from his home to his office, and on the
way he met a man named Hatch. Hatch was
a poor man who lived on the edge of the town,
and he was now proceeding in the direction
of his home, carrying upon his shoulder a carpenter's adze.

"Good-morning, Hatch; are you going to
build a house?" said Mr. Shallcross.

"Oh, no," replied the other, stopping, "I
haven't got so far as that yet. All the im-

provement I'm plannin' for this season is a
new step for my back door, and I've got a
log up there that I'm going to hew square.
That's the cheapest way of makin' a step when
you've got the log. I've just been up to Mr.
Kefford's to borrow his adze."

"Mr. Kefford's!" said Shallcross. "What
is he doing with an adze?"

"Oh, he's got a regular carpenter's shop
in his yard," said Hatch, "and I often go up
there to borrow his tools. It's a lot cheaper
than buyin' 'em."

"For all that," said Shallcross, taking the
adze from the man and looking at it, "I should
think it would pay you to keep tools like this.
You would make up the cost by saving time."

"But I haven't got the cost, and I have got
the time," said Hatch, smiling good-humored-
ly. "There's where the difference comes in."

As the two spoke, Mr. Shallcross carefully
examined the adze. On one end of its large
iron head was a curved blade, while the other
was shaped like a hammer. The striking surface of the hammer-end was round and measured about two inches in diameter. Making a
mental calculation of the length of the handle,
he thought it was a little over three feet.

" There is some sense in what you say, Hatch," said Mr. Shallcross, returning the tool. " Anyway, you get a doorstep for nothing."

As soon as Mr. Shallcross reached his office, which was in the same building as that of Mr. Kefford, he went into his back room and opened his window, which looked out upon Decatur Street. Then from some umbrellas and canes which stood in the corner he selected a walking-stick a little over three feet long, and with a large, heavy head. Stepping to the open window Mr. Shallcross put his arm out of it, holding the cane by its lower end, and found that he could easily extend the head of the stick to the middle of the sidewalk. It would require a strong arm to handle an adze in this way, but Mr. Shallcross believed that a man meditating murder and standing at a window expecting the approach of his intended victim, who would be likely to make this short cut from the station, would be so excited as to be fully able to strike such a blow as that which felled Reuben Farris to the ground.

In the matter of the will, Mr. Kefford was the client of Mr. Shallcross. Moreover they were very good friends, and it could not be supposed that the latter gentleman would rush into the office of the first named and explain to him his suppositions and experiments regarding the adze, but he did speak of them to some people; his conscience would not allow him to keep silent, and—why this should have been I could not imagine—I was one of those persons.

When Mr. Shallcross had spoken to me of what he had done, and of what he felt bound to suspect, I became exceedingly angry. It seemed to me that people—even the kindest and most honorable—were racking their brains to make horrors out of trifles. I concealed my feelings as well as I could, for I did not wish to quarrel; but with the intent to prove to Mr. Shallcross that the blow he had summoned out of the regions of his imagination could not have been made with an adze, I went to a hardware store. There I found that the adze heads were sold separately from the handles, and while I was looking at some of the former I noticed that their hammer-ends had square surfaces. I looked at others and others; the hammer-ends were all square. Then I asked the dealer if he had any with round hammer-ends, to which he replied that they were not made in that way.

At another place where they sold hardware
I examined adze heads; their hammer-ends
were square. I went into a carpenter's shop
and talked to the man about putting up some
shelves in my office. While we were speaking, my eyes rambled about in search of adzes.
I saw one; its hammer end was square.

I did not return to Mr. Shallcross's office.
Depressed, instead of encouraged, I went to
my own. From what I had seen of adzes and
from what I knew of the length of their handles, I could not but believe that a strong man
could reach out of the window and strike a falling blow with one. It was certain that Mr.
Archibald Kefford owned an adze the hammer-
end of which had a round surface about two
inches in diameter, and which was unlike any
other in the town. For an hour, at least, I
sat and thought. To suspect the father of
Natalie of a murderous assault was impossible
for me, but it was plain as daylight that other
people were doing that thing. The conse-
quence of their suspicions would be terrible,
would be awful beyond comprehension, if Reuben Farris should die!

In the case of his assault it was not probable that I would be asked to take part in any

way, but in it I determined to take part. I would devote myself entirely and wholly, by night and by day, with mind and body, even with money if necessary, to the discovery of the assassin of Reuben Farris and to the removal of every suspicion from the father of Natalie. I knew as well as I knew anything that these two objects were the same.

The business of a detective is fascinating to a great many people, and it had always been so to me, but now it possessed an interest which overshadowed every other earthly purpose. Apart from my desire to further the ends of justice, I was going to enter the field in defence of the future of Natalie, in defence of my own future. If unjust fate crushed her father, it would, through her, crush me. She might never know it, but I should be crushed. I rose to my feet and swore that I would find the man who had committed the dastardly crime.

In planning my search for the assassin, my mind naturally inclined to the direction of Doctor Latimer, but reason soon told me this was foolish. The man had been at home in Satbury during the whole of the night of the assault. But he might have employed some one to do the deed! This, to my mind, was the most natural aspect of the case.

As a probable instrument of Latimer's villainy, I thought of the man Hatch. It would have been a good scheme for Hatch to station himself in the back office of Mr. Kefford, into which he could easily have climbed from outside, and it would have been very prudent for him to supply himself with a peculiar adze belonging to Mr. Kefford. Of course he would have returned it after he had used it, so if an immediate search were made it would have been found in Mr. Kefford's possession. But I also considered that a little later, Latimer might have thought it wise to prevent Mr. Kefford from concealing this adze and to have it removed to Hatch's house, where it would be kept ready to produce in case Mr. Kefford should be brought to trial for the assault upon Farris.

That afternoon I walked out to Hatch's house. He was not at home, but in the backyard there was a log, one side partly hewn, and by it stood the adze which he had borrowed. I went to it; I examined it; I measured the diameter of its hammer-head. Mr. Shallcross had been correct—the diameter was about two inches.

I stood and looked at the adze. The thought came into my mind that perhaps it would be a good thing to take it and hurl it into a creek which ran near by, to do anything to hide it and get rid of it. But a moment's reflection told me that this would be foolish, and in the next moment an incident made me understand that it would be impossible. A man dressed in ordinary clothes, but whose face was familiar to me as a policeman, approached me and carelessly remarked that he supposed I had come out to look at the adze. The lawyers had been talking a good deal about it, he said, and he had been sent out there to keep an eye on it.

" There is nobody at home, now," said he, " but I shall stay around here, keepin' out of sight, and watch for anybody who comes to talk about it. I guess there will be somebody or other who will take enough interest in that adze to come soon and see Hatch about it; at least, that is the opinion in town."

I made some casual remarks about the advisability of keeping an eye upon everything that might possibly be connected with the case, but I said nothing which might help anyone who had suspicions of Hatch. If he had anything to do with the assault, I wanted to be the man to find it out and fix the crime upon him. I spoke as if I thought the adze of little importance, and soon left the place.

I continued my walk for a little distance and then crossed the creek by a bridge, in order that I might return to town through the woods. On the bridge was a boy, fishing. From my early youth I had been fond of fishing, and I stopped to watch him. The stream was quite deep here and he was fishing for catfish, which swim near the bottom.

Presently he felt a bite and gave a jerk. Then he began to haul up his line.

" I guess I've got one," said he.

" From the way you pull up," I remarked, " it must be a pretty big fish."

" Don't know about that," said the boy; " I've got to pull this line hard whether any-thing is on or not." And as he said this the end of his line came up above the water and he swung it onto the bridge. Fast to the hook was a little catfish seven or eight inches long.

" You see," said the boy, " why it is a pretty heavy line to pull up."

The boy took off his fish, and I stooped and examined the fishing-tackle, which lay on the floor of the bridge.

"Where did you buy this?" I asked the boy, who was putting his fish upon a string with a few others.

"I didn't buy it," he said; "I found it."

"Where?" I asked.

"In a gutter," said he.

I asked a few more questions and then I said: "I'd like to fish; will you sell me your line? I'll give you fifty cents for it." The boy looked at me, astonished. If I had said ten cents he would probably have thought it a good offer.

"All right," said he, "you can have it for that."

I handed him a half dollar, and then, apparently afraid that I might reconsider the bargain, he said that he guessed he had better hurry home if he wanted to get his fish cooked that day, and he forthwith departed.

I stood upon the bridge, seeing nothing that was about me, but with my brain filled with a tumultuous crowd of ideas which seemed intent upon driving out my reason and my senses. These ideas soon formed themselves into a regular sequence with a horrible and awful conclusion which chilled me as if I had been suddenly turned into ice.

I now knew that my work as a detective had suddenly come to an end. I had succeeded in my search for the man who had stricken Reuben Farris to the earth, who, perhaps, had murdered him.

That man was no other than *myself*.

II.

Motionless, I stood upon the bridge, holding in my hand the fishing-tackle I had purchased from the boy, still that awful procession passing through my brain, always ending with the figure of Reuben Farris stretched on his bed in the hospital. My mind was stunned. I seemed to have lost the power of thinking; I was merely the prey of thoughts which came to me unbidden and relentless.

Suddenly I heard a rustling sound; I started, frightened; it was but a bird flying out of a bush, but it startled me into my senses. I knew I was frightened. Quickly I cut the leaden sinker from the fishing-line and threw the latter with its hooks into the water. Then with the sinker in my hand, and my hand in my pocket, I walked toward the town.

No chain of events could be clearer or better defined than those which led from me to the man in the hospital. I had always been fond of fishing, and before I came to Camborough I used to fish a good deal for perch in the Delaware River, using a very peculiar tackle called a bow line or dipsy line. This apparatus, which was intended to catch several fish at once, was lowered to the sandy bars frequented by perch, by means of a leaden sinker, generally called a dipsy lead, very heavy and of conical form, its broad base enabling it to rest upright upon the bottom. I did not use a bow line, but among my effects I had found a dipsy lead which for some time had done service in my office as a paper weight.

On the evening of August 21st I had been sitting in my office, which was on the third floor of the building in which the rooms of Mr. Kefford were situated. I was not in a pleasant humor; my mind was irritated, and it annoyed me to think that it was so. I had been more deeply touched by the manner in which I had been ignored in the matter of Nicholas Kefford's will than I had supposed. With the Kefford family and with everyone else, I had endeavored to treat the matter as if it were

quite natural that I should not be retained or
consulted regarding the affair; but when I
found myself alone in my office, I could not
treat it in that way. I was very much vexed
and piqued.

Suddenly my cogitations were broken in
upon by the lugubrious wail of a cat in the
street below me. This sound was a disagreeable one to me at all times, but in my present
state of mind it enraged me. I seized the first
heavy object which came to hand—which happened to be the dipsy lead—and rushing to
the open window I looked out. There I saw
in the darkness below a light-colored object
moving on the sidewalk. Instantly I hurled
my dipsy lead at it with all my strength. I
heard a thud, but whether my missile had hit
its object or had merely struck the sidewalk,
which in this back street was not paved, but
covered with gravel, I did not know, nor did I
care. I could not see into the darkness, and if
I had driven the cat away I was satisfied. I
returned to my table and my thoughts, and
soon afterward went out.

Not until I had stood on the bridge by the
side of the boy, gazing with astonishment at
the heavy lead which was attached to his little

line, and which I knew to be my own as soon as my eyes fell upon it (for I had moulded it myself, after a fashion which suited me), had I remembered what had occurred in my office on that fatal evening; but when the boy had told me that he had found this dipsy lead in a gutter, and when, upon further questioning, he said that it was in a gutter in Decatur Street, just back of the office buildings, and that he had found it on the day after what he called " the Farris murder," I had remembered everything.

Reuben Farris had worn a light-colored felt hat, and when I had looked out into the darkness below my window I had seen nothing but this hat moving beneath me. At this hat I had hurled my dipsy lead, and it had struck Farris fair on the top of the head, the broad, flat bottom of the leaden cone coming horizontally downward because it was the heaviest part of the sinker. It had broken through the skull of the unfortunate man, forcing downward not only a circular piece of the skull but that part of the hat with which it came in contact. As I had noticed when examining the hat, the impression of the heavy object with which Farris had been struck down was well marked. The lead had rolled off into the gutter, where the boy had found it the next day.

I reached the town and hurried to my office, fortunately meeting no one. I went into the building by a back way, and as I passed the place where Farris had fallen, I shuddered as if I had seen the accusing blood from the wound of a corpse.

The first thing I did when I reached my room was to measure the lower surface of the dipsy lead. It was exactly one inch and seven-eighths in diameter. This, allowing for a thickness of felt all around the bottom edge of the lead, would probably make a fracture two inches wide. With Mr. Kefford's adze the circular fracture would have been somewhat larger. Every link in my chain of events was perfect.

The dipsy lead still in my hand, I sat in my room and asked myself what I was to do now. My first impulse after measuring the lead had been to hurry to the court-house and tell the sheriff exactly what had happened; to free the father of Natalie from all suspicion, and to show that the blood of Reuben Farris was on my hands—innocent hands as I had always supposed them to be.

But the remembrance of the words used by the boy made me hesitate. If this should be murder, if Reuben Farris should now be dead, or should die, what then?

What I had done was a piece of criminal and unpardonable carelessness, followed by the most terrible injury to a fellow-man. If the case should be regarded in that light by the authorities, I ought to be willing to suffer any punishment which the law might inflict, and if this punishment should be in the shape of damages to Farris should he recover, I would most cheerfully accept the penalty and sacrifice, if necessary, all the property from which I derived my income.

But if Reuben Farris did not recover, the case would be very different. Then it would be a matter of life and death to me to prove that when I hurled from my window that heavy leaden missile, I thought I was throwing it at a cat, and not at the head of a man. It was generally believed that the assailant of Farris had been waiting for him at an open window, knowing that he would probably come along Decatur Street. Why should not I have been waiting for him at an open window far above him and safe from observation? Everybody knew that I had a great interest in the Kefford will case, and consequently in the appearance or non-appearance of the man who had been sent for to testify in that case. I had frequently discussed the matter with my acquaintances in the law and out of it, and I did so the more zealously because by avoiding the subject I might have led persons to suppose that my feelings were hurt. It was known, too, that I was paying attentions to Miss Kefford, and that I was a warm friend of the family; and, in fact, the more I thought of it, the more plainly it seemed to me that it might reasonably be suspected that I might have been actuated by a very strong desire that Farris should not testify regarding the Kefford will. If he should swear that he had witnessed the will, the fortune of the dead Kefford was lost to his relatives. There were chances that he might so swear, and I was known to be a young man of quick temper.

Why should not the story of the cat appear absurd and ridiculous? What man of average sense would stand at a third-story window on a rainy night, when footsteps could scarcely be heard, and when it was so dark that people on the sidewalk could not be plainly discerned, and hurl more than a pound of lead at something which might possibly be a cat? What reason had I to expect that I should be able to convince a court that I was a silly fool and not an intending murderer?

When my thoughts had gone thus far, I put the dipsy lead in a drawer, which I locked, and then I hurried to the hospital. I had been there before, and had shown, I hoped, a creditable interest in the unfortunate man, and now I tried hard to calm myself down into the appearance of one influenced by such creditable interest and nothing more. It might have been better for me to have stayed away from the hospital, for when I was told that, although the operation had been considered successful, the patient was still in an insensible condition, with vitality so low that at any moment he might cease to breathe, I feared that I showed an agitation scarcely less than that which would have been produced by the news of the dangerous condition of a loved relative. It might well be asked why, under ordinary circumstances, I should be so affected by the danger of a person with whom I was not acquainted.

All that night I considered from every possible point of view my terrifying situation. New reasons for suspicions of me constantly cropped up. If I had accidentally struck a man senseless, why should I have waited five days before I announced the fact? Why should I have allowed one of the best men in town, a man whose son-in-law I hoped to be, to rest so long under the suspicion of a foul crime? Why should I wait until I should see whether the man died or not, and whether Mr. Kefford was likely to get into serious trouble, before I came forward with this trumped-up story of a cat?

And there was Natalie! If she had by this time found out that suspicion was gathering around her father, what would she say when I told her that I had waited five days before avowing myself to be the culprit? If she believed I had entirely forgotten what I had done, then it would almost be as bad as if she did not believe. A lawyer whose business it is to discover criminating facts, but whose judgment and memory are so frail as to make him overlook the all-important facts in such a case, must be almost as despicable as a man who commits a crime and lies about it!

I became indignant at fate. Why should I lose everything worth having in this world? Why should I give up my love, my prospects, my life, because I had committed a careless fault? Why should I suffer the terrible punishments which might follow the avowal of my part in this tragedy, of which tragedy, at the time it was committed, I was absolutely ignorant?

In the town of Camborough, in fact in the whole world, there was no one who could help me answer these questions. If I told my secret to anyone, I would have no right to ask him to keep it a secret, and he would have no right to do so. How I cursed myself for the egregious vanity which had urged me to push myself into this affair! Of course it was a good motive which prompted me to give all possible assistance in the search for a criminal and to clear a good man from suspicion, but that had not been all my motive. I had wanted to show Camborough what I could do by myself. I had wanted to produce the criminal, and now that I had found him I was afraid to produce him. If I had kept in my proper place no one would have ever known that I had done the deed, for I should not have suspected it myself. It was as if a native Australian had proudly hurled a boomerang at an enemy and the murderous missile had returned, striking him fair in the forehead.

I had reached the point, now, when I considered only myself. The thought that my avowal would relieve Mr. Kefford of suspicion grew of less and less importance. I said to myself that there was really nothing positive to connect him with the crime. He might suffer, but not as I should suffer. I could not make up my mind to shatter my life.

I rose in the morning without having decided whether I would continue to live among the citizens of Camborough as a free and respectable man, or whether I would deliver myself into the hands of the law for a crime of which I knew I was not truly guilty. I was sitting in my office that morning about nine o'clock when my friend, Craig Wilson, came in. He was a young lawyer about my age, but he had been longer in the profession, and had had some experience. Wilson had scarcely seated himself when he exclaimed:

" Old boy, you are not looking well! Have you been reading all night, studying up wills and assassinations? I think you are putting too much of your nerve power into this business. Everybody knows you are interested, and that is all right, but there is such a thing as going too far, even in a good cause. You want a rest. What do you say to going out fishing this afternoon?"

"Fishing!" I exclaimed.

"Yes," said Wilson. "I had an idea you were going into that line again. I know you used to be a great fisherman, and Billy Saunders, the son of our gardener, told me that yesterday you bought a fishing-line of him and paid him some fabulous price—a dollar or two I think he said—for one of his old lines. That looked to me like a bad attack of fishing fever, and my opinion is that it is the sort of disease that would do you good. Shall we start out after luncheon?"

"No," said I, "I cannot possibly do it; it will be utterly out of the question." I think I said something about an engagement, but I do not remember. My mind was entirely occupied by a new fear—a fear that this crime might be fixed upon me without my confessing it. The boy would be a witness to prove an extraordinary desire on my part to possess myself of the missile with which Farris had been struck. I did not want to talk, but I must say something.

"Is there any news," said I, "about—the man in the hospital?"

"No good news," replied Wilson. "In fact there doesn't seem to be anything good about this unfortunate affair, and I must admit it has an effect on me as well as on yourself, although you have much more reason to take it roughly than I have. I stopped at the hospital late last night and learned that Farris had had a very bad turn. At one time they thought he was dead, but he picked up a little as if his life was doing its best to stick to him. It would be very bad if he should die, for, between us, things are looking very shady regarding Kefford. Of course the evidence against him is very slight, but it is all the evidence there is against anybody. I am very much afraid, very much indeed, that if the man dies it will be absolutely necessary to take Mr. Kefford into custody."

"Never!" I exclaimed, springing to my feet. "He is as innocent as a babe; and the thing was not done with an adze."

I was on the point of saying more, but I restrained myself. This was not the place to tell my story.

" Cool yourself down, my boy," said Wilson, also rising; " it is all right for you to think that way, and I give you credit for it. I know you have been making experiments with hammers and things, and I know how you feel toward that family; but don't get yourself excited. That will do nobody any good."

When Wilson left me my mind was made up. Every suspicion must instantly be cleared from Natalie's father. I took the dipsy lead from the drawer and put it into my pocket. Then I arranged some of the papers in my desk, which I closed and locked; I put in order the things on my table; I closed the window and went out of the office, locking the door behind me. I might never see that room again.

When I reached the street I started toward the court-house, but I stopped; I could not do that just yet. I must see Natalie first. It was impossible for me to tell my story until I had seen her once again. I did not intend to tell her anything; I had no right to shock her with the terrible words which I must say. If she had been engaged to me things would have been different; but alas! I was the only one engaged. But I must see her; there was work before me which would admit of no delay except to see her once again. Everything must bend to that.

I could not have called upon Natalie at a more auspicious time; her father was at his office, and her mother and sisters were out. If my situation had been different, I believe I should have proposed to her that morning. We had a shaded piazza to ourselves; she was more charming, apparently more tender in manner, than I had ever seen her. If it had not been for this weight upon my soul, I know I should have proposed to her; but between me and Natalie now stood, solemn and inflexible, my knowledge that I was an object for the action of criminal law. No matter how the crime might be considered, I was that object. Being such, I could not talk to her of love.

I spoke to her, indeed, of very little. In fact I think she must have wondered why I came at such an unusual hour. I said some things of no importance, and then I listened a little and talked of some other trifles. Natalie seemed to be waiting, as if she expected there was something I would soon say; but she waited in vain. What made it all the worse, so very much worse, was the feeling, which I could not repress, that if I said the thing she expected me to say, she would be glad to hear it. I rose to leave, having come for nothing, so far as she knew. She must have perceived that something serious affected me, but of course she could not ask me what it was, for why should it not have been that thing which she had expected to hear, but which I appeared to be afraid to say?

As I took leave of her, I held her hand longer than usual in mine, and I could not help pressing it. I am not sure, but I think there was a slight pressure in return. When I looked at her to say good-by, I think my eyes must have been wet; I am sure hers were. It was her beautiful sympathy with something unknown, but which affected me, which showed itself unbidden in her eyes.

I hurried away, and walked resolutely to my fate. On my way to the court-house I became possessed by a singular fear. Mr. Kefford lived in the suburbs, at some distance from the centre of the town. I was afraid that something might happen to me, that I might be run over, that something might fall on me, that in some way I might be prevented from ever telling my story, and that the sorrow, the shame, and the misery that were rightfully my own would come upon Natalie's father, and therefore upon her. Sometimes I walked very fast; sometimes I ran.

When I reached the sheriff's office I found him there, but he was not alone, as I had hoped. There were, perhaps, half a dozen persons in the room, but this did not deter me; I could not wait until the sheriff was at leisure; I must speak at once; he might be on the point of issuing some terrible order. In fact, as I had entered the building I had almost closed my eyes for fear I should see Mr. Kefford in custody. I stepped up to the little group and boldly broke into the conversation.

" Mr. Harriman," said I, " you must excuse me for interrupting you, but I have something of the greatest importance to communicate, which should be brought to your notice at once. It is in the case of Reuben Farris."

At these words everybody stopped talking and all eyes were fixed upon me. Among the persons present, I perceived Messrs. Shallcross & Dorman, Mr. Kefford's lawyers in the will case. I was glad to see them here; I wanted them to hear what I had to say. I had not liked the conduct of Mr. Shallcross and wished him to know that Mr. Kefford had a better friend than he was.

Now that everyone was ready to listen to me, I did not know exactly how to begin, but I felt I must tell a clear story.

"Gentlemen," said I, "I have been for days engaged in the search for the man who committed the assault upon Reuben Farris. I had no commission to make this search, no authority in any way, and was actuated solely by my desire—my determination I might say —to remove suspicion from anyone on whom thoughtless and wicked suspicions might rest."

"Turned detective on your own account, eh?" remarked Mr. Dorman. "We have heard about that. The virtuous Hatch was the last man you shadowed, I believe?"

I had always disliked Dorman. He was cynical and rude, and my anger had frequently risen against him when I had heard him in court badgering a witness, but he should not badger me.

"You are mistaken, sir," said I, with a certain severity; "Hatch was not the last man I shadowed. The last man I shadowed was the

man who did the deed. I have found the culprit and I am here to tell the sheriff, and anyone else who may care to hear, who it was who
broke the skull of Reuben Farris."

To my utter amazement this statement was
greeted with boisterous laughter.

"You found him, did you?" cried Dorman.
"All alone, by yourself? Didn't you have
anybody to help you?"

And to this insult someone added the jeer:
"And what did you do with him after you
caught him? Got him outside?"

My eyes must have blazed as I stood and
confronted that group of men. I could not
have imagined that when I came here to tell
a story so heart-rending to myself that I
should be greeted with ridicule.

I knew I was regarded as a young man with
a very high opinion of himself, and I knew
that there were men in the town who would
be glad of any chance to put me down and
mortify what they were pleased to consider my
vanity; but that my present action should have
given them their opportunity seemed to me
the super-cruelty of fate. More than any con-
demnation of my actions which I had reason
to expect, I now feared that when I had made

my statement somebody would sneeringly say something about a boomerang. For an instant I thought that I would leave the room and let my story remain untold. If I did not tell it, it could never be known. But I peremptorily banished this idea.

"Gentlemen," I said, "you may laugh if you please, but I would like to say, without interruption, what I came here to say. I know who it is who struck Farris to the ground. I did it myself."

These words created the most sudden sensation: every face became serious, every eye · was fixed upon me in amazement, and not a sneer, a comment, or even a word, interrupted my story as I told it rapidly and clearly. In conclusion I took the dipsy lead from my pocket and handed it to the sheriff.

"This," I said, "is the missile with which Farris was struck. The bottom of it, you will see, with something added for the thickness of the felt of his hat, is exactly the measurement of the fracture in his skull. The only round-headed adze in town would have broken out a large piece.   ·

"Now, then, I have set the whole of this dreadful affair before you from beginning to end, and you can see plainly that no one had anything to do with it but myself. As to myself, I have nothing at all to say. What I did was an accident without intent of evil, but it was followed by such awful consequences— how awful I do not know—that I deserve severe penalties and am ready to submit to them.

" But if what I say in regard to the innocence of my intentions should be doubted; if it should be believed that I really wanted to kill the man; if the charge should be brought against me that I waited so long before making my confession because I hoped to find some scent which would put justice off my track, and that I did not tell what I had done until danger to another absolutely forced me to do it, and if the man should die and I should be held liable for his murder, still I have nothing to say, and shall submit to whatever may happen. I did not come here on my own account; I came solely to right another man. I have cut loose from everything which gives me an interest in life, and I put myself into the hands of the law; then if anyone chooses to laugh at me for.doing that, he can do it, and I shall say nothing."

For a few moments not a word was said

in that room. Several persons were looking
with great interest at the dipsy lead which was
passing from hand to hand; then Mr. Shallcross stood up and addressed me.

" My young friend," said he, " may I ask
where you have been this morning? "

This question enraged me. Was I to meet
with nothing but ridicule and insult? Did
this man think that I had been dissipating,
and had concocted this story under the influence of drink? It seemed to me as if his question implied such a suspicion. What business
was it of his where I had been? I was about
to refuse to answer, but conquered the impulse.

" I have been in my office," I said, the
words almost sticking in my throat, " and—
in one other place."

" Then," said Mr. Shallcross, " it appears
that you have not heard that this morning,
about ten o'clock, Reuben Farris recovered
from his delirium, became conscious and sensible, and told who assaulted him. That man
was Doctor Latimer; he has been arrested and
is now in jail."

I stood stunned and aghast. I saw before
me Mr. Shallcross with a beaming face and a

hand outstretched; I saw other hands and other faces; they all seemed coming toward me. Suddenly some great tension within me seemed to give way; the room rocked. I think I sat down, or perhaps I fell.

When I recovered my senses I was sitting in an armchair and I perceived the smell of whiskey. It came from a glass held toward me by Mr. Dorman.

"Take some of that," he said; "it will stiffen you up."

It would have been impossible for me to imagine before that hour that men, ordinary, common men, some of them rough-mannered, all of them men who took no interest in my affairs, some of them men who did not like me, and not one of whom I had ever thought of as a friend, should now gather around me and speak as those men spoke. It astonished me as much as anything else that had happened that morning. Mr. Shallcross held me by the hand while he spoke to me, but it was Mr. Dorman who had the greatest influence upon me. It was he who slapped me on the shoulder and spoke of the good stuff that was in me. He was generally rough in speech, but his manner now told me what he meant. Other people came up, and they shook hands with me, and said things which flushed my cheeks. The news of my fainting in the sheriff's office must have spread all about the court-house.

I made few answers to what was said to me, scarcely comprehending what I heard, and what I saw about me. I was delighted and excited. Generous, friendly feeling, although I might not know what it meant, could have no other effect upon me after what I had passed through. But my mind was not upon all this; something else engaged it absolutely and wholly; I wanted to get away. I told Mr. Shallcross that it was absolutely necessary for me to attend to something.

As I left the room other people came to me and shook my hand. One was a hack-driver who had a stand near the court-house; another was a man in town taking orders for trees and shrubs, whom I scarcely knew. It was all very strange to me; it seemed as if I had just been elected to an office.

At the door of the court-house a man came up to me and said that Mr. Kefford wanted to see me at his office. I stopped, I looked at my watch without noticing what time it was, and then, in a hesitating but hurried manner, I said that I could not go to Mr. Kefford's just now but would see him very soon. He really must excuse me for a little while, and with that I hastened down the street. I could not go to Mr. Kefford's office, but, as fast as my legs would carry me, I went to his house.

The one idea which now possessed me was to see Natalie. I had left her as if I had been leaving the world behind me, and now I was going to her as i fI had suddenly come to life. Just outside of the Kefford's front gate I met her. She was on her way to the town. It was a wonderful piece of good fortune. Had I delayed any longer at the court-house, she would have been lost to me in some side street.

"Come back with me," I exclaimed; "please come back with me. I have something to say to you."

She was very much surprised—it was easy to see that—but she turned back without asking questions, and we went into the library. There was no one there, and I closed the door.

Half out of breath, for I had been running part of the way, I told her all the things that had happened. I did not try to put them in order. I let the things I had to say come in their own order, and the strongest pushed themselves to the front. Everything I had done, everything I had thought, everything I had suspected, I told her hurriedly and hotly. I had had a feeling that I would keep her father out of the matter, but I could not help speaking of him. Allusion after allusion forced itself from me in company with something else, and so I might as well have told her the whole talk of the town. But this did not seem to affect her more than anything else. She must have heard something of the talk of the town, or suspected it.

There were tears in her eyes, but they were a different kind of tears from those I had seen before. She said scarcely anything; in fact, I gave her no chance to speak. I feared somebody might interrupt us, and now that I had her here I must tell her everything. She was deeply interested in all I said. Sometimes she flushed a little, and sometimes she turned a little pale, and once or twice she looked at me inquiringly; but still I went on galloping and plunging ahead with my story. Not a thought of the night or a deed of the day did I leave out, even when I had to go back for them and bring them up from the very beginning.

When I first perceived how she sympathized with me, and how deep was her interest, I had taken her by the hand, and this she did not appear to notice; as I warmed up with the description of my feelings when the conviction forced itself upon me that I was the man who had done the deed, I took her other hand, and this I continued to hold as I went on.

When I reached my statement in the sheriff's room, she leaned forward a little and said,

" And it was for my father! "

Then it was that I released one of her hands and put my arm around her. Then I kissed her once, twice, I do not know how many times.

" Yes, it was for your father," I said. I did not attempt to depreciate anything I had done; I accepted her gratitude just as she evinced it, which she did, not with words, but with her eyes and with the parting of her lips. There is nothing in this world which can give a man such rapture as to press to his heart and to his lips a beautiful woman whose father he has saved—or intended to save, which is the same thing. She asked me to go on and tell her the rest. I told it as quickly and as briefly as I could. It all seemed of such little importance that I could not spare the time for it. Suddenly a thought flashed upon me. Here I was holding a beautiful woman to my heart; I was kissing her eyes, her lips, her cheeks; I was holding one of her hands which tightly clasped my own, and I had never proposed to her! I had intended to do that before I began my story, so that she might better understand it.

I drew back a little and told her what it was that I had forgotten. She looked into my eyes with a smile.

" I think we can easily dispense with that," she said. At that moment I felt as if I could dispense with the whole of this rolling globe except that which I held tightly clasped in my arms.

It was not long after this that her mother came in, not knowing that there was anyone in the room. She was very much surprised to see us, and of course, under the circumstances, everything had to be told to her. I do not mean told as I had told it, for it was Natalie who did most of the telling; and she did it so clearly and put some things in such strong relief that all I could do when she finished was to ask Mrs. Kefford if she wondered that I had come there and that I had told her daughter everything that was in my soul.

Mrs. Kefford did not wonder. She cried quietly as if she had heard the news of the death of somebody, but I do not think she grieved; she was a very sensitive woman.

It was not long after this that Mr. Kefford came home to his two-o'clock dinner.

" Upon my word! " he exclaimed, " is this where you are? I have been waiting and waiting for you in my office. I did not want to talk to you in the court-house." And with this he began to say things which in my ordinary state of mind would have confused and embarrassed me very much; but my soul was so filled with the daughter that nothing the father could say, be it good or bad, could make very much impression upon me. I hope I was grateful for his gratitude, but I am not sure that I really showed that I was. I am certain, however, that I showed that I was very happy.

How Mr. Kefford became aware of our engagement I do not know. His wife or Natalie may have taken him aside and informed him of it. At any rate, he seemed to consider it a matter of course. It was certainly wise in him to do this, and I do not think it would have been of any use for him to consider it in any other way.

After dinner, Mr. Kefford asked me to go back with him to the court-house; he was anxious to hear if there were any further developments in the Latimer affair. I did not care to go with him, but of course I was obliged to consent. His talk on the way to the court-house was mostly about his daughter, and the manner in which he spoke of her made me love him very much.

When we reached the court-house we found that there had been developments of great importance. Farris had been well enough to make a legal deposition, in which, in addition to what he had said before, he declared, and swore to it before a notary, that he had never witnessed the signature of Mr. Nicholas Kefford to a will, that he had never heard of such will during his residence with the old man, and that his signature to any such document must be a forgery.

When this development was read to Doctor Latimer in the jail, he gave way entirely. He saw that it was of no use for him to try to de-

fend himself, and that it would be far wiser
for him to submit at once, hoping thereby to
lighten his penalties. He was tired of strug-
gling, he said; his Institution was deeply in
debt, and he had failed in every effort, good
or bad, which he had made to save it.

He had been very intimate with old Kefford
during the last part of the latter's life. The
will which had been found in the desk was an
exact copy (excepting certain names) of a will
that Latimer had found in that desk. He
had written the copy in a back-hand which
he was sure would never be taken for his own,
and, as I had supposed, was afraid to make any
changes in it for fear of fatal errors. He had
traced the signature of Nicholas Kefford, and
for witnesses had chosen two persons, one of
whom was dead, and the other far away, nobody knew where. He had copied the signa-
tures of both these from receipts for wages,
found in Mr. Kefford's desk. Although the
false will was dated a year back, it had been
made during the old man's short sickness, and
had not been finished very long when he died.

Naturally Doctor Latimer had been very
anxious to see Reuben Farris before anyone
else in Camborough should meet him. He

had been perfectly willing for him to come on, because what he had to say to the man could not be written and he could not leave the Institution.

Soon after supper on the day of the expected arrival of Farris, Doctor Latimer remarked to the two assistants who still remained with him that he was going into his office to attend to some important accounts, and he did not want to be disturbed. He had frequently told them this before, when he was engaged in his labors upon the will.

Leaving his office lamp burning, he went into his bedroom, which was on the lower floor, and adjoined the office, and then got out of a window, and, in the darkness of the stormy night, walked to Camborough and proceeded direct to the railroad station. There, outside in the rain, he waited until Farris arrived.

The doctor stated his business at once. Accompanying Farris as he walked from the station platform, he began by offering him a hundred dollars if he would swear that he had witnessed the will of old Kefford. Farris did not understand this proposition, but when it was explained to him he flatly declined it. Then the doctor increased his offer by degrees until at last he made it five hundred dollars.

But Farris would not agree; he would not swear falsely for any money. Then the doctor made him an offer to go away and stay away; that need not trouble his conscience, he would do nothing wrong himself and would not meddle in the affairs of other people. This made Farris angry and he spoke very sharply to the doctor, who also became angry.

Farris now walked very fast, wishing to hear no more, and the doctor had some difficulty in keeping up with him. Hurrying behind him and becoming more and more enraged as he thought of what awaited him when this man should swear to the truth, he was filled with a furious desire to punish the obstinate fellow; if he could have knocked him down with his fist he would have done it.

Suddenly, in the darkness, the doctor's feet struck against something which was heavy and which moved. Instinctively he stooped; he wanted a missile. He picked up the objcet, which seemed to be a piece of lead, and, holding it in the palm of his hand with the largest end downward, he ran up behind Farris and struck him on the top of the head.

Being a tall man, he dealt the blow very fairly. Farris dropped, and the doctor threw the piece of lead into the road. Then he left the spot, and hastened homeward as fast as he could. It was not half-past ten o'clock when he got into his bedroom window, and, putting on his slippers and dressing-gown, he went out of his office door, and entered the room where his two men were busy with their usual game of cards. Remarking that his eyes were tired and that he should go to bed, although it was rather early for him, he left them, and when the messengers from Camborough came to inquire about him, his assistants were positively certain that he had been at home all the evening and had gone to bed early.

Doctor Latimer had been greatly troubled about what he had done; he had feared that Farris would die and he would be a murderer, and when the patient recovered there was perhaps no one in Camborough who was so truly glad as Doctor Latimer. He had a conscience of a peculiar sort, and, now that it had ceased to prod him on the subject of taking the man's life, the doctor gave it a holiday, and in his relief he cared little what might happen next.

The next morning Craig Wilson found me in my office; I was there because it was too early to go anywhere else.

"Now, then," said he, "since you have proved that you are such a shockingly bad shot that you can't even hit a cat under your window, I think you would better give up that sort of thing and take to fishing again. It suits you better. Suppose we go this afternoon; we won't take any of those murderous dipsy leads you seem to fancy, but we'll have decent tackle."

I instantly declared I could not go fishing with him that day. I had something I must attend to, and really I had not a bit of time for that sort of thing.

"Come, come, now," said Wilson, "that won't do. She's going to the Culture Club this afternoon and my sister has made an engagement to go with her, so you might as well come along with me. We are all trying to do as much as we can for you, considering how you must feel about missing the cat, and the best thing I can do for you is to take you fishing."

Reluctantly I consented to accompany Wilson. I would have preferred to stay at my office and write a letter, but considering that I could say some things a great deal better than I could write them, and not wishing to make myself a subject for raillery—I had had enough of that—I agreed to go with him.

" By the way," said Wilson, as he was about to leave, " we have been discussing the matter of your dipsy lead and the cat. In the first place, you must have attempted the poor creature's life some time before Farris came along, for Latimer says that when he threw away the weapon you so kindly provided him with, he glanced up at this building and there was no light in any window; and, in the second place, you could not have struck anybody fair and evenly on the top of the head with the broad end of that dipsy. We have tried experiments with it, and when it is thrown from any height it always turns over and over and comes point end down, so that if you had hit Farris with the thing, you would have killed him dead, and, what is more, if you had struck the cat you might not have killed it—for that is no easy thing—but you would have hurt it dreadfully and have made yourself an object for the Society for the Prevention of Cruelty to Animals. But, fortunately, you are a bad shot, and no wounded cat has been found."

This was Craig Wilson's way of comforting people who had been under a nervous strain; but I needed no comfort, and we had a good time together that afternoon.

It is years since all this happened. As there was no true will signed by Nicholas Kefford, the original of the forgery having been destroyed by Doctor Latimer, the old man's property came to Mr. Archibald Kefford and Mrs. Crown. I married Natalie, and it was not long before we were living in a house of our own. I have had very good success in the law, but for some years I never pressed an investigation, never endeavored to find out the origin of some evil action, without stopping to consider whether it might not be possible that under some peculiar circumstances, and in some way I did not understand at the time, I might not be the man I was looking for, and that the legal blow I was about to deliver might not be turned, boomerang-like, upon my astonished self.

THE SKIPPER AND EL CAPITAN

THE SKIPPER AND EL CAPITAN

EARLY one summer morning there sailed into the harbor of Yakonsk, a seaport on the far northwestern edge of the Pacific Ocean, the three-masted schooner Molly Crenshaw, of Gloucester, Mass.

The skipper of this vessel, Ezra Budrack by name, of domestic proclivities, had with him his family, consisting of his wife and daughter. The Molly Crenshaw was the Budrack home. In this good craft, which Ezra owned, they had sailed to many ports, sometimes on one errand and sometimes on another. They were now entering the harbor of Yakonsk, hoping to do a little trading. They had visited the town before, and the Commandant of the Russian garrison stationed there was glad to see them.

That night, before the moon had set, there steamed into the harbor a Spanish merchant vessel, the Reina de la Plata, of about seven hundred tons. She dropped anchor near the entrance to the roadstead, and early the next morning one of her boats started for the shore. In the stern sat Matias Romino, captain of the steamer. As the ship's boat neared the Molly Crenshaw, a clear, strong voice rang out from the schooner's deck:

"Hello, el Capitan! I am glad to see you. I made up my mind that was your vessel the moment my eyes fell upon her, before sunrise."

The captain in the stern of the little boat gave a start. He was a handsome, well-made man, to whom much of his youth remained. His hair was black and his eyes were bright.

"Hello!" he cried, and ordered his crew to make for the schooner.

In a few minutes the two men were shaking hands on the deck of the Molly Crenshaw. They were well acquainted, having frequently met at ports where they had been trading, and they liked each other. El Capitan, as Ezra always called him, spoke English with an accent, now scarcely noticed by the Budrack family, and almost the first thing he did was to ask after the skipper's wife and daughter, and to hope that they were very well.

" They are all right," said Ezra, " and they'll be on deck in no time, when I tell them you're here."

Drusilla Budrack was a pretty girl and a good one. She had dark eyes, which she owed to her mother, and an embrowned complexion, which had been given her by the sea air. She was very glad to see el Capitan, although she did not say as much about it as her parents did. As for the Spaniard, he was delighted. For more than two years he had been in love with Drusilla. He had been in port with her for weeks at a time, and he had never met a Spanish woman who suited him so well. He longed to follow the example of the good Ezra Budrack, and sail the seas with a wife on board his ship. All these things were known to the Budracks, but nothing definite had been done in the matter.

As the Budracks and el Capitan were talking pleasantly together, relating their experiences since they had last met, they perceived a little gunboat approaching from the town.

" The Commandant treats you better than he treated me," said the skipper to the Spaniard; " I had to go in to see him and report my arrival, but he is coming to meet you."

" Perhaps he will do some fault-finding with me," replied el Capitan, with a smile, " because I did not go direct to pay my respects instead of stopping here."

In a few minutes the gunboat lay to near by, a small boat put out from her, and the Russian Commandant boarded the Molly Crenshaw. He was a stout man, with a countenance which was mostly hair, but he had a pleasant smile. He shook hands with el Capitan and the skipper, and bowed to the ladies.

" It astonishes me," said he to the two captains, " to see you consort in such a friendly way. Do you not know that your nations are at war? "

The three Budracks and el Capitan started in simultaneous amazement.

" What! " exclaimed the skipper. " I don't understand you! You said nothing of this to me yesterday."

" No," said the Russian; " I supposed, of course, you knew all about it, and when I was going to refer to the subject I was interrupted."

" I never heard of it! " cried Ezra. " It was not known at the port where I last stopped."

"No!" el Capitan cried, "I have had no news like this! War! I cannot believe it."

Then the Commandant drew from his pocket a despatch he had received from his government, and read it. It was a fair account of the war between the United States and Spain.

The two women began to cry. The skipper walked to and fro across the deck in great agitation.

"It is amazing!" he exclaimed. "They must have been fighting for a long time. And I knew nothing about it!"

El Capitan stood up, tall, erect, and almost pale. His eyes were fixed upon Drusilla.

"My country at war with the Americans!" he groaned.

"Yes," said the Commandant; "and she has been getting the worst of it, too."

This further information did not affect el Capitan. The fact that his people were fighting Drusilla's people was all the bad news his soul could recognize at that moment.

"You are enemies," said the Russian, "and your ships and their officers and crews should be kept apart. It is my duty to keep you apart!"

"We are not enemies!" cried el Capitan. "No war can make us enemies."

Mrs. Budrack looked at him with tearful gratitude. By nature she was afraid of all Spaniards, but she had learned to make an exception of el Capitan, and if he continued their friend what could there be to fear? Drusilla's eyes were downcast; she trembled with emotion, and if they had been alone she would have thanked her lover with a shake of the hand.

The skipper was not a sentimental person, and he was not in love with any Spanish woman; he had patriotic principles, and they came to the front.

"You are right, Mr. Commandant," said he; "if the United States is at war with Spain, and if the two countries are now fighting as hard as they can, of course el Capitan is my enemy and I am his. There is no other way of looking at it. It is hard lines for me, for I've liked him ever since I first knew him, and my wife and daughter will be very much cut up, I know, but there's no getting around it. He is my enemy and I am his."

"But what of all that?" cried el Capitan. "A country does not mean every single person in it. In every nation there is always some one who is different from the rest. I cannot be an enemy to my friends."

"But you will have to be, el Capitan," said the skipper. "You are a good man, and I have a high respect for you, but your country has made you my enemy. You have nothing to say about it, and you can't help it."

"That is right," said the Commandant. "The rulers of your nations have made you enemies. You must submit. If one of you commanded a man-of-war it would be his duty to capture the other one as a prize. If both ships were war vessels, it would be your duty to fight. Your governments have arranged all that."

At the mention of fighting Mrs. Budrack went below. She could hear no more. Drusilla, however, remained, silent, pale, with eager eyes.

The skipper knitted his brows and reflected. "Look here, Mr. Commandant," he said; "my vessel is liable to be taken as a prize by the Spanish, is she?"

"By a Spanish war vessel, yes," was the answer.

"But if there are no war vessels in the

case," said Ezra, " it seems to me that enemies should fight. If my vessel is liable to be taken as a prize, so is that Spanish vessel. How is that, according to your constitution? "

" My country has no constitution," said the Commandant; " her rulers decide according to circumstances."

" Do you sometimes have to decide according to circumstances? " asked the skipper.

" When I cannot communicate with my government I sometimes have to do so," answered the Russian.

" Well, then," said Ezra, " how do you decide now? "

" I must think," said the Commandant.

During this conversation el Capitan was silent, but looked very black. To be at war with Drusilla's country—it was a horrible fate.

" I have thought this," said the Commandant, presently: " I will have nothing to do with either of you, except to preserve strict neutrality. This is the order of my government. You are enemies, and at any moment you may begin to fight. I have nothing to do with that, but in this harbor you cannot fight. The laws of neutrality will not permit it."

The countenance of el Capitan began to

brighten. Suddenly it beamed. "I will fight," he cried. "I am ready to do battle for the honor of my country. Since there is no war vessel here to uphold her honor, the Reina de la Plata will do it. I will sail outside the harbor together with the Molly Crenshaw, and I will fight her."

El Capitan was a good man, but a wily Spaniard; his vessel was larger than the schooner, he carried more men. If he could capture the Molly Crenshaw he would capture Drusilla. Then let the war go on; what mattered it to him! He would have her, and everything else could be settled afterward.

"No," said the Commandant, "you cannot sail out of this harbor with this vessel. You are enemies, and the laws of neutrality demand that one of you must remain here for twenty-four hours after the other has departed."

Drusilla wept, and went below to join her mother. If in this time of war the Molly Crenshaw should sail away in one direction and the Reina de la Plata in another, when would she ever see el Capitan again?

The Spaniard approached the skipper and extended his hand. "I will go outside," he

said, " and wait there twenty-four hours until
you come. Then I will fight you."

" Very good," said Ezra, giving his hand a
hearty shake; " you may count on me."

" I do not think you have a right to fight,"
said the Commandant to Ezra, when el Capitan had departed for his steamer. " You are
both merchant-men."

" But we are each liable to be taken as a
prize," said Ezra, " and I think that makes
it square."

The Commandant shook his head. " Even
if my country had a constitution," he said, " I.
do not know that it could settle that point.
But I shall take no responsibility; all I can do
is to preserve strict neutrality."

The next morning the good schooner Molly
Crenshaw, with a fine breeze, sailed out of the
harbor of Yakonsk, and she had scarcely
reached the open sea before she saw, a few
miles away, the smoking funnel of the Reina
de la Plata. The Spanish vessel immediately
changed her course and made directly for the
Molly Crenshaw.

El Capitan was in high spirits. He had had
twenty-four hours in which to reflect upon the
state of affairs, and to construct a plan of bat-

tle, and he was entirely satisfied with the
scheme he had worked out. As has been said
before, he was so much stronger than his new
enemy that he thought there would be very
little trouble in capturing her, even if her
skipper and her crew should make some show
of resistance. His steamer rode much higher
out of the water than did the schooner, and if
he should lie alongside of the latter, which he
could easily do, she, depending entirely upon
the wind, while he possessed all the advantages
afforded by steam, his men could easily slip
down on her deck and quell any disorder which
might be occasioned by his action.

Then, as soon as the schooner's company
had surrendered and good-fellowship and
order had been restored, he would take Skipper Budrack and his family on board his own
steamer, where they would have the very best
accommodations. He would put a prize crew
on the Molly Crenshaw, and the two ships
would sail away to a Spanish port. On this
voyage, which naturally would be somewhat
long, he would settle matters with Drusilla
and her parents. He had no doubt that he
could do so. He believed he knew a good deal
concerning the young lady's state of mind, and

her parents would not be in the position to resist his entreaties which they would have occupied had they been sailing in their own vessel, and able, whenever they chose, to put thousands of miles between him and the object of his hopes—of his life.

When he finally arrived at a Spanish port, and if the prize he had captured should be formally adjudicated to him, he would then make the Molly Crenshaw a wedding present to Drusilla. He would take command of the schooner, and his parents-in-law should sail with Drusilla and himself, if they so chose, or, if they liked it better, they should spend their declining years in any pleasant spot they might select, receiving regularly a portion of the profits of the voyages which he and Drusilla would make to various ports of the world. His face beaming with happy anticipations, he leaned over the rail as the steamer rapidly approached the schooner, which was now lying to.

Before the two vessels were within hailing distance, Skipper Ezra Budrack displayed a large flag of truce.

" You needn't do that! " roared el Capitan, through his speaking-trumpet. " I am not going to fight you without notice. I make for you only that I may plan the battle with you."

Now the two vessels lay, gently rolling, side by side, as near as safety would permit.

"Before we begin," shouted Ezra to el Capitan, "I want you to look at this pistol," and with this he held up a large revolver; "this is the only shooting-iron on board this vessel, and, as I don't want any accidents or unnecessary bloodshed, I am going to throw it into the sea. Look now! Down she goes!" And with that the skipper hurled the pistol into the water below him with such force that it must have made a hole in the bottom of the sea. "Now, then, el Capitan," cried he, "what are you going to do about fire-arms?"

The Spanish captain disappeared, but in a few moments he returned, bearing a large carbine. "This is the only gun we've got," said he, "and down she goes!" With these words he pitched it into the sea.

"That's all right," said the skipper; "and now, whenever you're ready to come on, we're ready to meet you. Of course, as you're a steamer, you'll have to do the coming on."

"I'll do that," said el Capitan; "but before we begin, I, too, have something to say. I shall subdue your men and capture your ship with as little violence as possible, but still there will be a scuffle, and there may be blows and a good deal of general disorder. That is to be expected, and I do not think either of us can prevent it. Therefore, I beg of you, my dear skipper, that you will keep your wife and daughter safely shut up in your cabin. I shall tell my men not to go aft if they can help it, and on no account to go below, and as I shall be on board I shall see that my orders are obeyed. Of course I shall allow no injury to come to the two ladies or yourself, but I do not wish that they shall even be frightened. I hope, if it can be so managed, that the whole affair may be transacted so quietly and promptly that it will seem to them like an ordinary nautical manœuvre."

"His English is wonderfully improved," thought Skipper Budrack; "when first I knew him he could not express himself like that." Then, with a gradually expanding grin, he called out to el Capitan: "I am much obliged to you for your kind consideration for my family, but you must not suppose that I would take my wife and daughter on board my vessel when I was going out for a fight. I left

Mrs. Budrack and Drusilla in the town. They are staying with the Commandant's family, who gave them a very kind invitation."

Now el Capitan stamped his feet and swore many Spanish oaths. Every plan he had made had been swept away as if it had been struck by a typhoon. If he could not capture Drusilla, what would a victory be worth to him? He was mad with rage and disappointment. All the time he had been talking his eyes had been scanning the cabin windows in the hope of seeing a fair face or a waving handkerchief. It was a vile trick the skipper had played on him. He had had such kind thoughts; he had planned to be so magnanimous; he would have taken the schooner so gently that the most tender heart would not have been made to flutter. But now everything was different. He would not say another word to that deceiving skipper. But suddenly an idea came into his fiery brain. "I will run down his schooner," he exclaimed. "I will utterly destroy it. I will sink it to the bottom. But I will be merciful; I will save his life; I will save all their lives if I can. But his vessel will be gone. Then I will take him on board my steamer, and I will keep him here. His wife and daughter must come to him; they cannot be left in Yakonsk, and there is no other ship in which they can get away. On the voyage I will plead my cause; I will make everything all right. I shall have time enough to do that before we reach port. Things will be not so good as they would be otherwise; I shall have no schooner to present to my wife on her wedding day, and I may not be able to do much for Skipper Budrack and his wife, but I will do what I can; they will be my parents-in-law."

He gave orders that the Reina de la Plata should be again put about and headed for the schooner under full steam. He put men in the bow with life-preservers, and two boats, with their crews, were made ready to be dropped from the davits the moment the two vessels should strike.

On board the Molly Crenshaw there was great stir of preparation. The skipper knew that if there was to be a fight at all the steamer must make the attack, and there could be no doubt that her best method of doing so would be to ram her antagonist. Therefore, he had spent the greater part of the preceding day in preparing for that contingency. His men were now placed in suitable positions on the deck, some armed with marline-spikes, some with capstan-bars, and a few with axes.

As the Spanish steamer came rapidly on, some of the men in her bow perceived something on the schooner which they had not noticed before. She appeared to have four masts, although one of them was much shorter than the others. They spoke of the matter to each other, but did not understand it.

Among the preparations the skipper had made for the approaching fight was this apparent fourth mast, which stood about midships, and consisted of a very large and strong spare spar. Its small end had been sharpened and shod with iron, while the other rested in a heavy socket, in which it could be moved at pleasure by means of blocks and tackle.

On came the Spanish steamer, heading directly for the Molly Crenshaw, and aiming to strike her about midships. On she came until the bright eyes of el Capitan could be seen shining over the rail. On she came, with the men in the bow ready to throw over their life-preservers, and the men in the boats ready to drop to the water and pull for any unfortunate American sailors who might rise to the surface after their vessel had sunk. On she came until she was within a few hundred feet of the schooner. Then, suddenly, down dropped the big spar into an almost horizontal position; it was pulled a little forward in obedience to a quick command from the skipper, and pointed directly at the steamer's starboard bow.

El Capitan saw his danger and shouted to the steersman—but it was too late; the Reina de la Plata could not change her course, but went straight on. As the schooner was so much lower than the steamer, the iron-shod spar struck the latter about half-way between her water-line and her rail. It crashed through her sides and ran for nearly half its length into the vessel.

The force of the concussion was so great that both vessels went dashing through the water for a considerable distance, and if the spar had not held her in position the schooner would have been capsized, even if she had received no other damage. As they moved together they naturally swung toward each other, so that when the motion had nearly ceased they were lying side by side, the spar having accommodated itself to this change in position

"CRASHED THROUGH HER SIDES AND RAN FOR NEARLY HALF ITS
LENGTH INTO THE VESSEL."

by ripping a larger hole in the wooden side of the steamer.

Now there was a great yell on board the Reina de la Plata, and many heads appeared above her rail.

" Stand by to repel boarders! " shouted the skipper. But before any of his men could gather around him a dozen or more Spaniards were on his deck; they jumped, they slid down ropes, they dropped like cats. Capstan-bars and marline-spikes were raised high in the air, but not one of them was brought down upon the heads of the enemy, for the skipper and his men were astonished to see that the Spaniards were unarmed. As soon as they reached the deck of the schooner they took off their caps and, bowing very low, approached the skipper. More Spaniards dropped down from the larger vessel, and some of them, who could speak English, explained why they came.

They were glad to be made prisoners; they did not wish to fight the Americans; all they asked was good and sufficient food and the payment of their wages, which were now a long time in arrears. These things were not to be obtained on the Spanish ship, and they were delighted to have an opportunity to surrender.

When his men had left him, el Capitan, disheartened and with downcast visage, slowly let himself down from the side of his vessel. He was dressed with unusual care, for he had expected to act on this occasion the part of a conquering hero in the presence of his mistress, and had arrayed himself accordingly. In his earlier days he had been an accomplished horseman as well as a seaman, and as a cavalier garb was more picturesque than that of an officer of a merchant vessel, he wore a broad hat with a feather, a bright-colored sash, and high boots, to which were attached a pair of jingling spurs. He was, perhaps, the only man who had ever fought a marine battle in spurs.

El Capitan stalked toward the skipper. " I am your prisoner," he said. " I am disgraced. I have lost everything. I have no ship; I have nothing. Now I cannot ask you for your daughter."

" You are right, there," said the skipper, with a grin; " this isn't the time nor the place for that sort of thing. But what am I to do with all these fellows of yours? I don't want them on board my schooner."

" Send them back to my ship," said el Capitan, in a sombre voice. " Send me back to

join them, if you please. Cut that spar in two with axes, push away from my poor, wounded craft, and set your sails. The force of the concussion has sent everything on board my ship to starboard, and as soon as you loose yourself from her she will list, she will take in water through that great hole, she will go to the bottom—down to the bottom with me and my men, and that will be the end of us. We will trouble you no more."

" No, sir," said the skipper; " that's not my way of doing business. I have made a prize of your steamer, and I am going to keep her. The hole in her bow can be repaired, and then I shall have a good vessel. I am going to make fast to her bow and stern, and that spar will keep her on an even keel until we get into port and ground or dock her."

" Have your own way," gloomily replied el Capitan; " take her into port, exhibit me as a captive at the tail of your chariot. Nothing matters to me. The best thing I can do is to jump overboard."

" No, sir! " cried the skipper; " you are my prisoner. You belong to me. You have no right to jump overboard. If you should do that you would not be honest. After surrender it is cowardly to resign or run away."

The Spaniard put his hand upon his heart. " I have nothing left but my honor," he said; " you may trust that."

" Now, el Capitan," said the skipper, " you can see for yourself that although your ship is my prize I cannot take her into port. She must take me. My sails are no good for that purpose. Tell your engineers and firemen to go on board and get ready to steam into the harbor. You, with your engine, will tow me along, and I, with my spar, will keep you from capsizing. We will make our vessels fast fore and aft, and then we'll get under headway as soon as possible."

Side by side, like a pair of nautical Siamese twins, the schooner and the steamer slowly approached the harbor of Yakonsk, but before they were in sight of the town they were met by the little gunboat, with the Commandant on board. They lay to and the Russian boarded the schooner. When the situation was explained to him, he was very much interested.

" I am amazed," said he to the skipper. " I did not suppose you could do this. And now what is your next step? "

" I want to take my prize into your port,"

said Ezra, " and have her repaired. Then I'll put a prize crew on board of her, and take her away with me."

" No, sir," said the Commandant; " the laws of neutrality forbid that!"

" But what am I to do?" exclaimed the skipper. " If I separate from her she will list to starboard and go down, and if a gale comes up while we are fastened together in this fashion we shall both be wrecked."

" I am very sorry," said the Commandant, " but all I have to do is to observe the laws of neutrality. It is a bad way to capture a vessel, but I cannot help it. The laws of neutrality must be observed. Only one of the vessels can enter the harbor of Yakonsk."

El Capitan looked down over the side of his vessel, but said nothing. His heart was heavy, and he took but little interest in what might happen next.

The skipper was angry, and vehement in his expressions. He had always disliked war, and had accepted it only when it had been thrust upon him; but at this moment he hated neutrality worse than war, and was willing to accept none of it.

The Commandant stood in deep thought,

and brushed his countenance with his hand. " There is one thing you can do," he said, presently. " Your two vessels can proceed together as near the mouth of the harbor as the laws of neutrality will allow. Then you can set the steamer's crew to work to shift everything movable to the port side, and when you have cut away your spar I think she will be able to steam up to the town, as the sea is tolerably smooth. Then I can set all the ship-carpenters in Yakonsk to work on her. There are a good many of them, you know, for building small vessels is the main industry of our place. And you, Mr. Skipper, can cruise out here until she is repaired, after which she will leave and you can come in and join your wife and daughter."

" And how long will it take to make the repairs? " impatiently asked the skipper.

" I will put the carpenters on her as close together as they can work, inside and out, and, from what I can judge of the damage, I think they can have her ready to sail in a week."

The skipper grumbled savagely, and wished he had not captured the Spaniard, but he made up his mind that he would have to be satisfied with things as they were, and he determined, if he must cruise for a week, to sail for Petri-metkoff, and try to do a little business there. This would occupy just about a week.

The two vessels moved on toward the harbor's mouth, the great spar was cut in twain, the Reina de la Plata steamed slowly toward the town, and the Molly Crenshaw set sail for Petrimetkoff.

It was nine days and twelve hours later when Ezra Budrack's three-masted schooner arrived at the port of Yakonsk. The skipper was very late; he had been detained by unfavorable winds and the exigencies of trade; but, dark as was the night, he entered the harbor, dropped anchor, and waited for daylight. Then he went ashore, and knocked at the door of the Commandant before any of the family was up. It was not long before that high official opened the door himself, still wearing his nightcap.

"I may be a little early," said the skipper, "but you must excuse me. You know a man who has not seen his wife and daughter for nearly ten days, and at a time when everything is in such an upset condition, is naturally anxious. Can I go to Mrs. Budrack?"

"Your wife and daughter!" cried the Commandant. "They are not here! They sailed away in the Spanish vessel yesterday afternoon. They were so anxious about you, when you did not return at the time you fixed, that they determined to go to Petrimetkoff and join you. If you had left there they were sure they would meet you on the way."

"Did my wife and daughter hatch up that plan?" shouted the skipper. "I don't believe a word of it! It was that wretched el Capitan! It is a scheme worthy of a crafty Spaniard! He wanted to have them on board with him! That is all he cared about! He persuaded them to go; I am as sure of it as if I had been here and heard every word that was said! But I can wait no longer. I must put on every stitch of sail I can carry and go after them. When they find I am not at Petrimetkoff I don't know where he will take them."

"No, sir!" said the Commandant; "you cannot leave this port until twenty-four hours after they sailed. The laws of neutrality demand that you remain in the harbor until five o'clock this afternoon, and as that's the case you might as well come in and take breakfast with us."

The skipper expostulated violently, but it was of no use, and he went into the house and took breakfast.

At about noon, the Commandant and the skipper were standing on the pier of the town, when they saw in the offing the smoke of a steamer. In a few minutes they descried the Reina de la Plata coming in under full steam. The Commandant gave a great shout.

"The unprincipled Spaniard!" he cried. "He knows he has no right to enter this harbor until he is sure your vessel is not here. I must go and stop him. He must go back and lie outside until the laws of neutrality permit you to go out to him."

What the skipper then said concerning the laws of neutrality need not be recorded here, but the air quivered with the intensity of his ejaculations. "Make him go back!" he cried. "Do you suppose I am going to let that Spaniard steam away again with my wife and daughter? I shall row out to her, and you can do what you please with your gunboat." Then he shouted for his men, but only one of them was in his boat, which lay at the pier. The others were up in the town.

The Commandant ran to his gunboat, but

steam was not up in that little vessel. He gave his orders and hurried back to the pier to prevent the skipper from holding communication with the Spanish vessel.

"What do you mean?" shouted the angry Ezra, when he saw three soldiers arrive on the pier. "That's my vessel—my property. She's no Spaniard now. And she has my wife and daughter on board."

"It is my duty," said the Commandant, "and I can't help it."

"Duty!" exclaimed the skipper. "If you are so particular about duty, why did you allow her to lie here for a week to be repaired? Do you call that neutrality?"

"I don't call that anything," said the Commandant. "I know of no decree issued by my government which would prevent my giving work to the ship-carpenters of this town. As soon as steam is up on my gunboat I shall go out and make that Spaniard turn back. Confound him!" he continued, "he is coming too far, and he is about to drop anchor."

"Yes!" exclaimed the skipper, "and they are making ready to lower a boat. Perhaps my wife and daughter will come ashore."

"They shall not do it!" roared the Commandant. "There shall be no communication. O that my gunboat were under steam! I would sink that little boat. It is making directly for the pier."

"You'd better not try that," cried the skipper. "That would be a worse breach of neutrality than anything that has been mentioned yet. But mind you, Mr. Commandant, that steamer does not leave this port until I get my wife and daughter. If I can't hinder it any other way I'll sink my schooner across the mouth of the harbor."

The Commandant paid very little attention to these words. The boat from the Reina de la Plata was approaching rapidly. El Capitan sat in the stern, and as he came nearer it was seen that his face was beaming.

"Keep off!" shouted the Commandant. "Don't try to land here, or——"

El Capitan may have been deaf with excitement, but, whether this was the case or not, he was standing on the pier in less than a minute after the Commandant had shouted to him.

"This is intolerable," said the Russian, advancing. "The laws of neutrality forbid communication——"

"Down with the laws of neutrality!" shouted el Capitan. "I trample them under my feet! I have nothing to do with them!"

The countenance of the Commandant bristled with rage. "Nothing to do with the laws of neutrality?" he yelled. "I will show you——"

"Ha!" cried el Capitan. "You cannot show me anything. To be neutral there must be enemies; to enforce neutrality there must be war. There is no war, therefore there is no neutrality. Peace has been proclaimed between the Spaniards and the Americans. I have the news. I got this Russian newspaper from a steamer I spoke, bound for Petrimetkoff, and I immediately put back here at full speed, Mr. Budrack, because I wanted the Commandant to know everything in case you should arrive without my sighting you, which you did."

During this speech the skipper stood amazed. The war ended! Peace! What complications did this news bring with it! He wanted to row out to his wife and daughter, but he must wait and find out how matters stood. The Commandant had been reading an account of the peace protocol, and he now translated it into English for the skipper.

" Well? " said the Commandant, looking at el Capitan.

" It is well," said the Spaniard, " very well. There is no war; I am no longer a prisoner. There is no war, and my ship is no longer a prize."

" Stop there! " shouted the skipper. " I don't agree to that."

" But you must agree," said el Capitan. " Your prize has not been adjudicated to you, and I am sure no court would give it to you now."

" He is right," said the Commandant. " I am afraid he is right. But tell me this," said he, addressing the skipper: " if that ship is not your prize, who is going to pay the ship-carpenters for her repairs? "

It was el Capitan who made answer. " I do not know," he said, shaking his head; " but one thing is certain: I ordered no repairs."

" And I would not have had them made if you had ordered them," said the Commandant. " I do not believe you have any money. I set those carpenters to work because you ordered it, Mr. Budrack."

"But if it is not my prize," said the skipper, "what had I to do with it, then, and what have I to do with it now?"

"Gentlemen," said el Capitan, "do not let us dispute about who shall pay those wretched carpenters. Do not let us give them a thought when there are so many joyful things to talk about. It is right that you should know, sir," he said, turning to the skipper, "because you are her father. And you, sir," to the Commandant, "because you are the chief official of the place, and there may be constitutional laws which would compel you to make some kind of a legal entry."

"We have no constitution, as I told you," said the Commandant; "but we have laws which compel the payment of mechanics."

"What are you talking about?" cried Ezra to el Capitan.

"It is this," answered the Spaniard. "When I took your wife and daughter on board the Reina de la Plata I considered their wishes as commands. I was a prisoner; I belonged to the husband of the one and the father of the other. The steamer was his property—I remembered my position. I said no word to them of what was in my heart. But this morning, when I heard that I was free, that I stood on the deck of a vessel of which I was commander, then all was changed. I had a right to say what I pleased, and I told your daughter that I loved her. I will not speak of the details, but she accepted me, and my soul immediately floated as bravely as that proud flag of Spain you see upon my vessel."

"And her mother?" inquired the skipper. "What did she do?"

"She shed tears," replied el Capitan, " but I am sure they were tears of joy. She said she did not believe you would allow your daughter, sir, to wed an enemy, but she was sure you would not object to an alliance with the subject of a friendly power."

The skipper made no further remark, but got into his boat and was rowed to the steamer.

El Capitan, being a man of discretion, did not go to the vessel until half an hour later. The skipper met him at the rail.

"I have settled the whole matter," said Ezra. "I expected you to marry my daughter because my wife had made up her mind that it should be so. If your ship had been my prize I had intended to sell the Molly Crenshaw, and we would all have sailed on the Reina, because, in these days, a steamer is better for trading than any three-masted schooner, no matter how good she may be. Things are changed, but I shall still carry out my plan. I shall sell my schooner, and buy the steamer, if your owners will act reasonably about it. And then, of course, I will pay for the repairs, and I suppose I must settle the back wages of the sailors, if I expect to keep them."

That evening the three Budracks and el Capitan dined with the Commandant and his family. They spent a pleasant evening, and when they had returned to their schooner the skipper and his wife sat up for awhile in their little cabin, to talk over matters and things.

" This has all turned out very well for Drusilla and el Capitan," said Mrs. Budrack, " but if we sell the Molly Crenshaw we shall lose a very pleasant home.

" Yes," said Ezra. " I don't suppose that Spanish steamer can be made to take her place as far as our comfort goes."

" And it may end," she continued, " in our buying a house on shore, somewhere, and living there. I don't believe el Capitan will be wanting us to be sailing about with him all the time."

"No," said Ezra, "and I don't believe we would like it, either." ·

"The Commandant was in a very good humor to-night," remarked Mrs. Budrack. "He seemed to think it a fine thing for the town that his ship-carpenters had such a good job."

"Oh, yes," said Ezra, "I don't wonder he was pleased; but if I had known I should have to pay for that hole I made in that Spanish vessel, I would not have punched it."

"And listen to those sailors," said Mrs. Budrack, "over there on the steamer. They are all singing. I expect it's the thought that they are going to get their back-wages that makes them so happy."

"Yes," said Ezra, somewhat dolefully, "and, from what el Capitan told me this evening, some of their wages must be a long time in arrears. It will be a pretty heavy drain on me, but as that's going to be my ship, and as el Capitan is going to be my son-in-law, I suppose I've got to pay them, and make things square for him and Drusilla."

Mrs. Budrack reflected for a moment. "Now, Ezra," said she, "let me tell you something. The next time you get mixed up in a war I'd advise you to get on the side that's beaten, or else on the side that's bound to preserve the laws of neutrality. It doesn't pay to conquer."

"COME IN, NEW YEAR"

"COME IN, NEW YEAR"

IN a fine old country mansion, commodious, somewhat imposing and positively heavy in its style of architecture, resided the Hon. Horace Brunder, now an elderly man, and Mrs. Brunder, his wife. For several years these two had made up the family—a very small family for so large a house. They had no children, and, although they were very good company for each other, they felt as they daily grew older that they could not of themselves make their home as cheerful and as pleasant as they would have it. They felt this the more forcibly because there had been many years when that house was very cheerful and very pleasant. Therefore it was, about six months before this story opens, this all too quiet couple had taken into their home a young girl, Margey Griffith, the niece of Mrs. Brunder and one of a large family of fatherless boys and girls.

247

The Hon. Horace had never been fond of children, and at one time in his life it might have been said that he absolutely disliked boys and girls, but now, since he had ceased to go out in all weathers and was feeling a growing dependence on the indoor pleasures of his home, he had agreed with his wife that it would be a good thing to have some young life in the house, and that of all the persons they knew the niece Margey was best adapted to supply the missing and needed element in their household life.

It had been considered by Margey's family that it was a most fortunate thing that her rich uncle, who did not care for young people, should take her into his house, and for a time the girl herself was very well satisfied with the change from the somewhat contracted suburban house and the active bustle of a large family to the quiet rural beauty of the old mansion, its garden, its lawn, and its woodland. But as summer passed and as autumn, with its bright-hued foliage, came and went, and as the rigors of winter settled themselves upon the land, Margey often thought of the stirring life which was going on at home, where winter was the liveliest time of the year. Here, when the snow was deep, she could not walk much, and, although she sometimes went sleighing, it was not a very exhilarating thing to sit wrapped in furs by the side of her aunt, who seldom spoke when she was out in the frosty air, and who would have been unpleasantly agitated if the horses had broken into the fine spanking gait at which Margey would have driven them had she had command of the reins, or even command of the coachman.

At last Christmas came, but it was a dull time for Margey. There were neighbors invited, but they were all elderly people and of a reposeful turn of mind. Margey received several presents, among them a beautiful little watch from her uncle, and, although she had never received anything which could compare with these Christmas gifts, they did not compensate her for the loss of the holiday atmosphere of her home. During the whole day she felt as though she were attending the funeral of Santa Claus.

But on the last day of the year her spirits sank still lower. With her brothers and sisters and the elderly members of the family she had been accustomed ever since she could remember to make a great deal of New Year's Eve, and among the observances which were never omitted was the traditional custom of opening the front door of the house exactly as the clock struck the hour of midnight, in order to let the New Year come in. Then, altogether, young and old, they would shout, as the door swung back: " Come in, New Year! Welcome, New Year! " And when it was considered that the newcomer had really crossed the threshold they would turn to each other, each wishing all a happy New Year and many more to come. This time-honored ceremony was to Margey one of the most pleasant features of the holiday season, for it concerned not only the joys of the moment, but those of happy days to come.

On this New Year's Eve Margey felt herself in a truly doleful mood. Her uncle and aunt had gone to their room at ten o'clock, and not one word had they said which indicated that they considered this evening to be in any way different from the ordinary evenings of the year. To Margey this seemed like a sort of domestic sacrilege. If she could have done so, she would have sped away to her home, even if it had been necessary to speed back again before the cock should crow.

She went to her room not because she

wanted to do so, but because the lights were all put out down stairs; but she did not go to bed. She sat thinking of all the lively scenes that were going on at home. Most likely they were playing charades, but they would be sure to stop them a little before twelve. Her mother and one of **the** girls would be getting things together for a little supper, for they always began the New Year with something to eat, drink, and be merry over. In this big, old house it would be high-treason to eat between twelve and one o'clock at night.

The hands of Margey's new watch moved on and on until they pointed to a quarter of twelve, and then the eyes of our young lady opened wider and wider as she sat and gazed at the wall and saw the family at home. She could see them just as well as though they were there.

"They are all looking at the clock," she said, "watching and waiting and talking. They always begin too soon for fear of being too late. Tom is standing at the front door now, so that nobody shall get ahead of him when the time comes."

For a few moments she sat as though her eyes were fixed on the energetic Tom, when suddenly she rose to her feet.

"I'll do it," she said, "even if I have to do it all by myself in the dark. I'll go down and let the New Year in."

Slowly and on tiptoe she descended the softly carpeted staircase. At the landing which overlooked the hall there was a round window, through which came the rays of the full moon, lighting the hall and stairway, so that Margey could see her way without the slightest trouble. The big clock was in the shadow, but she knew it was not yet twelve, and, stepping lightly to the great hall door, she went quietly to work to unfasten it. There was a bolt and a chain and a lock. The first slipped back easily and without any noise, and the chain was removed in a moment, but the lock turned hard, and as she forced the big key around she was afraid that there might be a sudden click which would be heard on the floor above. It would be a dreadful thing if her aunt should hear it, for it had been thoroughly impressed on her mind that if that good lady should be suddenly startled nobody could know what might happen. But, although she moved the big key slowly and with much difficulty, she moved it steadily, and finally it went around as far as it would go, without a click.

The door was unfastened. She turned the knob and stood, holding it firmly, waiting for midnight. Very soon she heard a whirring sound in the big clock on the landing. Then there came the first stroke of twelve, and with that Margey stepped back and opened wide the door.

"Come in!" she said, but before she could utter the words "New Year" she stopped suddenly, for on the portico in front of her she saw a man. The girl was on the point of screaming, but even at this dreadful moment she remembered that if her aunt should be startled nobody could know what might happen, and so she clapped her hand to her mouth. She sprang back, however. She could not help that, and at the same moment the man stepped into the hall.

"You are right," he said in a whisper, and looking at the hand which was still over Margey's mouth. "I understand. I won't make the least noise in the world. Let me shut the door. I can do it very quietly."

If the cold air which rushed in through the open doorway had frozen Margey as stiff as a statue she could not have been more incapable of speaking or moving than she was at that moment. If she had dared to cry for help or tried to run away, she would not have been able to do either. She stood and stared, whiter than the moonlight. The man was refastening the door, and as he did so a ray of blessed relief came into the mind of Margey. He had put down on the floor a valise and an umbrella. Surely no burglar, no wicked man of any sort, would go about with a valise and an umbrella, and he seemed to know all about fastening doors without making a noise. This ray of relief was a very little ray, but it revived Margey sufficiently to enable her to drop her hand from her mouth.

The man now stepped toward the library door, and with one finger on his lip he beckoned to Margey. She was so astonished at this action that, almost without volition, she followed him. She was so thoroughly frightened that she could do nothing herself. She had not even the strength to disobey, but as she stepped into the library she hugged to her heart the thought of the umbrella and the valise. The man took from his pocket a box of matches, and, striking a match, he stepped, without the slightest hesitation, to the corner of the mantel-piece, on which stood a great candlestick, and lighted the candle. Then he quietly closed the door.

"I do that," he said, "because if your aunt should hear our voices and be startled, there is no knowing what might happen."

"How could he know that?" Margey asked herself, and a third ray of comfort was added to that furnished by the umbrella and valise. In the light of the candle Margey could see that the man was rather short, very well wrapped up, and wore a fur cap, which now, however, he removed, showing a head of reddish brown hair a little curled, and with some streaks of gray on the temples. His face looked as if he had lived out of doors a good deal, in all sorts of weather, but his eyes were bright, and there was a pleasant expression about the mouth, as if he would be glad to laugh if there were anything to laugh at.

"It was very, very good of you," he said, still speaking in an undertone, "to come down and let me in. You must have seen me from your window. I was afraid there was no one awake in the house. I heard you at work at the bolt and the chain, and I knew why you were so slow and so quiet. Of course I cannot be mistaken in supposing you to be Miss Griffith?"

Now Margey found her voice—that is, a little of it. " Yes," she said, " and who, I beg of you, sir—who are you? "

" I am John Brunder, your uncle's brother. Surely you have heard of me? "

" A very little," said Margey.

" And how much, may I ask? " he said, showing some surprise.

" I never heard you mentioned but once," she replied, " and that was one day when I found Aunt Ellen in one of the bedrooms which I had not seen before, the door having always been locked."

" Had it a bedstead in it," said he, " with a curved footboard? "

" Yes, it had," said Margey, more and more relief coming into her mind each moment.

" And did you notice anything in the way of sporting articles—guns, boxing gloves? "

" Yes," said Margey. " There were boxing gloves and foils on the wall at the head of the bed and two guns on a rack, and there were some cases in the corner which looked as if they held fishing-rods. I was surprised to see these things, and asked Aunt Ellen to whom they belonged. She said that the room used to be occupied by Uncle Horace's brother John, but that he did not live here now."

" Is that all she told you? " he asked.

" Every word," said Margey.

He gave his head a little nod. " Perhaps it was as well," he said. " There's no use in raking up disagreeable things before young people. But I am glad to hear that my old room is kept just as it used to be. That's a good sister-in-law of mine, and I hope I may not do a thing to startle her, knowing as I do that no one could tell——"

" What might happen," added Margey, involuntarily.

" But you ought to know all about me," said he. " It will not do for you to be ignorant any longer, especially as you were so good as to come down to let me in."

" But I didn't," said Margey. " I didn't come down to let you in."

" Then who, in the name of common sense, did you ask to come in? There was nobody but me on the porch."

" I opened the door for the New Year to come in," said Margey.

John Brunder stood and looked at her in amazement, and then Margey, who had almost recovered her self-possession, told him all about it.

"Well, well, well!" he exclaimed, "you're the kind of girl I like. I knew that a niece of my brother's wife was living here, but I had no idea she was such a—such a girl as you are! What is your name?"

"Margey."

"Miss Margey," said John Brunder, extending his hand, "I wish you a very happy New Year."

"The same to you, sir," said she, giving him her hand.

"And now you want to know why I don't live here," said John Brunder. "You certainly have a right to know, and I will tell you in as few words as possible. I was born in this house and have lived here a good deal, off and on, and the last time I took up my abode in the room with the bedstead with the curly footboard I thought I was settled for life, but my brother and I are very different in disposition. He is more sober and quiet than I am, and I am a great deal more lively and restless than he is, and there you have our characters in as few words as possible. About six years ago we had a misunderstanding. I will not say anything about it, because he is not here to present his side of the question, and under the circumstances it would not be fair for me to present mine. However, I am very hot-headed at times—not always, mind you, for generally I am very mild indeed, but at this particular time I ignited and went off like a fire-cracker, and you know that when a fire-cracker goes off it doesn't come back again."

Margey was listening with great interest. She and her companion had seated themselves, and she was rapidly losing all fear of him.

" As I told you," he continued, " I went off and did not intend to come back, but gradually my ideas began to change. My brother was getting old—so was I, for that matter— and I determined to try to be reconciled with him. I started out this day thinking it would be a good thing to begin the New Year in harmony and brotherly love. I expected to be here early in the evening, but my train was detained for a long time, and I really did not know how late it was when I walked up here. I was dumfounded at finding the house all shut up and dark, and I could not think what to do, for I knew very well that if I rang the bell I might startle your Aunt Ellen, in which case nobody could know what might happen. So I stood there deliberating, and I really believe

I was on the point of walking back to the village when I heard someone opening the door so gently and quietly that I was positively certain it was highly desirable not to make a noise. So, you see, I was not surprised when the door opened. I supposed that someone, probably Joseph Buckle, had seen me arrive. By the way, is Joseph still here?"

" Oh, yes! " said Margey.

" I am glad of that," said John Brunder. " Joseph was always a good friend of mine. Now you see," he continued, " just how things stand. You come down to let the New Year in, and in I pop. I hope the New Year came in with me, and that it will prove to be the happiest that any of us has yet known."

" So do I," said Margey, but she had always wished that ever since she had known what a New Year meant.

John Brunder rose. " My dear young friend, Miss Margey," he said, " what are we going to do next? And if you will allow me to answer my own question I will say that the very best thing you can do for me is to give me something to eat, or, if it will please you better, allow me to get it myself, for if the pantry of this house is still under the charge of Joseph Buckle I know where to find the eatables."

For a minute Margey stood and looked earnestly at the good-natured gentleman. She believed, just as firmly as she believed anything, that he was Mr. John Brunder, the younger brother of her Uncle Horace, but still she had no positive proof of the fact; she had only his word for it. Was it right for her to allow him to go about the house and eat things without giving the family notice of his presence? But if she were to go upstairs and knock at her uncle's door, her Aunt Ellen—oh, no; she could not do that at this time of night.

He laughed. He was almost on the point of laughing aloud, but he checked himself. " I know what you are thinking about," said he, " and it is perfectly right for you to think so."

" Oh, I don't really think," said Margey apologetically, " but, you see, I——"

" Of course I see! " he answered. " I see, perfectly. Just wait a minute." So saying, he picked up his umbrella. " Now, please look at the name on this silver plate," said he, holding it close to the candle.

Margey obeyed. " But that isn't your name! " she exclaimed in surprise. " That is my uncle's name, Horace Brunder! "

" To be sure it is! " ·said he. " I took it away by mistake and left mine. If he refuses to be reconciled with me, we can change umbrellas anyway, so that my time will not be entirely lost."

Margey smiled. " I think that is a queer way to prove your identity," she said, " but as I truly believe it doesn't need any proving it does not matter."

" It is a very good proof," persisted the other. " If I were an improper person and had taken that umbrella, do you suppose I would have brought it back? And now let's go into the pantry. I'm nearly famished."

So saying, he picked up the candlestick, and, shading the flame so that no ray of it should go upstairs, he crossed the hall into the dining-room. Margey followed, and as she saw how deftly he made his way around the furniture and toward the pantry she felt positively assured that he must at one time have been very much at home in that house. In the pantry John Brunder put the candlestick down and looked about him.

" Do you still eat Albert biscuit? " he asked.

" Oh, yes! " replied Margey.

" Then I know where Joseph Buckle keeps

them. Joseph never changes. If a thing belongs in one place, it belongs there always. There," said he, opening a dresser drawer. " Here is the tin box, just where I have found it hundreds of times before."

Margey now thought she ought to help a little. To be sure, this genial gentleman seemed to know so well where to find the eatables that she might have gone to bed and left him to take care of himself, but this did not suit her ideas of propriety or proper hospitality, so she opened another closet.

" Do you eat cheese at this time of night, sir? " she asked.

" Oh, yes," he replied, " when I am as hungry as I am now! And isn't that a box of sardines? Open, too! Now, let us take these things over to the table. No, I don't want any plate. All I want is a knife to cut the cheese." And as he spoke he opened a drawer and took out a knife. " Now, my dear," said he, " if you will look in the corner of that second shelf and see if there is not a box of preserved ginger there I shall be much obliged to you. Joseph always kept preserved ginger in that corner."

Margey laughed as she produced the tin

box. "You do seem to know where things are kept in this house," she said, "and I don't believe anybody has eaten cheese and sardines at this time of night since you went away."

"No," said he, seating himself at his impromptu meal; "my brother Horace never indulges in such improprieties, but I was always much more imprudent. But, so far as I can see, my imprudences have agreed with me."

"Perhaps that is because you are so much younger," said Margey.

"Younger, yes," said John Brunder, "of course I am younger, but perhaps I ought not to fall back too much on my youth, for I am fifty-six. However," he added, "so long as I am able to eat cheese and sardines in the middle of the night I am not going to complain of my age."

Margey was looking at him with great interest, thinking it must have been a long time since he had had anything to eat, when suddenly she heard a little noise. It was like a person coming cautiously down stairs. She started and listened earnestly. There could be no mistake. She heard footsteps on the backstairs, the door of which opened not far from the place where she stood. John Brunder stopped eating, and half rose from his chair.

" Somebody coming! " he whispered.

Now the door of the stairway slowly opened, and from behind it protruded the head of Joseph Buckle, the butler. His face was pale, his eyes and mouth were wide open, and a big club, which he thrust out in front of him, trembled in his hand. John Brunder rose to his feet and pushed back his chair.

" Jo-seph! " he exclaimed. " Upon my word, it is the same old Joseph! I say, Joseph, how do you do? "

The old butler stepped down and stood motionless on the floor, his big stick in one hand and a lantern in the other. He looked at Margey, and then he looked at John Brunder.

" Mr. John! " he exclaimed in a voice muffled by fright, caution, and amazement. Then, turning his head, he added, " And Miss Margey! "

" Give me your hand, my good Joseph," said John Brunder. I don't wonder you don't believe your senses. But what are you doing with that club? Did you think we were burglars? "

"I did, sir," said Joseph. "I heard voices, and I was sure there was somebody in the house, and so I came down."

"Why didn't you bring a pistol? What would you have done with that club if we had really been burglars?"

"Oh, I couldn't bring a pistol, sir," said Joseph. "If I should fire a pistol and Mrs. Brunder should hear it, there's no knowing what might happen. So I had to come down with nothing but a club."

"You're a brave fellow," said John Brunder, "and a loyal one, and I am glad for your sake as well as for our own that we are not robbers. You see, Joseph, I have not forgotten where you keep the good things to eat."

Margey now took pity on the bewildered butler and told him everything that had happened.

"Well, well!" exclaimed Joseph. "I'm wonderfully glad to see you, Mr. John. It's been a different house here since you went away, sir. Don't you remember, sir, we used to open the front door for the New Year when you lived here?"

"Of course I do," said John Brunder. "I always used to have some youngsters here, and we had fine times."

"And if I had had any idea, miss, that you were used to that sort of thing I'd have come down to help you."

"Oh, she didn't need anybody's help," said Mr. John. "She did it as well as an angel could have done it. If I had gone back to the village, I believe I should have been so cross that I would have started for the city early in the morning. You know that's my way, Joseph."

"Yes, sir," said the old man, "and sometimes it has been a pity that it was your way. But would you like me to go and waken Mr. Brunder, sir? I think I can do it without making any stir."

"Oh, no, no, no!" exclaimed Mr. John. "Don't think of it. If either of you ever wants to be reconciled with anybody, don't make him get out of a warm bed of a cold night to do it. No, I'll wait until morning. You can get me into my old room, can't you, Joseph, without disturbing anybody?"

"Of course I can," said Joseph. "We'll go up the backstairs."

"Then I'll bid you good-night," said Margey, "as I can do nothing more for you."

"More!" exclaimed Mr. John. "If it is

all right between my brother and me to-morrow morning, there isn't a being on earth who could have done as much. And I am very sorry, indeed, that I have kept you up so late." With this he picked up the candle, and he and Joseph escortèd Margey to the foot of the great stairway, where she bade them good-night and went quietly up in the moonlight.

When Margey reached her room, she did not go to bed. It was very late, not far from one o'clock, but she did not mind that. Some of the family at home were up yet. It was the most natural thing in the world to sit up late on New Year's eve. Then she began to think of all that had just happened. It certainly had been a good thing that she had been loyal to the old custom of the family, a wonderfully good thing, for she was sure if Mr. John were as good-natured and as jolly in the morning as he had been that night his brother could not help being reconciled. She would be very glad, too, if he should come back and live there. It would be so pleasant to have such a jolly person in the house.

As she thought and thought the affair of the evening seemed like a romance to her. If all turned out well, it would really be a holiday story. And yet there was an imperfection in the romance. It was not altogether the sort of story she would have made if she had been writing it, and neither was it exactly the sort of real happening that it would have been if she had arranged it. Mr. John was as bright and as cheery as anybody could be, but still if she had had the management of everything and was going to make a romance in real life, which it might just as well have been, her own personality would not have been the only element of youth in this pleasant invention. Margey was capable of being very fond of elderly people, but still she was young—she was not yet twenty—and if the person who came with the New Year had been just like Mr. John, only younger— But she would not think such thoughts as these. She ought to be ashamed of herself. Still, for all that, fifty-six was pretty old. Everybody in that house seemed to be so old! Her favorite maid, Mary, had a married daughter, and, so far as the romance of the evening was concerned, things might have been different just as well as not.

When at last she pressed her face to the pillow, she was still thinking.

" Fifty-six," she said to herself, " and it might just as well have been—have been "—And she had not decided upon the exact age it might have been, when she dropped asleep.

The next morning Margey was downstairs very early, nearly a quarter of an hour before breakfast, for she was anxious to know everything which should happen. In the hall she met Joseph.

" I wish you a very happy New Year, miss," he said. " I forgot it last night, being so rattled, and if anybody deserves a happy New Year you do, miss."

All the romance had gone out of Margey's mind, and things seemed very commonplace to her in the cold light of day.

" I don't believe I had anything to do with anything," she said. " Mr. John Brunder would have waited a little while longer, and then he would have rung the bell, even if it should startle my aunt."

" Oh, no, no, no! " said Joseph. " He wouldn't have done that. Nobody knows what might have happened if he had done that. But you'll be glad to hear, miss, that everything is all right. They've been up since a quarter past seven, for I told Mr. Brunder the news when I first went into his room. I have not known such early goings-on since Mr. John went away."

"And they are truly reconciled?" asked Margey.

"Indeed they are!" answered Joseph. "They're all upstairs in the study now, as merry as crickets. Even Mrs. Brunder wasn't a bit startled, or if she was it didn't hurt her. There, miss, that's the study door now. They're coming down and in a family party, just as they ought to be." And with this he retired to the dining-room door.

Margey waited in the hall. It delighted her to know that her Uncle Horace and his brother were good friends again, and that her aunt was happy, and that the house would be more cheerful, and if she had done anything to help bring this about she was very glad of it, but the vague and wandering thoughts which had filled her mind the night before had all gone. The romance of the affair had vanished.

Downstairs came the happy party, merrily talking. Her Uncle Horace was first of all, his face brighter than she had ever seen it, and as soon as he perceived her he called out, "Happy New Year, Margey!" in a voice so strong and hearty that she could scarcely believe it belonged to him. Then her aunt, who seemed really in a hurry to come downstairs, gave her the same greeting, which was echoed loudly by Mr. John, who was a little in the rear.

"Happy New Year to"—you all! she was about to add, but she did not. She simply stood and gazed, her face turning now a little pale and now a little red, and her eyes wide open with wonderment. The last person of the party coming down the stairs, a little behind Mr. John, was a man evidently young. He had no beard, and his face was very fresh-colored. He was tall, too; taller than her Uncle Horace. She thought he looked as though he wanted to bid her a happy New Year, too, but he did not do it.

Now Mr. John laughed aloud, and they all laughed, excepting the young man, who apparently knew what they were laughing about, and who turned a little red, and excepting Margey, who did not know what they were laughing at, and who turned somewhat pale.

"Ah, Margey," shouted Mr. John, "I know what you are thinking about! You're wondering where he came from—you're won-

dering where he came from a good deal more
than you are wondering who he is. You don't
know whether I brought him in my valise or
folded up inside the umbrella."

"Now, John," said Aunt Ellen, " you are
positively cruel. Margey, this is Arthur, your
Uncle John's son. And, Arthur, I must make
you acquainted with my niece, Margey Griffith."

The young people silently shook hands,
harmonizing in color as they did so, for the
recollection of her romantic fancies suddenly
came across Margey's mind and flushed her
face.

"Oh, I am not going to be cruel! " cried
Mr. John. " This young man made the trip
with me yesterday, but I thought it better for
me to leave him at the village and to come to
the house by myself; for when Arthur went
away he was nothing but a boy, scarcely fifteen, and I did not know how he might be
received."

"Which was all stuff and nonsense," said
Mr. Horace Brunder. " You ought to have
known that he would be welcome."

"Well," said Mr. John, " I thought I could
manage things better by myself, and as you

sent for him early this morning he has nothing
to complain of.   Moreover, if I had brought
Arthur along with me I don't believe I should
have had enough to eat last night, for he's a
great deal worse in regard to cheese and sardines in the middle of the night than I am; but
everything's all right now, and as this young
lady is really to consider me as one of her
uncles she might as well begin instantly, and
so I am going to bid her a happy New Year
again, and give her a kiss," which he did without delay, and then Aunt Ellen kissed her, and
then Uncle Horace did so.

No, not Arthur.   It was not until the
seventh of April of that year that he found
himself entitled to that inestimable privilege.

There were a great many things which had
to happen before the seventh of April.

In the first place, Margey had to learn all
about the trouble which had resulted in Mr.
John's leaving the old family home, and when
she discovered that the quarrel between the
brothers had been caused by some mad pranks
of the boy Arthur she set herself earnestly to
work to analyze the mind of the young man
Arthur and to find out for herself the interesting series of developments which must have

taken place in his character to change him from the reckless youngster to the exceedingly kind-hearted and considerate young man that he now was.

Like many other persons in this world, Margey was very fond of the study of human nature: meaning thereby, as is often the case, that she had formed an ideal concerning a certain subject, and that she hoped to be able to convince herself that the subject was equal to her ideal.

She did not have uninterrupted opportunities for continuing her study, for after a week or two Arthur was obliged to go away, but he came back as soon as he could, and he assisted her so much in coming to a satisfactory conclusion in regard to himself and his relation to her ideal that by the time the seventh of April came around her education in this branch was entirely finished.

On the next New Year's eve, a little before twelve o'clock, every member of that family, including Joseph Buckle and some other household servants, assembled in the great hall to invite the New Year to enter. To Margey was assigned the duty of opening the door, and she did it all herself, refusing any assistance, even from the very urgent young man who stood close beside her.

When the great door was opened wide and everybody all at once cried out cheerily, " Come in, New Year! " there entered nothing but a great blast of cold and frosty air, but everybody knew that the New Year had come in, and the door was closed.

" Now," said Mr. John, " this is all very well, but I can tell you, my good relatives and friends, that no happier New Year will ever pass that threshold than when Last Year and I came in together."

Margey and Arthur had some doubts about this, for they were to be married in the spring.

A SAILOR'S KNOT

A SAILOR'S KNOT

SIDE by side with Florence Brower, I stood upon the sea-sands. We had been walking along the beach, and now we had stopped to look out over the ocean. I had known this beautiful girl for about a year, and the love for her which had been gradually growing up in my heart had become so absolutely irresistible that, the day before, I had come down to the little seaside village, where Florence and her aunt were spending the summer, on purpose to tell her that I loved her, and to end, in one way or another, the suspense which tossed my soul in a storm far more violent, I believed, than any which had ever broken upon this coast.

If, up to that moment, Florence had not known that she loved me she had no doubt of it when I had finished speaking. She could not conceal the truth from herself, and she did not try to do it. She withdrew her gaze from the sea and dropped it upon a little strip of sand between us. In a very few words, but as plainly as I had spoken in many words, she answered me. She gave me the heart which I had just taught her to know.

In the beautiful world in which we walked together, or stood together, during the next hour, there were many wonderful things—the sky, the sea, the sparkling air, the scent of the pine woods on the bluff; but there was nothing so wonderful as the great knowledge that Florence was mine. I could scarcely understand it; I did not try to comprehend it.

At last the time came when we must go back to the village. We walked slowly, sometimes, in the lonely stretches, hand in hand.

On the outskirts of the village we met a jolly old sea-captain, retired from active service and known to us both—Captain Asa Lopper by name. When his eyes fell upon us a curious grin came over his wrinkled face as he gave us an abbreviated greeting. My response was so loud, so hearty, so cordial that the old man must have known that something extraordinary had happened to me; but it struck me with surprise that Florence scarcely spoke to the captain at all. In fact, when she saw him

she gave a little start, and after that, for some minutes, she did not say anything. She soon recovered herself, however, and talked cheerfully until we reached the cottage where she and her aunt were staying.

I wished to go into the house, that together we might tell the glorious news to Miss Moulton, but Florence gently objected.

"It would be better," she said, "if I were to tell her myself. Of course it will be a great surprise to her."

That evening when, at the earliest justifiable moment, I called at the cottage I did not see Miss Moulton. Florence told me that her aunt had a headache and begged to be excused.

"You have told her of our engagement," I said; "what does she think of it?"

Florence smiled.

"I am bound to say," she answered, "that she does not like it; but you must not mind that. Any engagement I might make would be a great shock to her. Ever since my mother's death, when I was five years old, my aunt and I have lived together. She has no control over me; I am of age, and I am entirely my own mistress, but it is natural enough that the news I gave her would shock her."

Then my dear girl changed the subject, and the world was very bright.

The next morning I hoped to see Miss Moulton as well as Florence and to make my peace with the older lady. Of course she could have no personal objection to me, and I knew she was a good woman; so, filled with the courage of the morning, I did not fear that I could make it possible for her to see me without a headache. But when I neared the cottage I saw that that was no place for me that morning. There were summer dresses and straw hats upon the piazza, a good many of them. Some of the village ladies were making a call.

After an early dinner I was smoking a cigar in a little summer-house at the bottom of the hotel garden, when a boy came to me and told me that a gentleman wished to see me. I was surprised at this, for I was but little acquainted in the village, and when I reached the hotel I found in the office a middle-aged man whom I had never seen before. He was a serious-visaged person with gray whiskers and introduced himself by means of his card as Romney C. Lloyd, attorney-at-law, of New York, and then asked me if I would be kind enough to allow him a private conversation.

I conducted him to the reading-room, which during the day was seldom tenanted. Here we sat down and he opened the conversation.

"I am here, Mr. Radnor," he said, "on account of a telegram which I received last night from Miss Hester Moulton. I took an early train this morning, and am very glad I found you at home, sir, for I wish to return to-day."

"Do you mean," I exclaimed, "that Miss Moulton telegraphed you to come to see me?"

"She did," Mr. Lloyd replied, "and on very important business, I assure you, sir."

"And what is your business?" I asked. "Has it anything to do with my engagement to Miss Brower?"

"It most certainly has," said he. "But before I enter upon the subject, let me ask you if you have any knowledge of Miss Brower's father, Gideon Brower?"

"I know nothing about him," I replied, "except that he has been dead for a good many years."

"Nine years, sir, in September next. And as you know nothing about him I will give you some information. He was a very eccentric person, but his eccentricity was not of a character which could give any reason to doubt the perfect soundness of his intellect. He had his own ideas, and he carried them out without regard to the opinions of other people. For the greater part of his life he was a sea-captain. He commanded fine merchantmen, and came to own them; he invested wisely and amassed a large fortune. But he never changed his habits or his mode of life; he was greatly attached to the sea, and his compauions and friends were men who in some way were connected with the sea. He married a lady of excellent family, a Miss Moulton, of New Haven, who was a passenger on a ship which he commanded on a voyage to the Mediterranean. After the marriage his wife sailed with him on nearly all his voyages, and when she died old Captain Brower declared that as soon as Florence was old enough she was to sail with him on every voyage he made, and when she got married she was to marry a sea captain.

" When the old man died he left a will, made not long before his death, which contained some peculiar provisions relating to the manner in which his daughter should inherit his property, and it is due to you that you should be made acquainted with these provisions. The most important clause is that which declares that the testator's entire fortune is devised to his daughter, Florence, on condition that she shall marry a sea-captain."

At this I started. " Marry a sea-captain! " I exclaimed.

" I beg that you will not interrupt me, sir," said Mr. Lloyd. " Let me put the case plainly before you, and then you will know better what to say. I will not go into the details of the will, but its import is simply this: So long as Florence Brower remains unmarried the property left by her father is to remain in the hands of trustees, and the interest and gains accruing from its investment shall be paid to her. When, according to the desire of her father, she shall unite herself in marriage to a sea-captain, then the whole fortune shall be made over to her. But if she shall marry, and not marry a sea-captain, then her interest in said fortune shall immediately cease and determine, and the whole of the estate shall be appropriated in a manner which is afterward set forth, and which is mainly for charitable objects connected with mariners and their families. This same disposition is arranged for if she dies a single woman."

I could not repress an expression of surprise and anger.

"Excuse me, sir," said Mr. Lloyd, "but I beg you will give me your attention a little longer. I have set before you the conditions of the will of Gideon Brower, and I now wish to set before you your own position in this case. You have engaged yourself in marriage to Florence Brower. You are not a sea-captain. It is impossible that, by any pretense, or even the honest adoption of a seafaring profession, you can entitle yourself to be considered a sea-captain in the sense in which such a person is referred to in the will. The old man was very wary, and a whole clause is devoted to the purpose of making it impossible for anyone, who is not really and truly in the strictest sense of the word a sea-captain by profession, to marry Miss Brower, and enable her to inherit the fortune of her father. So you see that Captain Brower tied a good, strong sailor's knot around his daughter's future.

"Now, sir," he continued, "should you marry her the consequences are immediate. She inherits nothing of her father's estate, and, more than that, she loses all interest in it; and the income, which she now receives, will cease. May I ask you, Mr. Radnor, if you have a private fortune which will compensate Miss Brower for the absolute loss of her father's estate? I do not ask you, you will observe, if you are engaged in a business which is likely to yield you an income which will make up for her loss, for I possess full information upon that point." It seemed to me as if my crushed condition did not admit of words, and yet this last remark stung me into speech.

"What do you mean?" I asked. "My business?"

"In this case, as the legal representative of Miss Brower, I have made your business mine. I know that you are the junior partner in the linen importing house of Woodruff & Radnor. This morning, before I took the train, I went to the Mercantile Register Office and investigated the commercial rating of your firm. I find that the credit of the house is very low. In fact, you have a very poor commercial standing in business circles. You need not get angry, sir. In cases like this we deal only with facts and there is no need of our forming opinions; so, unless you have a private fortune, or expect one, you are now asking Miss Brower to give up a present competence and a future fortune, and you have nothing to give her in return. Now, sir, I have put the case before you, and you can decide for yourself whether or not you are going to insist upon the disastrous engagement you have ignorantly made."

There was absolutely no answer I could make to the man, and I felt, too, that when I should become able to answer it would not be to him.

" Tell me this," I said, in a choking voice: " What has Miss Brower's aunt to do with this matter? How does it concern her? And why should she send for you? "

" I will tell you," he said. " Miss Moulton is a lady without property. Since the death of Captain Brower she and her niece have lived together, and she has shared the benefits of the very handsome income derived from the estate. In fact, she acts as head of the little family and assumes its responsibilities. When her niece marries anyone, other than a sea-captain, she will be entirely without support, unless, indeed, that support shall be assumed by the person who marries her niece.

Naturally enough, sir, she is deeply concerned in the matrimonial actions of Miss Brower."

My head swam; my blood boiled. I rose and pushed back my chair.

" I do not want to talk about this now," said I, " and I do not say that I believe a word of it; but one thing I will say—if what you tell me is true, it is the most abominable piece of business I have ever heard of. It is unnatural, vile, incredible." And with that I strode out of the room and into the open air. In what state of mind I left the prying, brutal lawyer I did not know or care. My first impulse was to rush to Florence, but I changed my purpose. I was not in a fit state of mind to meet her. I walked with rapid strides on the beach, but in an opposite direction to that which Florence and I had taken the day before.

I knew now why she had started when she had met Captain Lopper. The dear girl had so loved me, when she pledged herself to me to be mine forever and ever, that she had not thought of the wicked conditions of her father's will, and they had not come to her mind until we encountered that old sea-captain. Then suddenly she remembered, and of course it affected her.

Now, too, I understood all about her aunt. Poor Florence! What a time she must have had with that sordid woman!

In the evening I repaired to the cottage. I had not made up my mind what I was going to say, but there seemed to be no reason for doubt as to what I ought to say. However, love is above everything, and I would come to no conclusion until I had seen Florence.

I met her on the piazza.

" You know everything that has happened! " I exclaimed. " Tell me what you think about it."

" Don't be excited," she said. " Let us sit down and talk. I do not think there is much to consider. We have engaged ourselves to each other, and that is the main point; everything else is secondary. For myself, I will merely say that under no circumstances would I refuse to engage myself to a man for the reason that I might lose money. I made up my mind about this, long ago. In fact, I had ceased to consider the matter altogether. Now, then, sir," she said, with a smile, " what do *you* think about it? "

I could not answer. I felt as if I could tear the hair from my head; again was this terrible responsibility of deciding cast upon me.

During my hesitation I saw a quick shade pass over Florence's face; it was gone in an instant.

"No," I exclaimed, "you need not think that!"

"I do not think it," she said quickly. "A devil thrust the idea into my mind, but I would not let it stay. I know as well as I know anything that I am the same to you, whether I have money or not."

Now I rose and stepped toward her, with arms outstretched. I had not determined to accept her sacrifice; I had determined upon nothing; but love is stronger than all besides. I stopped suddenly; there was a sound of footsteps in the hall and someone was about to enter the parlor.

But Florence was very quick of action. She stepped closer to me and said in a voice low, but perfectly clear and distinct, "It is settled; we are to marry."

All that night, in my waking hours and in my dreams, the angels sang to me a song of heaven, the words of which were these: "We are to marry." And all night long, sleeping or waking, I heard the devils sing another song, the words being: "You rob her of her fortune." I awoke the happiest man in the world, and the most distressed one.

I knew now what I had not appreciated before—that Florence was a rich woman. In town she and her aunt lived in a handsome house; they had horses, carriages, opera-boxes —all that rich people have. When I had thought of these things at all, I had supposed that Miss Moulton was wealthy; now I knew that she had nothing, Florence everything.

As never before had I appreciated Florence's wealth, so never before had I appreciated my comparative poverty. I was young and enthusiastic, and had high hopes of a successful mercantile career. But when I came to look at my prospects in the cold hard light which Mr. Lloyd had thrown upon them, I saw that it would be a long time, if that time ever came, before I could offer Florence even a small proportion of what I would take from her if I married her.

Business had not been good of late, and my partner, Woodruff, who was the capitalist, in a very small way, of the concern, had become despondent. I was indeed a poor young man, and I had had no right to ask a girl like Florence to marry me. But love is above everything, and love had met love, and Florence had said we were to marry! These words, for the time, swept doubt and conscience to the right and left, but doubt and conscience never failed to come rolling back.

I spent that morning with Florence, much to the discomfiture of Miss Moulton, who supposed that we would have settled everything on the evening before, and that I would have gone away by an early train. Florence was a brave girl that day. She saw how happy I was and how miserable I was, and she tried hard, in every gentle and sensible way, to bring me into her frame of mind; but this was a difficult piece of work. I was not sure she was capable of understanding the position in life which I could offer her, and if I dilated too much upon this point, I feared that again the suspicion might come into her mind that I did not want her without her money.

Before I left the cottage she proposed that we should take a sail in the afternoon. We would get Captain Asa to take us out in his boat, and the fresh air would clear our brains. Of course I agreed, but I said to myself that the longer I stayed here the harder it would be for me to decide; after all, perhaps the best

thing I could do might be to go away and write
to her.

There was a good wind and Captain Asa's
boat soon left the village far behind her. We
were on a long tack, Florence and I sitting
together on the windward side, the captain at
the tiller. For some time he had been looking
at us with a certain whimsical but benignant
expression, and now he spoke.

"You two young people seem to have run
into a streak o' bad weather, eh? Kind o'
rough and lookin' like as if there was goin' to
be a heavy blow. Isn't that about it?"

We both gazed at the old man in astonishment.

"What do you mean?" I exclaimed.

"Well, there ain't no use o' makin' no bones
about it," said he. "I know what's the matter with you. I knowed it day before yesterday mornin' when I met you walkin' along
the beach. I said to myself, 'There now,
it's come at last. She's goin' to be married,
and it ain't to a sea-captain.' Now don't jump
like that; you might go overboard before you
know it. I know all about your father's will,
miss. I knowed the old captain very well. I
never sailed with him, but I met him on shore

lots o' times; and I've heard about the queer will he made."

"Does everybody in this place know about my father's will?" asked Florence, indignantly.

"Some does," replied Captain Asa, " but the most of 'em doesn't. I heard about it a long time ago, but I never thought of it agin till the other day. I knowed what had happened when I saw you two walkin' together, and I wasn't a bit surprised when that lawyer got here, nor when I saw your doleful face, sir, after seein' him, when you was a-walkin' on the beach, goin' along at about six knots an hour. Well, I've had you two on my mind ever since, and I'm glad to have a chance o' tellin' you what my thinkin' comes to. Would you like to hear?"

Florence and I looked at each other. These astonishing remarks of the old captain had a very strong flavor of impertinence, but it was such a good-natured impertinence that I did not know whether or not I was called upon to resent it. Florence appeared amused and curious.

"What in the world can you have been thinking about us, Captain Asa?" said she. " Of course we would like to hear."

"Well, then," said the captain, "I'll let you have it in as short order as I know how. Here you are, miss, with a fortune, which I've heard is a mighty big one, waitin' to jump into your lap the minute you marry a man that's a sea-captain, and, more than that, all ready to scud out o' sight the minute you marry anybody that ain't a sea-captain. Well, you made up your mind to marry a man that ain't a sea-captain, and while I don't want to say nothin' to hurt nobody's feelin's, I'm bound to say that I don't believe, judgin' by the looks of that young man's face when he was marchin' along the beach yesterday, that he's got a fortune to give you in place of the one that's ready to scud away. So you've got to give up either the man you want to marry or the money you ought to have, and it ain't an easy thing to make a choice like that."

Florence flushed.

"You are very much mistaken, Captain Asa," she said. "It is not at all difficult to make such a choice, and I have made it."

"Oh, that's all very well for you, miss," said the captain. "You're givin' up what's yours, but it's different with him. He's makin' you give up what's yours; and that must come dreadfully tough on a man who's any kind of a man. Now don't get mad, either of you. Just let me tell you how you can get out of the whole trouble without losin' any of the money and neither of you givin' up the other one. This is the way to do it: You, Miss Brower, you marry me."

At this I sprang to my feet.

"Look out, young man!" shouted the captain. "The next thing you'll be overboard, and that'll settle matters the wrong way."

"Sit down, Arthur!" cried Florence, "and don't interrupt him. This is the funniest thing I ever heard."

"Well," said the captain, "this is the way I'd do it: Some fine mornin', whenever you two are ready, I'll take you in this boat and I'll sail you over to Clamborough. Parson Mil- lick lives over there, and he and I 're good friends. He's married me twice a'ready and he'll do it again. Then, miss, we'll come back here and you will have your marriage cer- tificate in your pocket. Then you and your aunt can start for New York, and your fath- er's money will be yours—every cent of it. That'll be all fixed and settled. Now, as for me, it ain't in the course o' nature that I can last very much longer. I'm in my seventy-eighth year now, though, perhaps, I don't look it, and there ain't none of my family that's ever reached eighty, so it ain't nat'ral to expect that I'll be in the way very long; and all I want out o' this business is just two dollars a day as long as I'm survivin'. I did think o' puttin' it at two and a half, but two dollars is enough. Then when I'm out o' the way—and I'll put it in my will that you ain't to wear no black—all you've got to do, sir, is to wait a decent time and then step up and marry the widder."

At these remarkable words Florence looked at me and then at the captain and burst into uncontrollable laughter. I stared at her in amazement. What in the world there was to laugh at I could not imagine. My mind was filled with horror. To imagine Florence as a widow was to think of myself as a defunct consort. I was angry; I felt as if I would like to get up and throw the old man out of his boat, and yet there was something in his proposition which raised in my soul a feeling which was certainly not resentment, but which I would be ashamed to call hope, the result being that my mind was in a turmoil such as it had never known before.

" You are both young," said the captain, " and I expected you'd both bile over, but whether you bile out o' the spout or rattle the lid, it don't make no diff'rence. And when you come to think serious about what I've said, I know you'll cool down. You can laugh as much as you please, miss, but you know as well as I can tell you that here am I a-holdin' out to you the whole o' your father's fortune, and all you've got to do is to hold out your hand and take it, and pay me two dollars a day for nobody knows how short a time."

At this Florence laughed again.

" Captain," she cried, " I believe you'll live a dozen years! "

At this the old man almost lost his temper. " I don't want to be disrespectful, miss, but that's stuff. It ain't in natur' that I can do it, and, as to the gentleman, I put it to his own good-sense if he wouldn't rather wait a little bit so that you can have the money that's rightly your own than to take you now and strip you o' every copper. I've had my say, and I don't want to hurry you about your an-swer. You two are caught in a heavy blow and I've offered you a port of refuge. Now you can make up your minds whether you'll run in or not."

On the homeward trip I found myself in a very embarrassing position. I felt as if I could blaze and burst like a package of fire-crackers, but I also felt that I had no right to decide anything. It was not for me to say whether or not Florence should accept the fortune which was offered to her in this way.

" Captain Asa," she exclaimed, " you must not ask for an answer to your amazing proposi-sitiou. An answer would put an end to it, and it ought to live forever."

" That's not serious," said the captain, " and it don't mean nothin'. All I ask you is to think it over, and take it cool. Even if I did live to be eighty you two would only have to wait two years, and that's not as long as I waited the fust time I was married; and as to two dollars a day for two years, that's not much when circumstances are considered."

Florence and I did not say much to each other as we walked from the landing-place to the cottage. She was pale, and I could see by her nervous step that she was excited. Be-fore we reached the house she stopped.

" I am beginning to hate my father's

money," she said. "I believe it is a curse upon me." Then suddenly she looked me full in the face. "I wish you hated it as I do," she said.

This was a sharp thrust, and it hurt me. In my soul I knew I was not angry enough at the old sailor for the proposition he had made. I knew that, in spite of myself, I did not utterly repel his astounding proposition. I knew that the desire not to deprive Florence of her fortune was ready to rise above everything whenever the chance was given it.

"Don't look like that," she said, speaking more gently. "I know you are only a man, and that your every thought in this world is for me. Let us forget that old captain; let us forget everything in this world but each other. If we can do that, I think we may be very happy."

It was necessary for me to return to New York the next day, and I was glad that it was necessary. To decide the great question of my life was almost impossible. I knew that if I said the word, Florence was ready to marry me regardless of all consequences. But for me to accept this sacrifice was an entirely different thing.

In less than a week after my arrival in New York the question was decided for me. The firm of Woodruff & Radnor failed most disastrously. The senior partner was a rash and hopeful man; the junior partner was in love. The wreck had been complete; everything was gone; we had nothing left but our debts. I had a little income which came to me from my family—barely enough to support me in the simplest way of living. To ask Florence to give up her fortune and share my absolute poverty was simply impossible. I wrote to her and told her everything. I did not ask her to release me from my engagement; I simply withdrew from it. I knew that it would be kindness to her if I did that.

She did not write to me. What could she have said had she written? We simply parted without a word of regret, or a word of love. My letter to her was no more than a mere business note.

I went into the country to visit my family, and while there I received a letter from Miss Moulton. This surprised me very much. What could she have to say to me? It was now nearly two months since I had parted with Florence, and in all that time I had not heard from her. Miss Moulton's letter was a long one, and portions of it were written so well, and her statements were so clear and so plainly expressed, that I felt sure that much of the matter had been dictated, or at least suggested, by someone other than the writer.

The contents of the letter may be stated briefly: Miss Moulton informed me that before she and her niece returned to New York they had received news that things were going badly with the Brower property. Some of their legal friends had had their suspicions aroused by some very remarkable investments made by Mr. Lloyd, who was one of the principal trustees of the estate, and who seemed to have taken everything into his own hands, and they had therefore made some investigations into the state of affairs. The result showed them clearly that Mr. Lloyd was acting very injudiciously and rashly, and, although there was no proof of any actual dishonesty, there was every reason to fear that if he was allowed to keep on in his present speculative career, the Brower estate was in great danger.

After this there followed several pages of very careful writing, in which Miss Moulton endeavored to say what she had to say in the most delicate and sympathetic manner. But the sum of it was this: Florence had determined to accept the helping hand which Captain Asa had held out to her. It was necessary to do something promptly and immediately in order to save her estate, which, as Miss Moulton put it, was now all that was left to her. The only thing which could be done promptly and immediately was to marry Captain Asa on the terms which he had proposed.

This had been done. They had not called in the services of the captain's old friend, Parson Millick, but they had been married by the rector of the village church. Florence had wished to do nothing in an underhand way. She wished that all who cared to know should know everything she had done, how she had done it and why she had done it. After the simple ceremony Miss Moulton and her niece had repaired to New York and the captain had gone home to his cottage.

Florence had made immediate claim for her property and was now in full possession of what was left of her father's estate. The value of the property had been much impaired, but a handsome fortune remained.

"There is one thing," Miss Moulton wrote

in conclusion, "which Florence has said to me several times, and which I do not think I am violating any confidence in mentioning. She asserts that the marriage she has made is an honorable and straightforward one, with no afterthoughts. One or two of her friends have suggested that it would be possible, after a time, to terminate the connection by means of a divorce, which would be easy enough should both parties agree. But to this she declares she will never consent. Her respect for herself would not permit her to think of it." The letter ended thus: "I have written this at the request of Mrs. Lopper, who thinks that you should know everything that has happened, and that she would rather you should hear it from me than from anyone who might be apt to state it incorrectly."

Mrs. Lopper! This was too much. I laid my head upon the table before me and shut my eyes. But the world was no blacker to me with my eyes shut than when they were open.

For the greater part of the winter I lived an aimless sort of life, and yet not altogether aimless, for the great desire which now possessed me was to avoid a meeting with Florence. I knew very well that if I should meet her I would find her the same sensible, straightforward, noble woman that I had always found her, and that she would do everything to set me at my ease and to establish between us those relations which should exist between two persons situated as we were.

But I also knew very well that, so far as my feelings toward Florence were concerned, there was nothing noble, straightforward, or sensible about them. I thought that I could not meet her—I could not look at her. To take her by the hand and call her Mrs. Lopper—I would rather cut off my hand.

As the spring began to grow into summer a strange instinct seemed to possess me, and that was a desire to go to Captain Asa. Whenever I thought of the little village by the sea, of his cottage, and of himself, I imagined that I saw the only refuge which offered itself to me on the face of the earth. No matter how far I might go, where I might wander or travel, there was no other place in this country or in foreign lands where I might not meet with Flor—no, Mrs. Lopper and her aunt.

So down to the village by the sea I repaired with my baggage, and when I went to call upon Captain Asa he was delighted. I don't know why he should have been glad to see me, but he most certainly was glad. He would not allow me to stay at the little tavern where I had taken a room, but insisted on my coming to his house. If I wanted to pay him board I could do so. He would make no change in his way of living on my account, therefore he would not charge me much.

I found Captain Asa in fine condition mentally and physically. He did not hesitate to acknowledge that his regular income had had a most beneficial influence upon him. He did not work so hard—in fact, he did not work at all unless he felt like it. He lived better —his mind was always at ease.

Had I been asked at this time how long the good captain was likely to live, I might have said, judging from his general appearance, that there was no reason why he should not survive for ten years or more. He looked a great deal more hale and hearty than when I first knew him.

He was very jolly, and his enjoyment of my company seemed to increase. "I was gettin' mighty lonely before you came," he said, "for I'm bound to admit that a fellow that

hasn't anything that he's got to do is a good
deal more apt to get lonely than if he had something to do. And then, again, it seems the
comicalest thing in the world for you and me
to be living here together. I'm not going to
go into particulars, but it does seem comical."

He made this remark a good many times,
and he never made it without finishing off
with a good laugh. I saw nothing comical in
the situation; in fact, there was nothing in the
world at that time which seemed comical to
me, or very interesting. But I could not deny
that the old captain seemed to be some sort of
a connection between me and something which
had been all the world to me, and I do not
doubt that the captain thought I was some
sort of a connection between him and something which was the source of all the great
comfort and satisfaction which now pervaded
his life. So, although it might appear comical
that we should live together, it was natural
enough that we should like to do so.

Meanwhile, idleness pressed rather heavily
upon me, and yet I had no ambition for any
career in life but one. It had struck me in
my melancholy wanderings and cogitations
that if, in the future, circumstances should so

arrange themselves that—Mrs. Lopper should be free again to marry, it was more than probable that, with her conscientious feelings and constant desire to do what was honorable and right, she might feel that she could not carry out her father's wishes in regard to her, and especially could not rightfully enjoy the fortune he had conditionally left, unless she not only married a sea-captain but continued to be the wife of a sea-captain—that is, if she should choose to marry again. That might be a very finely drawn sentiment, but I could see that there would be ground for its existence, especially in the case of such a woman as the daughter of Captain Brower.

Now, when Captain Asa asked me to go out sailing with him I always consented, and I asked a good many questions about keels, rudders, and masts.

" Oh, ho! " said he one day, " you're beginnin' to catch the seafarin' fever. I don't wonder at that. A man's always in danger of gettin' it if he associates with them that's had it."

I answered that I did begin to feel an interest in nautical matters which I did not previously know. The captain looked at me steadily for some moments; then he said:

" Now, look here, young man. I don't think there's a better thing.in this world that you can do than to learn to be a sailor. From what you tell me, all you know of business is of no earthly use now, and so you've got to learn somethin' else. And if you've got to do that, why don't you take to navigation? It would be a good thing for any able-bodied man that hasn't a leanin' in another direction, and it would be a particularly good thing for you. Yes, sir," he repeated, " it would be a partie-ularly good thing for you. I don't want to go into any questions about how long it would take you to graduate, and that sort of thing, but I do say that I'm mighty glad to know that you take an interest in the sea."

After that Captain Asa lost no opportunity of instructing me in regard to all sorts of nau-tical points, even going so far as to endeavor to instil into my mind the use of the sextant. But I am afraid he found me a very dull scholar. I had inclination enough, but no apti-tude. It was evident that Neptune had had nothing to do with the stars that influenced my nativity.

The fact that a steady and regular income now rolled in upon the captain—in very small

waves to be sure, but in surf quite heavy
enough for the sort of beach he possessed—
made him feel that he could indulge himself
in little extravagances. He had a sum of
money hoarded by, but until now he had never
felt that he could draw upon it for luxuries.
Now he did feel that he could do so, and he
bought a better sailboat than he had ever
owned—making a very good bargain, by the
way, in trading off his old one.

One day when we were sailing on the bay,
a mile or two from shore, a very heavy wind
sprang up—it may have been half a gale, or
three-fourths of one, or perhaps seven-eighths,
for all I know—but it blew hard, and as his
new boat was furnished with a jib, to which
sail Captain Asa had not lately been accustomed, he thought it would be wise to take
it in.

I offered to go forward and lower the jib,
but this he would not allow me to do.

" You will fall overboard if you try that,
my boy," said he; " just you take hold of this
tiller and keep it exactly as it is, and I will go
for'ard."

The captain scrambled to the bow, as active
as a boy, and as I looked at him I could not

prevent a little feeling of despondency. My conscience was always ready to resist any such feeling as this, but sometimes it was taken unawares.

As Captain Asa crouched by the mast, lowering the jib, the wind gave a sudden leap against the sail—though this may not be a nautical expression—and the shock to the boat was so great that the tiller jerked itself from my hand. It is likely that I did not comprehend the necessity of grasping it firmly at such a time, but, at any rate, it was gone from my hand in an instant, and in that instant the boat swept around as though it would slide from under us.

It did slide from under the captain. Totally unprepared for such a motion, he slipped and went overboard. As I gazed with open-mouthed horror upon him as he toppled toward the sea, he turned his head in my direction and gave me a look which I shall never forget as long as I live. It was a look of suspicion, contempt, and hatred. It told me as plainly as if he had spoken that he believed I had purposely let the boat fly around. He knew very well that it would be everything to me if he should fall into the sea and be drowned.

He did fall into the sea, but not entirely. The accident was a much more terrible one than I thought it was going to be when I first saw him totter outward from the deck. He fell into the water with a great splash, but one foot was caught in some cordage, and so, instead of sinking out of sight and rising again head uppermost, which would have given him a very good chance for his life, he hung in the water head downward and unable to do anything to help himself.

Instantly I was at his side; clutching something on deck with one hand and reaching the other toward him, I seized him by his clothes and endeavored to pull him upward. But this I found almost impossible. The old man must have weighed nearly two hundred pounds.

Still, I must pull him out of the water. If he should hang thus a few seconds longer, he would be drowned. He must not drown! Again I lifted—I pulled—I strained every muscle, every sinew; I drew myself upward as though possessed with a giant's strength. My eyes were starting out of my head; my muscles were stretched as though they would crack. But the captain's head came out of the water; one of his arms came up, and with a sudden dash he caught the railing, now very near him—the weight of both of us keeling the boat over toward him—and then with a tremendous heave I had him on board. I rolled him over to a place of safety, and there, with purple face and glaring eyes, he lay in the bottom of the boat, puffing and spitting salt water from his mouth. He had held his breath and had not lost consciousness. In fact, he had been in the water but a very little time.

The boat lay with its head to the wind, pitching and tossing, and the mainsail flapped and fluttered in a terrible way. But as I did not know how to do anything to help matters, I did not try. In a few moments, however, the captain was himself again—at least enough himself to go to the stern and take the tiller. And then, dripping with water, he put the boat about and headed her for the village.

So far we had said nothing. Neither of us had breath enough for talking. But now Captain Asa turned his face on me with a very different expression from that which I had seen upon it as he went overboard.

" Bless my soul," said he, " I thought you would split yourself apart when you were pulling me in! You are a better fellow than

"AGAIN I LIFTED—I PULLED—I STRAINED EVERY MUSCLE, EVERY SINEW."

I took you for. Fact is, there ain't many men along this shore could 've done it."

I felt very much inclined to ask him if he had really suspected that I had purposely caused the accident, but I thought it would be better to keep quiet. He did not suspect me now, and that was enough.

Before we reached the shore I was shivering with cold, for the upper part of my body had been well drenched. As for the captain, he declared that he thought he was going to have a chill. We secured the boat and hurried home as fast as possible. The old man looked a little blue in the face, and I could see him shiver. It would be a bad thing for a man at his age to be taken with a chill.

I paid no attention to my own wet condition, but set vigorously to work to take care of the captain. I gave him a good rub-down and put him to bed. Then, at his request, I mixed him a dose of quinine and whiskey. There was a medicine chest in his room, and I weighed the drug in a little pair of brass scales.

"Make it sixteen grains," said the captain, his head just peering above the blankets. "That's a dose for a whole day, but I'll take it all to once."

When I had poured the whiskey into a tumbler he spoke again:

" Who's that for?" said he. " We don't take no infant doses in this house. Put in about as much again, if you please. Now stir in the quinine and get old Jane to fill it up with hot water, the hottest she's got."

When I brought this terrible decoction to Captain Asa's bedside he sat up, put the glass to his lips, and drained its contents in one draught.

" It's the only way to take that sort of stuff," said he. " If you stop once you'll never begin again." And then he lay down and covered himself up.

A little later I mixed myself a dose according to the captain's prescription, but with the proportions very much smaller, and when I had swallowed it I said to myself, contorting my face dreadfully, I am sure, " If I have poisoned that good old man I have done it at his own request."

Old Jane, the woman who came in from a neighboring house to attend to Captain Asa's domestic affairs, was very much concerned. About three years before, she told me, the captain had fallen into the water and had been very sick for a week afterward, and had to have a doctor.

As I lay in bed that night, unable to sleep on account of the taste in my mouth, distressing ideas came into my head. I could not help thinking that the captain was three years older than when he had fallen into the water before, and was therefore more likely to be affected by the drenching. Then I began to ask myself if it were possible that there could be anything which I ought to have done and which I did not do—if, in any way other than the carelessness which made me let the tiller slip from my hand, I could blame myself for what had happened and for what might happen.

I came down a little late next morning, and I found the captain on hand, as lively as a cricket, with a great appetite for his breakfast. My spirits rose and the meal was a very pleasant one. The captain seemed delighted to see me in good spirits. He talked gayly over our morning pipes, and, slapping me on the back, exclaimed, " You're a mighty poor sailor, I'm bound to say that, but you're a good fellow at a steady pull," and with that he gave me one of those glances of approval which had been quite frequent during breakfast.

I continued to go out with the captain, fishing and sailing, but my nautical education was brought to a close.

" I don't believe it's a bit of use," said he. " It ain't in you and it can't be put into you. You might as well take me up to New York to teach me to sell linen goods and ribbons. You were born for the land, and I was born for the sea, and we'd better stick to what suits us."

If the old fellow had known how earnestly and how often I had longed that I had been born for the sea, he would not have made that speech.

I knew very well that I now ought to go somewhere and try to do something, but I made no effort in any direction. The captain wanted me to stay with him and I wanted to stay. If I went into the busy world I felt that I was much more likely to meet with Florence than with any opportunity of making money. I believed that I would be involuntarily and unwittingly drawn in her direction. I could not even consider this without a chill in my heart, and I stayed with the captain.

I never saw anyone more determined to enjoy life than was Captain Asa Lopper at this time. Never before, as he told me over and over again, had his conscience allowed him to live up to his income.

Now he was careful not to go beyond it, but he lived up to it.

Among other comforts which he gathered about him was a cow. The captain was very fond of fresh milk, and he was determined to have plenty of it. Morning, noon, and night, he drank milk at his meals, and if he wanted more of the refreshing beverage between meals he went out into his little paddock and milked a glassful. If a friend stopped in in the daytime, or even in the evening, the captain was glad to milk him a tumblerful of fresh milk, if he would take it. On being told that this sort of treatment was rather bad for a cow, the old man replied, " It may be bad for her, but good for me. I bought her for my good, not for her'n."

He was also fond of what he called " garden stuff," and when his cucumbers were big enough to pick he had them on the table morning, noon, and night. I frequently remarked to him that it was a dangerous thing to drink so much milk and eat so many cucumbers at the same time. But he laughed at the idea.

"I've spent the biggest part of my life," said he, "in not havin' what I wanted, and now that I've got the chance to have what I want I'm goin' to have it. It's my opinion that cow's milk and cowcumbers go first-rate together."

This troubled me and it troubled old Jane. "It'll give him the cholery," she said, "and if he once gets took with that it's all up with him."

The next morning I got up very early, and, going into the garden, I picked all the cucumbers from the vines and gave them to the cow. She consumed them with rapidity and with evident gratitude, and I felt delighted to see them disappear. I had begun to feel that it was my paramount duty to take care of Captain Asa's life. If anything, in any manner connected with fatal results, should happen to him while I lived with him, what would—what would people say? In fact, what would I think if any sort of evil which I could avert should come to this old man who stood between me and all earthly happiness?

The captain said nothing about the loss of his cucumbers, at which I was a little surprised. But the next day he was very loud in praise of the quality of his milk. " I never tasted anything like it," he said; " it's better than any kind of drink I ever did drink. It's all nonsense about my way of milkin' bein' bad for the cow. I don't think that rich people who keep their cows in mahogany stalls has got milk like this."

The weather was bad that day and at night there was a regular storm. The wind was high and the rain was heavy. A little before bedtime the captain began to complain of not feeling well, and before long he was in great pain.

" I've got the cholery," he said, " or somethin' like it."

His face grew very gray and haggard. Old Jane had gone home, and I thought the best thing to do would be to go immediately for the doctor. So I clapped on my hat, and, not thinking it necessary to put on even an upper-coat, I hurried to the house of the only physician in the village. But he was away and was not expected back that night.

This was terrible. Something must be done immediately for the captain, and there was no use in going back to him without medical assistance. I did not know what to do; I did not know where to apply for help. Every house seemed dark and shut up, and, besides, it was not the assistance of neighbors, but a doctor, that the captain needed.

Two miles south of the village lived Dr. Story. I had often passed his house, and the thought now struck me that the proper thing to do was to go there as fast as I could go.

So off I started through the storm. If I should try to get a vehicle there would be a long delay. I could get there quicker on my legs than in any other way.

For a time I ran. Then I was obliged to content myself with walking rapidly. The rain beat down upon me, sometimes almost blinding me. The wind blew as if it would tear off my coat, and the road was so dark that I could not see how to keep out of the mud and puddles. Two or three times I came near going into a ditch.

I had gone about a mile when I began to feel tired and dispirited. I was walking in the very teeth of the storm, and it seemed as if it would be impossible for me to accomplish the rest of the distance. Besides, it might be of no use if I did succeed in reaching the doctor's house. He also might be out. If I turned, the wind would be behind me, and I should soon be back in the village. But I did not turn. I pressed on.

For the next ten minutes I might have imagined that some sort of a wicked angel was keeping company with me and whispering into my ear:

"Why do you do this, anyway?" it said. "You might drop down directly, utterly exhausted, and perish in this storm. Why do you do it at all? You have done already a great deal more than your duty. And, supposing you do not get a doctor, and he does die? You can't blame yourself, for you have done all you could. And then, and then, and then—think of what will happen then!"

As the wicked angel said this her voice became so alluring and charming that I believe I did make a sort of half stop. But I went on.

"Look over toward the right," continued the wicked angel. "Do you see that light? That house is only a little way from the road. The people are up. They doubtless have a fire and are warm. They would be glad to take you in out of this storm. They will let you go to bed. They will give you something hot to drink. In ten minutes you can be comfortable and warm in a bed which will be delightful to you, no matter what sort of bed it is. All you have to do is to turn and hurry to that house."

But I did not turn. There was a woman in this world to whom I could never confess that I had failed, in any way, to do my very best to keep Captain Asa Lopper in this world of life.

I was almost worn-out when I arrived at the house of Dr. Story. If it had been half a mile farther I could not have reached it. Fortunately the doctor was at home, and after I had told him my errand it was not fifteen minutes before we were both going back to the village in a covered vehicle.

We found the captain in a very bad way. He was almost unconscious. " If I had been an hour later," said Dr. Story, " I do not think I could have done much for him."

It was nearly a week before the captain was himself again, and during that time he sold milk to his neighbors. While he was confined to his house I was his constant companion, and my evident solicitude made an impression upon him. One evening—it was the first day he had been able to smoke a pipe—he said:

" I've been thinkin' a good deal about you

lately, and about me, too. We've got along in a number one fashion here together, and it seems to me as if we might get along together in some other way. You ought to be doin' somethin' for yourself, and you might as well give up all thought o' bein' a sailor; and as that's got to be given up, it ain't fair for me to be askin' you to stay here much longer. You've done a lot for me while you've been here, but you can't do nothin' for yourself. Now, what I've been thinkin' is this. I told you that I've money put by. That money is more'n you may suppose it is, and more'n anybody supposes it is. I've always been of a savin' turn of mind, and when I've got hold of a penny I've known how to turn it. Now, it seems to me that what I've got might as well be turned in the lump. And it strikes me that maybe you're the man to turn it."

I looked at him in surprise. I did not know what he was talking about, and told him so.

" Well," said he, " this is what I'm talkin' about. You're a linen merchant; that's what you are. And you're such a beastly bad sailor that I think you must be a pretty good merchant. From what you told me, the man that was your partner was a pretty shackling sort of a fellow, and I've no doubt that I would make a better partner than he was. Now, what do you say to goin' into business again, with me as partner? It couldn't be a very big business at the beginnin'; but if I 'tend to the money part, and you 'tend to the linen part, and if you do your part as well as I've seen you do things down here in this village —always leavin' out anything nautical, mind you—I don't see why we couldn't turn over the money I've got saved up, and divide what we make by turnin' it. Then you'd be in business, and I'd be what they call a sleepin' partner—a jolly good kind of a partner, for a man of my age. Now, what do you say to this?"

I shall not relate what I said to that, nor what was said in the many conversations on the subject which followed. But the end of it all was that I went to New York and made arrangements to go into business with Captain Asa as a partner, instead of Woodruff, the firm name being "Radnor & Co."

At the end of a fortnight I returned to the village to report to Captain Asa what I had done, and to inform him fully of the condition of our young business house, in every detail of

which I knew he would be greatly interested.
I myself was in fairly good spirits, better than
I had supposed it was possible for me to be.
Although I must have years of labor and anxiety before me—for the captain's capital was
small, and my credit had received a heavy
blow—and although there was no reason to
feel sure, now that I had given up all thoughts
of a nautical life, that I should ever be able to
attain that happiness which was the only thing
worth working for in this world, still I felt encouraged and, in a degree, cheerful. There
was something before me which I could do,
and I was doing it. Furthermore, I had won
the good-will of a good old man. That, in
itself, was enough to cheer my soul.

When I reached the captain's cottage I
found he was not alone. Sitting near him
on his little piazza, and smoking with him an
evening pipe, was a broad-shouldered, handsome young man, whom, after the captain had
warmly greeted me, he introduced as his
nephew Tom, the son of his youngest brother.

"Now, whatever you've got to say," remarked Captain Asa, "you can say just as
well before Tom as not. He's in the family,
and he's one of us. Now, you can see for your-

self that Tom is a sailor, a regular out-and-out mariner. He started out in life on shipboard just as soon as he left school, and he's worked his way up faster'n anybody I know of. Now, though he's barely thirty years old, he's the captain of as fine a four-masted schooner as you'll find on this coast, from Newfoundland to Florida."

At these words a horrible iciness pervaded my system. I could not tell myself why this should be so, but it was so. Captain Tom Lopper was nothing to me; at least, he should have been nothing to me. But the fact of his existence affected me to such a degree that Captain Asa had to ask me several times to tell him what I had been doing, before I could make him an adequate answer.

All the time that I was talking about the house of Radnor & Co. I was thinking of Captain Tom Lopper. He was a bright young fellow, with a bluff, hearty expression, with a more refined appearance and a more cultured method of expressing himself than I had been accustomed to in sea-going people. He was neatly dressed in a light summer suit, with nothing about his clothes to suggest the sailor. And yet he was plainly a sailor from crown to heel. He did not say very much, but he took an earnest interest in his uncle's affairs, and I perceived, with disapprobation, that all his remarks were sensible and to the point.

I stayed over Sunday with Captain Asa, and his nephew very soon made himself intimate with me. If he had confined himself to general subjects of conversation I should not have objected to this. But there was only one subject which seemed to interest him, at least when he and I were alone, and that was his uncle's marriage. Of course there could be no subject in this world which I cared less to discuss with him. But if he noticed this it made no impression upon him.

Now, all this was in very great contrast with Captain Asa's manner of treating his marriage. He frequently spoke of Mrs. Lopper to me, but always in a way which indicated that we were both to consider his matrimonial connection as a matter of course, satisfactory to all parties and needing no discussion; and he always avoided saying anything which might in any way wound my feelings. In fact, he showed a thoughtful consideration of which I had not believed him capable.

But it was very different with Captain Tom.

Coming toward me as I was standing on the beach, he laughed as he said:

"I can't help thinking all the time of this queer match that Uncle Asa has made. It's the funniest thing in the world to think of that old man swooping down upon an engaged couple, marrying the lady, and adopting the man. That's what it looks like to me. Upon my word I can't think of you in any other way than as my uncle's son-in-law. Of course, that's ridiculous, but it's the way it strikes me." And then he laughed heartily.

I could not resent this sort of thing. The young fellow was pleasant and good-natured, and I even fancied that he had conceived a liking for me. But I could not stand such talk—it was impossible; and if there had been a train from the village that Sunday evening I should have taken it.

The next morning, at breakfast, Captain Tom was in a very good-humor. He had a holiday, for his ship was in the docks for repair, and, after spending a few more days with his uncle, he told me he intended to run up to New York for a week or so.

"I want to see the town," he said, "and, more than that, I want to go and call on my aunt Florence. After all I've heard about her I've got the greatest kind of desire to see her."

He said a great deal more—something about seeing me—but I heard none of it.

As soon as breakfast was over I took my valise and started for the train.

All the way to the city I heard nothing and thought of nothing but these words, " my aunt Florence! " They seemed to be glowing in the sky, to be painted against the trees and rocks; and if I shut my eyes, they were burned into my brain. He was going to see his " aunt Florence! " It was enough to drive me mad!

What happened when Captain Tom came to New York I do not know. I know he did come, for he called upon me twice at my place of business and left his name; but, unfortunately, I was not in either time.

My mind seemed to be continually upon the subject of his visit, to the great injury of my business interest. Sometimes I imagined this thing, sometimes that. I knew very well that Mrs. Lopper was not obliged to receive all her husband's relatives, but I knew also that she was kind-hearted, courteous and civil to all. And why should she object to a visit from the nephew of that respectable old sea-captain whom she had known nearly all her life?

This latter view took the stronger hold upon me, and I painted a great many mental pictures based upon it.

One of these pictures—the one upon which I worked most frequently—was this: Mrs. Lopper had taken me completely and absolutely at my word. I had desired to withdraw from the engagement we had made, and she considered that as a thing settled forever. If I had been the man she would have liked me to be I would have thrown all money considerations in regard to her or in regard to me to the wild winds, and would have declared myself as ready to marry her as she was to marry me. But I had withdrawn definitely, no matter for what reason, and for the future I was entirely out of the question.

Here now came a fine young fellow, a real sea-captain. Of course, under the circumstances, she would not think of him as anything but her husband's nephew; as such, a relative by marriage. She would learn to like him—I did not believe it would be very difficult for her to do that—and when the time came when she should be free again, even if it should be years ahead, there would be the man who would occupy the exact position which her father desired should be occupied by her husband, when he made his last will and testament and conditionally left her his great fortune.

As for Captain Asa, it had seemed to me on my latest visit to him that he was growing younger. His face was filling out, some of its wrinkles had disappeared, his hair was not quite so gray, he stepped about as if he did not know what it was to be tired. There appears to be nothing which so promotes longevity as to go out of office. I considered Bismarck; when he retired from the affairs of state his life seemed to stretch out indefinitely before him. Captain Asa had retired from office. He was a man of leisure. He did nothing he did not want to do. He rested as much as he pleased, he ate and drank what suited him; all his time was his own, and he was happy and contented.

But the longer he lived the better acquainted would Mrs. Lopper become with Captain Tom. Relationship by marriage would gradually merge into friendship. Captain Tom would see to that. And when the great change in her affairs should come, the next change would be something which might be considered almost inevitable—at least from the point of view in which I regarded it.

In one of our conversations Captain Tom had said to me that I must not think that he was in the least degree jealous of me on account of what his uncle had done in the business way.

"Of course," said he, "you know that I am the old man's only heir, and that at his death I would have had that money he has scratched together. But he has talked over the whole thing with me, and I am perfectly satisfied. When he dies I will inherit his share in the business; and, from what he says about you, I have not the slightest doubt that that will be a great deal better thing for me than if I simply had the money, which I should not have known how to manage as you will manage it. So I want you to understand, Mr. Radnor, that I am with you and uncle, and am perfectly satisfied with everything that has been done."

This was all very well for Captain Tom, but if I had said I was not jealous of him I should have lied most shamefully.

Once or twice in the course of the early summer I went down to see Captain Asa. I found him a little more sedate than in former days. I could not gather from his conversation that there was any cause for this, but I could not help noticing it.

Captain Tom had not yet gone back to his ship, which appeared to take a dreadfully long time to repair; but I asked very few questions about him, and his uncle volunteered but little information. I knew he had been to see Mrs. Lopper—I steadfastly kept myself up to the point of thinking of her under that appellation—but what he had thought of her and what she had thought of him I did not know —and I did not want to know.

Once only did the old captain make a remark about his nephew which was of any importance to me.

"Tom's a wild sort of fellow," he said, " and he's got his head full of schemes, and wants to know what I thought of his askin' Mrs. Lopper and Miss Moulton to take a trip down the coast in his vessel, when she's refitted. He says they might make up a little party and have a jolly time."

"And what do you think of it?" I exclaimed, eagerly, my heart sinking as I spoke.

"I don't think nothin' of it," replied the captain, dryly. Then, with a touch of his old humor, he added, "Tom's a good deal better hand at a tiller than you are, but I wouldn't trust him to jump after a person overboard any more'n I trust you."

"But what did you say?" I interrupted, abruptly. "Did you advise him to ask her?"

"All I said was," replied the old man, "that if he asked her I wanted him to tell her at the same time that I was agin' it, dead agin' it. The fact is," said he, putting his hand on my shoulder, "that if Mrs. Lopper or you goes out on a sailin' vessel while I'm livin', I want to be at the helm."

This remark had a strange effect upon me. I could not understand it. It seemed to indicate an interest in me, coupled with another interest, which appeared inexplicable.

During the rest of that visit the old man did not talk much about his nephew, but when he did allude to him he spoke in a way which gradually produced a suspicion in my mind. Could it be possible that he was becoming jealous of his nephew?

When I took leave of the captain he was unusually friendly and cordial.

" I'm mighty glad," he said, " that you and me's gone into business together. It's a good thing for you because it keeps you in the kind of life that suits you, and it's a good thing for me because I feel that my money's goin' to grow till it gets to be worth somethin' to them that comes after me. As you know, I've fixed it with the lawyers so that, if I die sooner'n any of us expects me to, that money shan't be sudd'nly drawed out of the business, leavin' you swamped."

I told him that I had not forgotten all that, and I assured him that I would make it the object of my life to see that his money did grow as he hoped it would.

" That's right," said he, as he shook hands with me; " it's a good thing for a young fellow if at least one of his objects in life's like that."

There seemed to be a certain good fortune connected with the captain's money. The business began to look very promising. Of course, everything had to be done on a somewhat small scale, but I was naturally prudent and cautious, with an eye to a good bargain, and what the captain had said to me about his trust in my ability to make his money grow had produced a considerable effect upon me.

I felt it my duty to give up making imaginary pictures about what might or might not be happening here or there, with this person or that, and to devote my mind as much as possible to strict business. In spite of the dulness of the trade I made some very profitable contracts, and had good reason to hope that I should do still better later in the year.

Occasionally, however, I was obliged to allow my mind to wander in the direction of what was to me the most engrossing interest on earth, and in this connection I sometimes thought that it was my duty to take steps toward some sort of social intercourse with Mrs. Lopper. We had known each other as well as any two people on earth could know each other. Why should we now be strangers? The connection between us had been severed utterly, and did not that severance annihilate the past? Should not everything that was gone by be treated as if it had never been? Ought I to continue my friendly relations with the old captain and have nothing whatever to do with his wife? Did it not give reason to suppose that I still encouraged feelings which should be utterly suppressed? If there were overtures to be made, I ought to make them.

I had withdrawn—I was the one who should approach again. My heart might be broken, but that was no excuse for not behaving with courtesy.

I reasoned a great deal in this way, but it was absolutely useless. I knew that it would be impossible for me to appear before the woman I had once loved so passionately, and behave as if I had never loved her. I was willing to do my duty so far as I could, but if that should be my duty, I was not equal to it.

During the summer I applied myself most strictly to business, living in airy uptown lodgings, and not going to the country at all. But toward the end of the season I began to feel that I must see Captain Asa again. I still felt, in a way, that I must take care of him, that I must act the part of guardian-angel to the old man. I had no reason to suppose that he needed my protection, for in the few notes I had received from him during the summer he always said he was very well, and I knew that he had given up the cultivation of cucumbers, and that his cow had gone dry. In fact, my observation during my later visits had shown me that the old man was getting to be very careful of himself.

There was only one reason for my imagining that Captain Asa needed any sort of protection, and that reason seemed to lie in the direction of his nephew. I could not imagine what that young sea-captain might do which was not right and desirable, but it seemed to me that a man of his nature must be doing— or must want to be doing—things undesirable and not right.

Perhaps he might induce his uncle to take a cruise with him before he had made a trial trip with his vessel, and that something might be found to be wrong when they were far from land, and that they might all go to the bottom together. If such a thing had occurred, I should have looked upon Captain Tom as a murderer. I would not have taxed him with committing a murder in his own interest, because it would not be right for me to charge any man with such a crime as that.

But the thought of such an accident made me shiver. It is terrible to think of anyone, especially one honored and respected and loved, as living a life the loss of which would be an advantage to other people. If such a life should come within the scope of our action and influence, how careful we should be to cherish, protect, and defend it, in every way and at all times!

Thinking over these things, I journeyed down to the seaside village, and there, to my dismay, I found that Captain Asa was not at home. He had left his cottage about a week before, and old Jane could tell me nothing about his probable destination.

" He said he was goin' off for a holiday, and that's all he did say about his doin's," she told me. " But he left word that if you or Captain Tom came down here, you was to be taken care of just the same as if he was at home."

" And when does he expect to come back? " I demanded.

" I don't know no more about that," she replied, " than I know where he is. When the captain's got anything to do, he goes along and does it. Many a time, when he was a younger man, he's gone off on a cruise and nobody knowed where he'd gone to cruise to, and when he was coming back. But when he was ready his boat would sail into the bay, and that would be the end of it."

I stayed at the cottage that night in a state of great perplexity and anxiety. That the captain should go away in this manner, without telling anybody where he was going, and especially without telling me, his business partner, who ought to know all his movements, was something I could not comprehend. That Captain Tom was not with him was plain enough from his orders to old Jane. And that he had thought it probable that I might come down there seemed evident. There could be no doubt that he did not want me to know where he had gone.

A horrible idea crept into my mind. Could it be possible that for any reason the old man had determined to go away, not only from his cottage and the village, but from the world? At this thought a glittering, black-hearted demon of a possibility rose before me, but I am happy to say that I promptly assailed this accursed phantom and drove it out of my sight.

There was no use of my staying in the village. The captain might come back soon, and he might not; besides, there was reason to suppose that if he returned he would prefer that I should not be there upon his arrival. I made old Jane promise to write to me just as soon as he got back, and then I departed.

For a week or more I remained in New York. It was hot. It was oppressive. In mind and body I felt borne down, but I could not get away. While I was in this state of anxiety concerning the captain, old Jane had not written.

One morning I was sitting in my counting-house alone, for my bookkeeper had a holiday, when I was told that a lady wished to see me. Almost instantly the visitor entered the room. It was Miss Moulton! She was in a state of great agitation, and my heart sank as I beheld her. Had she heard some dreadful news about the captain?

"Mr. Radnor," she said, forgetting to shake hands with me, "I have something terrible to tell you. Please close the door, for no one should hear what I have to say."

"What!" I exclaimed; "has anything happened to——"

Miss Moulton interrupted me. She evidently misunderstood the object of my anxiety.

"Oh, Florence is well," she said; "there has been no accident."

I did not wonder at Miss Moulton's condition when I heard her tale. It was told in

many words and in a disjointed way, but the
substance of it was that the day before the mail
had brought to Florence a most dreadful communication. It was a legal document, which
informed her that Captain Asa Lopper had
gone out West and had there procured a divorce from her, on the ground of desertion.
He had gone off secretly to commit this horrible crime, but he had taken with him the
written testimony from people in the village
that he had been entirely deserted by his wife
ever since their marriage. The paper showed
that an absolute decree of divorce had been
obtained. Florence had been so shocked that
Miss Moulton thought at one time she would
have to send for a doctor. The blood raced
through my veins. My face must have blazed.

"What do you intend to do?" I cried.

"I don't know," she replied. "We have
sent for our lawyer, but he is out of town.
I thought I must come to you and tell you all
about it. There is no one else to whom I can
speak."

I sprang to my feet, furious with passion.

"What are *you* going to do?" she asked,
piteously.

"Do!" I cried, "I am going to see him. I

"IT WAS MISS MOULTON"

shall go to his cottage and shall wait there until he comes back."

Miss Moulton was evidently frightened. She begged me not to be violent, but I assured her she need have no fears of that kind.

Neither of us was in a condition to talk much further upon this subject. I promised that I would report as soon as I found out anything, and then she left me.

The first train down carried me to the village by the seaside—to the house of the man who had done this foul wrong to the noblest, the most honorable woman in the world.

I was at a white heat with rage. I forgot my relations with the old man. I only remembered how he had treated Florence. I did not know that he was at his home, but he must return sometime, and I would wait until he came.

It was a rainy day when I reached Captain Asa's cottage. I entered without knocking, and found the old man smoking his pipe before the kitchen fire. He arose and held out his hand, but I did not take it. I stood before him, trembling with the vehemence of my emotions. Without preface of any kind, or explanation of the manner in which I had

come to know of what he had done, I poured
out upon him all the contempt, all the indignation which had been gathering and seething
within me ever since Miss Moulton had spoken
to me. I made no allusion to anything that
he had done, except this one infamous act of
treachery, of insult, of cruelty, of dishonesty.

Soon after I began to speak the captain sat
down, held his pipe in his hand without smoking it, and listened attentively. When I had
finished, for want of words and breath, he
said, without any show of emotion:

" Now, I want you to know that I'm very
glad to hear you talk like that. If you had
talked in any other way I would have had a
very different opinion of you from what I've
got now. There may be some sense in what
you say, and it may be that there isn't any.
It shows you've got the right spirit, and I
wouldn't want to think of you as a fellow who
hadn't got the right spirit. And now, if you
are pretty well played out as far as talkin'
goes, I'll have a word to say; and I advise
you to take a chair." But I would not sit
down. I stood and listened to him.

" You're fiery mad," said he, " and I'm glad
of it. And I expect that Mrs. Lopper that

was is fiery mad, too. I'm sorry for that, for I wouldn't do anything to disturb her mind if I could help doin' it. As for her aunt, I expect she's simply blazin'. But it couldn't be helped. There wasn't no other way to do it. The whole business was goin' on in such a way that I couldn't stand it. I felt that I wasn't carryin' on my part of the bargain as I expected to carry it on. Every day I felt livelier and tougher. Every day my nephew Tom, when he was here, said to me in the mornin' when he come down, 'Uncle, you're lookin' younger than you was yesterday.' And I don't wonder that he said so, for I felt it.

"Now, I was mighty glad that all this was so. This world suits me fust-rate, and I want to stay in it as long as I can. But I felt kind o' mean. I knew that I wasn't standin' up to what might reasonably be expected of me, and that's a thing that's never happened to me before. But I want you to understand that when I was thinkin' in this way, I wasn't thinkin' of Mrs. Lopper that was, then, as much as I was thinkin' of you. For a good while I've had a powerful feelin' for you. It had a pretty bad upset that day when we were out on the bay, but after you fished me out of the water, and after you lived with me as you did live with me, and did the things you did do, that feelin' grew powerfuller and powerfuller.

" And then there was another thing that troubled me, and that concerned my nephew Tom. He's a good fellow, but I don't know so very much about him—he's been away to sea most of his life; and as to Mrs. Lopper that was, I don't know so very much about her. I knowed her father, and I'd seen her off and on ever since she was a little girl; but as for her inside mind, of course I couldn't be expected to know about that. And so, when Tom had been to see her two or three times, and come here talkin' about her as he did talk, it made me more uncomfortable than I was before.

" Now, Tom's got nothin' to complain of about me. When I die he'll have a share of the business, unless you choose to buy him out. So, as I felt that I didn't owe him nothin', I didn't like the idee of that young fellow gettin' any notions into his mind that wasn't intended to be there when I got up this plan of savin' Captain Brower's money for his

daughter, and givin' myself at the same time
a comfortable income without being obliged
to work or to draw on my savin's. I didn't
want Tom to put his foot into this business.
But the more I thought about it the more
likely it seemed to me that he might put his
foot into it.

"Then, again, it looked to me as if you were
gettin' a little more humble than you was—
a little more like not holdin' out—a little more
like givin' yourself up to your business and
tryin' to forget things which had gone wrong
and which might never come straight again.
I didn't want you to do that. It made me feel
as if I'd tried to mend somethin' and had
broken it all to smash.

"'So,' said I to myself, 'this thing's got to
be brought up with a round turn.' Then I
found out everything I could, went out West,
and brought it up with a round turn. I
didn't ask anybody to agree, because I knowed
nobody would agree. And I didn't tell anybody about it, because I knowed they'd try
to stop it; but I wanted to do it and I didn't
intend it to be stopped.

"Now it's done, hard and fast, and no
goin' back. That young woman you used to

walk about with on the sands down here hasn't got no husband. She's just as free as air— unless she considers herself bound to pay me two dollars a day for the rest of my life, and I'm inclined to think she'd feel that way, for our bargain said that I was to have the money as long as I live, without mentionin' anything that might happen in the meantime. And I'm just as free as—well—just as free as water. I can do what I please, and what anybody else does is no concern of mine—at least, I can't prevent it. As for you, I can't say that I consider you free at all—at least, accordin' to my way of thinkin'; " and as he said this he looked at me with a kindly grin. " No, sir, you're the only one of the whole business that's bound to do anything. And I don't think your duty is goin' to weigh very heavy on you."

It was impossible for me to be angry with this old marine angel. The crime with which I had come down here to charge him and to punish him for doing (if there were any way in which punishment could be inflicted) had been done for me. I held out my hand to him and begged his pardon for what I had said, at all of which he pooh-poohed, and filled me a pipe.

I stayed a day with Captain Asa, and then both he and I agreed that it was my duty to go back to New York and report the result of my interview with him. He did not give me many injunctions. I understood the whole story, he said, and I must make the best of it.

On my way back to the city my brain did as much working as the locomotive which drew the train. I was going to see Florence! And now that I had business with her—now that I had to explain a crime which had been committed against her, and to defend the perpetrator of that crime so far as I might—I felt that I could see her and speak to her.

As to the duty of which Captain Asa had good-naturedly twitted me, I determined to be strong and brave and to set that entirely aside. How Florence might feel toward me I could not tell. Perhaps she might charge me with complicity in this indignity which had been thrust upon her. But even if she held me innocent of this, she may have changed entirely her former opinion of me. I had deliberately renounced her. Now, even if it be for her own good, I know that a woman resents the rejection of her freely offered love. She would prefer to have that love accepted, no matter what misfortune it might bring upon her.

But, let Florence think of me as she would, I had determined upon one course. I would begin again, at the very beginning. I would consider all that had happened as something which had passed and which had no influence upon me. I would take no advantage of anything she had ever said to me. I would go to her as a friend—as an envoy. If afterward she would allow me to become her lover, this world would become Paradise. But I would presume upon nothing. One reflection gave me great comfort—I should not go to her as a pauper, asking to share in her fortune. The great goodness of the captain had made it possible for me to present myself as a young merchant with a fair chance of success before him.

With all these reasons and resolutions I thoroughly fortified myself. I had taken my position and I intended to make it plain exactly where I stood.

When I reached the New York house I inquired for Miss Moulton. Of course I must see her first, because she had sent me to the captain, and I must make my report to her.

But before I did anything else I must make inquiries about Florence. I had had many anxieties regarding the possible result of the great blow which had been dealt her.

Miss Moulton was at home. I sent up my card and was shown into the parlor. In a very few minutes someone entered by a side door. I turned quickly. It was Florence.

I stood speechless as she advanced. As all the events of his life rush to the mind of a drowning man, so into my mind rushed a long procession of the things which I had intended to say to Miss Moulton, and which I must now say to Florence. It was a terrible emergency. Without warning, without an instant to prepare myself, I must treat this heavenly beauty as a middle-aged spinster to whom I had come to make a report.

It is astonishing how I remembered everything that I had arranged to say; how all these statements, these reasons, these explanations, ranged themselves in perfect order according to their proper precedence. And it is still more astonishing how instantaneously, absolutely, and utterly they all disappeared from existence. In two seconds they had come and gone.

In her light muslins Florence was more lovely than ever. Her eyes were bright. She came to me with her hand outstretched. I put out my hand; then the other, without volition on my part, extended itself. I stepped to meet her, and in a moment she was clasped to my breast. As if it had been yesterday that we two had wandered on the sands, we sat down side by side, hand in hand. After a little she told me, with tears in her eyes, that nothing in this world could be more surprising than that this had happened as it did happen. But it had happened. It was something with which neither of us had anything to do.

It must have been half an hour after this that I felt myself bound to call together the array of statements and facts which I had come here to report. But as soon as I began to speak about the captain Florence stopped me. She would not hear of him. No matter what he had done or why he had done it, she could not forgive him. So curious is the mind of woman! She accepted the great happiness which he had given her, because there was nothing for her to do but to accept it. But she would not pardon him for having

given it. However, I pardoned him for both
of us, and I loved him for myself.

For some years after we were married Captain Asa Lopper continued to be a hearty old
man. He had an income of two dollars a day,
and appeared to be eminently satisfied with
what life had given him. I frequently wrote
him concerning our business, and I made it a
point to pay him an occasional visit. But
Florence never went with me. She never forgot that he gave us to each other, but also she
never forgot how he did it.

Good fortune seemed to attend the captain's
money. The affairs of the firm of Radnor
& Co. improved rapidly. Moreover, we had
another partner, for some of Florence's fortune was invested in the business.

I now felt quite able to buy out Captain Asa
and keep the business in my family. But I
would not do so. I knew that it delighted his
old soul to know that his money was gradually
increasing, without labor of his own, and I
would not deprive him of this reward for all
that he had done for others. When I visited

him he never complained of Florence's attitude toward him.

"I don't blame her," he once said; "in fact I wouldn't think as much of her as I do if she did different. I married her fairly and squarely, and I unmarried her unfairly. She's down on that sort of thing, and that's just what she ought to be, and we're satisfied all around."

All of this happened a good while ago, and the dear old captain is now dead. I have bought out his share of the business from Captain Tom, who was very glad to be thus enabled to become the owner of a new ship.

Florence and I have built a pretty cottage near the beach where we first found out what we were to each other, and if the marine angel who did so much for us during his life has any power to influence our welfare now, I am sure he is exerting it, for I don't see how any two people could be happier than we are.

THE GREAT STAIRCASE AT
LANDOVER HALL

THE GREAT STAIRCASE AT LANDOVER HALL

I WAS spending a few days in the little village of Landover, simply for the purpose of enjoying the beautiful scenery of the neighborhood. I had come up from Mexico because the weather was growing too warm in that region, and I was glad of the chance to vary my interesting and sometimes exciting travels with a little rest in the midst of this rural quiet.

It was early summer, and I had started out for an afternoon walk, when, just upon the outskirts of the village, my attention was attracted by a little group at a gateway which opened upon the road. There were two women and an elderly man. The women appeared to be taking leave of the man, and one of them frequently put her handkerchief to her eyes. I walked slowly, because I did not wish to intrude upon what seemed to be an affecting leave-taking; so when I reached the gate the women had gone, but the man was still standing there, looking after them.

Glancing over the low fence, I saw a very pretty grove, apparently not well kept, and some distance back, among the trees, a large, old house. The man was looking at me with a curiosity which country people naturally betray when they see a stranger, and, as I was glad to have someone to talk to, I stopped.

" Is this one of the old family mansions of Landover? " I asked. He was a good-looking man, with the air of a head gardener.

" It is not *one* of them, sir," he answered; " it is the only one in the village. It is called Landover Hall, and the other houses growed up around it."

" Who owns it? " I asked.

" That is hard to say, sir," he said, with a grim smile; " though perhaps I could tell you in the course of a couple of weeks. The family who lived there is dead and gone, and everything in it is to be sold at auction."

I became interested, and asked some questions, which the man was very willing to answer. It was an old couple who had owned it, he said. The husband had died the previous year, and the wife about ten days ago. The heirs were a brother and sister living out in Colorado, and, as they had never seen the house, and cared nothing about it, or about anything that was in it, they had written that they wished everything to be sold, and the money sent to them as soon as possible.

"And that is the way it stands," said the old man. "Next week there is to be a sale of the personal property—a ' vandoo ' we call it out here—and every movable thing in the house and grounds is to be sold to the highest bidder; and mighty little the things will bring, it's my opinion. Then the house will be sold, as soon as anybody can be found who wants it."

"Then there is no one living in the house at present?" said I.

"Nobody but me," he answered. "That was the cook and her daughter, the chambermaid, who just left here. There is a black man who attends to the horses and cows, but he will go when they are sold; and very soon I will go too, I suppose."

"Have you lived here long?" I asked.

"Pretty near all my life," said he.

I was greatly interested in old houses, and I asked the man if I might look at the place.

" I have not had any orders to show it," he said; " but, as everything is for sale, I suppose the sooner people see the household goods the better; there's many a bit of old furniture, candlesticks, and all that sort of thing, which strangers might like to buy. Oh, yes; you can come in if you like."

I shall not attempt to describe the delightful hour I spent in that old house and in the surrounding grounds. There was a great piazza in front; a wide hall stretched into the interior of the mansion, with a large fireplace on one side and a noble staircase at the further end, a single flight of stairs running up to a platform, and then branching off on each side to the second floor. On the landing stood one of the tallest clocks I have ever seen. There were portraits on the walls, and here and there a sporting picture, interspersed with antlers and foxes' heads mounted on panels, with the date of the hunt inscribed beneath. There was an air of largeness and gravity about the furniture in the hall, which was very pleasing to me, and when I entered the long drawing-room I found it so filled with books and bric-à-brac of the olden days, with many quaint furnishings, that, had I been left to myself,

even the long summer afternoon would not
have sufficed for their examination. Upstairs
was the same air of old-fashioned comfort.
The grounds—the grass rather long, and the
bushes untrimmed—were shaded by some
grand old trees, and beyond there were gardens
and some green pasture-fields.

I did not take the walk that I had proposed
to myself. When I left the old house I inquired the name of the agent who had charge
of the estate, and then I went back to the village inn, where I sat communing with myself
for the rest of the afternoon and all the evening.

I was not yet thirty, I had a good fortune,
and I had travelled until I was tired of moving
about the world. Often I had had visions of
a home, but they had been very vague and
fanciful ones. Now, for the first time in my
life, I had seen a home for which I really
might care; a house to which I might bring
only my wearing apparel, and then sit down
surrounded by everything I needed, not even
excepting books.

Immediately after breakfast I repaired to
the office of Mr. Marchmay, the lawyer who
had charge of the property. I stayed there a

long time. Mr. Marchmay took dinner with me at the inn, and in the evening we sent a telegram to Colorado. I made a proposition to buy everything for cash, and the price agreed upon between Mr. Marchmay and myself was considerably higher than could have been expected had the property been sold at auction. It is needless to say that my offer was quickly accepted, and in less than a week from the day I had first seen the old house I became its owner. The cook and the housemaid, who had retired in tears from its gateway, were sent for, and reinstalled in their offices; the black man who had charge of the horses and cows continned to take care of them, and old Robert Flake was retained in the position of head gardener and general caretaker, which he had held for so many years.

That summer was a season of delight to me, and even when autumn arrived, and there was a fire in the great hall, I could not say that I had fully explored and examined my home and its contents. I had had a few bachelor friends to visit me, but for the greater part of the time I had lived alone. I liked company, and expected to have people about me, but so long as the novelty of my new possessions and my new position continued I was company enough for myself.

At last the holiday season came around, and I was still alone. I had invited a family of old friends to come and make the house lively and joyous, but they had been prevented from doing so. I afterward thought of asking some of my neighbors to eat their Christmas dinner in the old house, but I found that they all had ties and obligations of their own with which I should not seek to interfere. And thus it happened that late on Christmas eve I sat by myself before a blazing fire in the hall, quietly smoking my pipe. The servants were all in bed, and the house was as quiet as if it contained no living being.

For the first time since I lived in that house I began to feel lonely, and I could not help smiling when I thought that there was no need of my feeling lonely if I wished it otherwise. For several years I had known that there were mothers in this country, and even in other countries, who had the welfare of their daughters at heart, and who had not failed to let me know the fact; I had also known that there were young women, without mothers, who had their own welfare at heart, and to whom a young man of fortune was an object of interest; but there was nothing in these recollections which interested me in these lonely moments.

The great clock on the landing-place began to strike, and I counted stroke after stroke; when there were twelve I turned to see whether I had made a mistake, and if it were now really Christmas day. But before my eyes had reached the face of the clock I saw that I was mistaken in supposing myself alone. At the top of the broad flight of stairs there stood a lady.

I pushed back my chair and started to my feet. I know my mouth was open and my eyes staring. I could not speak; I doubt if I breathed.

Slowly the lady descended the stairs. There were two tall lamps on the newel-posts, so that I could see her distinctly. She was young, and she moved with the grace of perfect health. Her gown was of an olden fashion, and her hair was dressed in the style of our ancestors. Her attire was simple and elegant, but it was evident that she was dressed for a festive occasion.

Down she came, step by step, and I stood

MR. MARCHMAY TOOK DINNER WITH ME AT THE INN.

gazing, not only with my eyes, but, I may say, with my whole heart. I had never seen such grace; I had never seen such beauty.

She reached the floor, and advanced a few steps toward me; then she stopped. She fixed her large eyes upon me for a moment, and then turned them away. She gazed at the fire, the walls, the ceiling, and the floor. There came upon her lovely features an almost imperceptible smile, as though it gave her pleasure thus to stand and look about her.

As for me, I was simply entranced. Vision or no vision, spirit from another world or simply a mist of fancy, it mattered not.

She approached a few steps nearer, and fixed her eyes upon mine. I trembled as I stood. Involuntarily the wish of my heart came to my lips. " If——" I exclaimed.

" If what? " she asked, quickly.

I was startled by the voice. It was rich, it was sweet, but there was something in its intonation which suggested the olden time. I cannot explain it. It was like the perfume from an ancient wardrobe opened a hundred years after a great-grandmother had closed and locked it, when even the scent of rose and lavender was only the spirit of something gone.

" Oh, if you were but real! " I said.

She smiled, but made no reply. Slowly she passed around the great hall, coming so near me at one time that I could almost have touched her. She looked up at the portraits, stopping before some old candlesticks upon a bracket, apparently examining everything with as much pleasure as I had looked upon them when first they became mine.

When she had made the circuit of the hall, she stood as if reflecting. Fearful that she might disappear, and knowing that a spirit must be addressed if one would hear it speak, I stepped toward her. I had intended to ask her if she were, or rather ever had been, the lady of this house, why she came, and if she bore a message, but in my excitement and infatuation I forgot my purpose; I simply repeated my former words—" Oh, if you were but real! "

" Why do you say that? " she asked, with a little gentle petulance. " I am not real, as you must know. Shall I tell you who I was, and why I am here? "

I implored her to do so. She drew a little nearer the fire. " It is so bright and cheerful," she said. " It is many, many years since

I have seen a fire in this hall. The old people who lived in this house so long never built a fire here—at least on Christmas eve."

I felt inclined to draw up a chair and ask her to sit down, but why need a ghost sit? I was afraid of making some mistake. I stood as near her as I dared, eagerly ready to listen.

" I was mistress of this house," she said. " That was a long, long time ago. You can see my portrait hanging there."

I bowed. I could not say that it was her portrait. An hour before, I had looked upon it as a fine picture; now it seemed to be the travesty of a woman beyond the reach of pigments and canvas.

" I died," she continued, " when I was but twenty-five, and but four years married. I had a little girl three years old, and the very day before I left this world I led her around this hall and tried to make her understand the pictures. That is her portrait on this other wall."

I turned, and following the direction of her graceful hand my eyes fell upon the picture of an elderly lady with silvered hair and benignant countenance.

" Your daughter?" I gasped.

"Yes," she answered; "she lived many years after my death. Over there, nearer the door, you may see the picture of her daughter —the plump young girl with the plumed hat."

Now, to my great surprise, she asked me to take a seat. "It seems ungracious," she remarked, "that in my own house I should be so inhospitable as to keep you standing. And yet it is not my house; it is yours."

Obedient to her command, for such I felt it to be, I resumed my seat, and to my delight she took a chair not far from me. Seated, she seemed more graceful and lovely than when she stood. Her shapely hands lay in her lap; soft lace fell over them, like tender mist upon a cloud. As she looked at me her eyes were raised.

"Does it distress you that this house should now be mine?" I asked.

"Oh, no, no," she answered, with animation; "I am very glad of it. The elderly couple who lived here before you were not to my liking. Once a year, on Christmas eve, I am privileged to spend one hour in this house, and, although I have never failed to be here at the appointed time, it has been years, as I told you, since I saw a fire on that hearth and a living being in this hall. I knew you were here, and I am very glad of it. It pleases me greatly that one is living here who prizes this old place as I once prized it. This mansion was built for me by my husband, upon the site of a smaller house, which he removed. The grounds about it, which I thought so lovely, are far more lovely now. For four years I lived here in perfect happiness, and now one hour each year something of that happiness is renewed."

Ordinarily I have good control of my actions and of my emotions, but at this moment I seemed to have lost all power over myself; my thoughts ran wild. To my amazement, I became conscious that I was falling in love— in love with something which did not exist; in love with a woman who once had been. It was absurd; it was ridiculous; but there was no power within me which could prevent it.

After all, this rapidly growing passion was not altogether absurd. She was an ideal which far surpassed any ideal I had ever formed for the mistress of my home. More than that, she had really been the mistress of this house, which was now my home. Here was a vision of the past, fully revealed to my eyes. As the sweet voice fell upon my ears, how could I help looking upon it as something real, listening to it as something real, and loving it as something real.

I think she perceived my agitation; she looked upon me wonderingly.

" I hoped very much," she said, " that you would be in this hall when I should come down to-night, but I feared that I should disturb you, that perhaps I might startle or———"

I could not restrain myself. I rose and interrupted her with passionate earnestness.

" Startle or trouble me ! " I exclaimed. " Oh, gracious lady, you have done but one thing to me to-night—you have made me love you ! Pardon me ; I cannot help it. Do not speak of impossibilities, of passionate ravings, of unmeaning words. Lady, I love you ; I may not love you as you are, but I love you as you were. No happiness on earth could equal that of seeing you real—the mistress of this house, and myself the master."

She rose, drew back a little, and stood looking at me. If she had been true flesh and blood she could not have acted more naturally.

For some moments there was silence, and then a terrible thought came into my head.

Had I a right to speak to her thus, even if she were but the vision of something that had been? She had told me of her husband; she had spoken of her daughter; but she had said no word which would give me reason to believe that little girl was fatherless when her mother led her around the hall and explained to her the family portraits. Had I been addressing my wild words of passion to one whose beauty and grace, when they were real and true, belonged to another? Had I spoken as I should not have spoken, even to the vision of a well-loved wife? I trembled with apprehension.

"Pardon me," I said, "if I have been imprudent. Remember that I know so little about you, even as you were."

When she answered there was nothing of anger in her tone, but she spoke softly, and with, I thought, a shade of pity.

"You have said nothing to offend me, but every word you have spoken has been so wild and so far removed from sense and reason that I am unable to comprehend your feelings."

"They are easy to understand!" I exclaimed. "I have seen my ideal of the woman I could love. I love you; that is all! Again

I say it, and I say it with all my heart: Would you were real! Would you were real!"

She smiled. I am sure *now* she understood my passion. I am sure she expected it. I am sure that she pitied me.

Suddenly a change of expression came over her face; a beaming interest shone from her eyes; she took some steps toward me.

"I told you," said she, speaking quickly, "that what you have said seems to be without sense or reason, and yet it may mean something. I assure you that your words have been appreciated. I know that each one of them is true and comes from your heart. And now listen to me while I tell you——" At that moment the infernal clock upon the landing-place struck one. It was like the crash of doom. I stood alone in the great hall.

The domestics in that old house supposed that I spent Christmas day alone; but they were mistaken, for wherever I went my fancy pictured near me the beautiful vision of the night before. She walked with me in the crisp morning air; I led her through the quiet old rooms, and together we went up the great staircase and stood before the clock—the clock that I had blessed for striking twelve and cursed for striking one. At dinner she sat opposite me in a great chair which I had had placed there—" for the sake of symmetry," as I told my servants. After what had happened, it was impossible for me to be alone.

The day after Christmas old Mr. Marchmay came to call upon me. He was so sorry that I had been obliged to spend Christmas day all by myself. I fairly laughed as I listened to him.

There were things I wanted him to tell me if he could, and I plied him with questions. I pointed to the portrait of the lady near the chimney-piece, and asked him who she was.

" That is Mrs. Evelyn Heatherton, first mistress of this house; I have heard a good deal about her. She was very unfortunate. She lost her life here in this hall on Christmas eve. She was young and beautiful, and must have looked a good deal like that picture."

I forgot myself. " I don't believe it," I said. " It does not seem to me that that portrait could have been a good likeness of the real woman."

" You may know more about art than I do, sir," said he. " It has always been considered a fine picture; but of course she lived before my time. As I was saying, she died here in this hall. She was coming down stairs on Christmas eve; there were a lot of people here in the hall waiting to meet her. She stepped on something on one of the top steps—a child's toy, perhaps—and lost her footing. She fell to the bottom and was instantly killed—killed in the midst of youth, health, and beauty."

"And her husband," I remarked, "was he——"

"Oh, he was dead!" interrupted Mr. Marchmay. "He died when his daughter was but a mere baby. By the way," said the old gentleman, "it seems rather funny that the painting over there—that old lady with the gray hair—is the portrait of that child. It is the only one there is, I suppose."

I did not attend to these last words. My face must have glowed with delight as I thought that I had not spoken to her as I should not. If I had known her to be real, I might have said everything which I had said to the vision of what she had been.

The old man went on talking about the family. That sort of thing interested him very much, and he said that, as I owned the house,

I ought to know everything about the people who formerly lived there. The Heathertons had not been fortunate. They had lost a great deal of money, and, some thirty years before, the estate had passed out of their hands and had been bought by a Mr. Kennard, a distant connection of the family, who, with his wife, had lived there until very recently. It was to a nephew and niece of old Mr. Kennard that the property had descended. The Heathertons had nothing more to do with it.

" Are there any members of the family left? " I asked.

" Oh yes! " said Mr. Marchmay. " Do you see that portrait of a girl with a feather in her hat? She is a granddaughter of that Evelyn Heatherton up there. She is an old woman now and a widow, and she it was who sold the place to the Kennards. When the mortgages were paid she did not have much left, but she manages to live on it. But I tell you what you ought to do, sir: you ought to go to see her. She can tell you lots of stories of this place, for she knows more about the Heathertons than anyone living. She married a distant cousin, who had the family name; but he was a poor sort of a fellow, and he died some fifteen years ago. She has talked to me about your having the old house, and she said that she hoped you would not make changes and tear down things. But of course she would not say anything like that to you; she is a lady who attends to her own business."

"Where does she live?" I asked. "I should like, above all things, to go and talk to her."

"It is the third house beyond the church," said Mr. Marchmay. "I am sure she will be glad to see you. If you can make up your mind to listen to long stories about the Heathertons you will give her pleasure."

The next day I made the call. The house was neat, but small and unpretentious—a great drop from the fine hall I now possessed.

The servant informed me that Mrs. Heatherton was at home, and I was shown into the little parlor—light, warm, and pleasantly furnished. In a few minutes the door opened, and I rose, but no old lady entered.

Struck dumb by breathless amazement, I beheld Evelyn Heatherton coming into the room!

I could not understand; my thoughts ran wild. Had someone been masquerading?

Had I dreamed on Christmas eve, or was I dreaming now? Had my passionate desire been granted? Had that vision become real? I was instantly convinced that what I saw before me was true and real, for the lady advanced toward me and held out her hand. I took it, and it was the hand of an actual woman.

Her mother, she said, begged that I would excuse her; she was not well and was lying down. Mr. Marchmay had told them that I was coming, and that I wanted to know something about the old house; perhaps she might be able to give me a little information.

Almost speechless, I sat down, and she took a chair not far from me. Her position was exactly that which had been taken by the vision of her great-grandmother on Christmas eve. Her hands were crossed in her lap, and her large blue eyes were slightly upraised to mine. She was not dressed in a robe of olden days, nor was her hair piled up high on her head in by-gone fashion, but she was Evelyn Heatherton, in form and feature and in quiet grace. She was some years younger, and she lacked the dignity of a woman who had been married, but she was no stranger to me; I had seen her before.

Encouraged by my rapt attention, she told me stories of the old house where her mother had been born, and all that she knew of her great-grandmother she related with an interest that was almost akin to mine. " People tell me," she said, " that I am growing to look like her, and I am glad of it, for my mother gave me her name."

I sat and listened to the voice of this beautiful girl, as I had listened to the words which had been spoken to me by the vision of her ancestress. If I had not known that she was real, and that there was no reason why she should vanish when the clock should strike, I might have spoken as I spoke to her great-grandmother. I remained entranced, enraptured, and it was only when the room began to grow dark that I was reminded that it was incumbent upon me to go.

But I went again, again, and again, and after a time it so happened that I was in that cottage at least once every day. The old lady was very gracious; it was plain enough that her soul was greatly gratified to know that the present owner of her old home—the house in which she had been born—was one who delighted to hear the family stories, and who respected all their traditions.

I need not tell the story of Evelyn and my-self. My heart had been filled with a vision of her personality before I had seen her. At the first moment of our meeting my love for her sprung into existence as the flame bursts from a match. And she could not help but love me. Few women, certainly not Evelyn Heatherton, could resist the passionate affection I offered her. She did not tell me this in words, but it was not long before I came to believe it.

It was one afternoon in spring that old Mrs. Heatherton and her daughter came to visit me in my house—the home of their ancestors. As I walked with them through the halls and rooms I felt as if they were the ladies of the manor, and that I was the recipient of their kind hospitality.

Mrs. Heatherton was in the dining-room, earnestly examining some of the ancestral china and glass, and Evelyn and I stood to-gether in the hall, almost under the portrait which hung near the chimney-piece. She had been talking of the love and reverence she felt for this old house. " Evelyn," said I, " if you love this house and all that is in it, will you not take it, and have it for your own? And will you not take me and love me, and have me for your own?"

I had my answer before the old lady came out of the dining-room. She was reading the inscription on an old silver loving-cup when we went in to her and told her that again Evelyn Heatherton was to be the mistress of the old mansion.

We were married in the early winter, and after a journey in the South we came back to the old house, for I had a great desire that we should spend the holidays under its roof.

It was Christmas eve, and we stood together in the great hall, with a fire burning upon the hearth as it had glowed and crackled a year before. It was some minutes before twelve, and, purposely, I threw my arms around my dear wife and turned her so that she stood with her back to the great staircase. I had never told her of the vision I had seen; I feared to do so; I did not know what effect it might have upon her. I cared for her so earnestly and tenderly that I would risk nothing, but I felt that I must stand with her in that hall on that Christmas eve, and I believed that I could do so without fear or self-reproach.

The clock struck twelve. "Look up at

your great-grandmother, Evelyn," I said; " it is fit that you should do so at this time." In obedience to my wishes her eyes were fixed upon the old portrait, and, at the same time, looking over her shoulder, my eyes fell upon the vision of the first Evelyn Heatherton descending the stairs. Upon her features was a gentle smile of welcome and of pleasure. So she must have looked when she went out of this world in health and strength and womanly bloom.

The vision reached the bottom of the stairs and came toward us. I stood expectant, my eyes fixed upon her noble countenance.

" It seems to me," said my Evelyn, " as if my great-grandmother really looked down upon us; as if it made her happy to think that——"

" Is this what you meant? " said I, speaking to the lovely vision, now so near us.

" Yes," was the answer; " it is what I meant, and I am rejoiced. I bless you and I love you both," and as she spoke two fair and shadowy hands were extended over our heads. No one can hear the voice of a spirit except those to whom it speaks, and my wife thought that my words had been addressed to her.

" Yes," said my Evelyn; " I mean that we should be standing here in her old home, and that your arm should be around me."

I looked again. There was no one in the hall, except my Evelyn and myself.

THE GHOSTS IN MY TOWER

THE GHOSTS IN MY TOWER

A^T one corner of the house I once lived in is a tall, wide tower, rising high above the trees which surround it. In one of the upper rooms of this tower I worked and thought, and here, in the evening and early part of the night, I used to be quite alone, except for the ghosts.

Before I had come to this house I knew that the tower was haunted, but I did not mind that. As the ghosts had never done anyone any harm I did not believe they would do me any harm, and I thought I should really be glad of their company, which must certainly be different from the company of ordinary people. So, when I had arranged an upper room in the tower so that I might pleasantly work and think therein, I expected the ghosts to come to me, and should have been very much disappointed if they had not.

I did not exactly understand these ghosts,

of which I had heard nothing definite, except that they haunted the tower, and I did not know in what way they would manifest themselves to me. It was not long, however, after I had begun to occupy the room, before the ghosts came to me. One evening, a little before Christmas, after everybody in the house but myself had gone to bed, and all was quiet, outside and inside, I heard a knock, and was on the point of saying, " Come in! " when the knock was repeated and I found that it did not come from the door, but from the wall. I smiled.

" You cannot come in that way," I thought, " unless there are secret doors in these walls, and even then you must open them for yourself."

I went on with my writing, but I soon looked up again, for I thought I heard a chair gently pushed back against the wall in a corner behind me, and, almost immediately, I heard a noise as if some little boy had dropped a number of marbles, or perhaps pennies, but there was no chair in the corner at which I looked, and there were no pennies nor marbles on the floor.

Night after night I heard my ghosts—for

I had come to consider them as mine, which I had bought with the house—and although I could not see them there were so many ways in which they let me know they existed that I felt for them a sort of companionship. When, in the quiet hours of the early night, I heard their gentle knocks I knew that, were the circumstances different, they would have been glad to come in, and I did not feel lonely.

Now and then I thought I heard the voices of the ghosts, sometimes outside, under my window, and sometimes behind me, in a distant corner of the room. Their tones were low and plaintive, and I could not distinguish words or phrases, but it often seemed as if they were really speaking to me, and that I ought to try to understand and to answer them. But I soon discovered that these voice-like sounds were caused by the vagrant breezes going up and down the tall chimney of the tower, making æolian tones, not of music, but of vague and indistinct speech.

The winter passed, and at last there came a time when I saw one of the ghosts. It was in the dusk of an evening, early in spring, and just outside of an open window, that it appeared to me. It was as plain to my sight as if it had been painted in delicate half-tones against a sombre background of tender foliage and evening sky.

It was clad from head to foot in softest gray, such as the phantoms of the night are said to love, and over its shoulders and down its upright form were thrown the fleecy folds of a mantle so mistily gray that it seemed to blend into the dusky figure it partly shrouded. The moment I saw it I knew it saw me. Out of its cloudy grayness there shone two eyes, black, clear, and sparkling, fixed upon me with questioning intensity. I sat, gazing, with checked breath, at this ghost of the tower.

Suddenly I leaned forward—just a little— to get a better view of the apparition, when, like a bursting bubble, it was gone, and there was nothing before me but the background of foliage and evening sky.

Frequently after that I saw this ghost, or it may have been one of the others, for it was difficult, with these gray visions, with which one must not speak or toward which it was hazardous to move even a hand, to become so well acquainted that I should know one from another. But there they were; not only did I hear them; not only, night after night, did my ears assure me of their existence, but in the shadows of the trees, as the summer came on, and on the lonelier stretches of the lawn I saw them, and I knew that in good truth my home was haunted.

Late one afternoon, while walking in my grounds, I saw before me one of the spectres of my tower. It moved slowly over the lawn, scarcely seeming to touch the tips of the grass, and with no more sound than a cloud would make when settling on a hill-top. Suddenly it turned its bright watchful eyes upon me, and then, with a start that seemed to send a thrill even through the gray mantle which lightly touched its shoulders, it rose before my very eyes until it was nearly as high as the top of my tower!

Wings it had not nor did it float in the air; it ran like a streak of gray electricity along the lightning-rod, only, instead of flashing down it, as electricity would pass from the sky, it ran upward. I did not see this swiftly moving spirit reach the topmost point of the rod, for, at a point where the thick wire approached the eaves, it vanished.

By this time I had come to the conclusion, not altogether pleasant to my mind, that my

ghosts were taking advantage of my forbear-
ance, with their mystic knocks and signals in
the night and their visits in the daylight, and
that there must be too many of them in my
tower. I must admit that they annoyed me
very little, and I was not in the least afraid of
them, but there were others who came into
my tower and who slept in some of its rooms,
and to the minds of visitors and timorous maids
there was something uncanny and terrifying
in these midnight knocks and scratches.

So, having concluded from what I had seen
that day that it was the very uppermost part
of the tower which had become the resort of
these gray sprites, and from which they came
to disturb our quiet and repose, I determined
to interfere with their passage from the earth
to my tower-top. If, like an electric current,
they used the lightning-rod as a means of
transit, I devised a plan which would compel
them to use it in the conventional and proper
way. The rod was placed there that lightning
might come down it, not that it might go
up, so I set myself to put the rod in a condition
that would permit the ghosts to descend as the
lightning did, but which would prevent them
from going up.

Accordingly I thoroughly greased the rod for a considerable distance above the ground.

" Now," said I to myself, " you may all come down, one after the other, whenever you like. You will descend very quickly when you reach the greased part of the rod, but you will not go up it again. You are getting very bold, and if you continue your mad revels in my tower you will frighten people, and give my house a bad name. You may become dryads if you like and shut yourselves up in the hearts of the tall and solemn oaks. There you may haunt the bluejays and the woodpeckers, but they will not tell tales of ghostly visits which may keep my friends away and make my servants give me warning."

After that there were no more gray flashes up my lightning-rod, though how many came down it I know not, and the intramural revels in the tower ceased. But not for long. The ghosts came back again; perhaps not so many as before, but still enough of them to let me know that they were there.

How they ascended to their lofty haunts I could not tell, nor did I try to find out. I accepted the situation. I could not contend with these undaunted sprites.

One evening, in the autumn, outside the same window from which I had seen the first ghost of the tower, I saw another apparition, but it was not one of the gray spectres to which I had become accustomed. It was a jet-black demon. Its eyes, large, green, and glaring, shone upon me, and it was as motionless and dark as a statue cut in coal.

For only an instant I saw it, and then in a flash, like the apparition I had first seen from that window, it disappeared. After that, I saw the demon again and again, and strange to say the ghosts in my tower became fewer and fewer, and at last they disappeared altogether. The advent of the black spirit seemed to have exerted an evil influence over the sprites in gray, and, like the Indian in the presence of the white man, they faded away and gradually became extinct.

The last time I saw one of my ghosts it appeared to me late on a November afternoon, among the brown foliage of an aged oak, just as a dryad might have peeped forth from her leafy retreat, wondering if the world were yet open to her for a ramble under the stars. The world was open to my gray ghost, but only in one direction. Between it and me could be seen, among the shadows of the ground, the dark form of the demon, trembling and wait-ing. Then away from the old oak, away from my house and my tower, along the limbs of trees which stood on the edge of the wood, slowly and silently, my ghost vanished from my view like a little gray cloud, gently moving over the sky, at last dissolving out of my sight.

Now, in the early hours of the night my tower is quiet and still. There are no more knocks, no more wild revels in the hidden pas-sages of the walls. My ghosts are gone. All that I hear now are the voices in the chimney, but I know that these are only imaginary voices, and, therefore, they produce in me no feeling of companionship. But my ghosts really existed.

THE LANDSMAN'S TALE

OSMANS TALE

THE LANDSMAN'S TALE

INTO a little town on the New England coast there came one day in mild October weather a quiet man without an object; at least, this was the opinion of the villagers.

This opinion was not formed until the stranger had lived for five or six days in their midst, having lodgings at the inn, but spending his days and even parts of his evenings in the open air; sometimes in the village streets, sometimes in the surrounding country, and very often on the sands and among the rocks of the ocean beach.

It was his manner of spending his time which proved that he was a man without an object. At first it was supposed that he was an artist—so many wandering strangers are artists; but he never sketched and it did not appear that he had brought with him even an umbrella or a camp-stool. He had probably not come for his health, for he seemed in good physical condition, and he had not come for the usual seaside society, for it was not the time of the year for that. All the summer boarders had gone and there was no one left in the little village but the regular inhabitants thereof.

The water was now too cold for sea-bathing, and, besides, he had casually mentioned that he did not care for that sort of thing; and, what was stranger than all, he had not come there to sail upon the ocean. Several times it had been proposed to him that he should go out in one of the numerous cat-boats or sloops which were idly lying at anchor in the little bay, for, in the middle of the day, the weather was just as good for a sail as it had been in August or September.

But only once did the stranger heed such suggestions, and then he hired the best boat in the bay, which was sailed by one of the oldest skippers, assisted by a weather-beaten mariner, and it may be therefore supposed that it was very well sailed; but whether the stranger liked the little excursion or not, it was impossible for the skipper to say. He had expressed no opinion on the subject, either while he was in the boat or after he landed, but as he did not go out again during his stay in the village, it was generally believed that he had not liked it.

It might have been supposed that he came to this quiet little place for the sake of living cheaply, had it not been for the fact that he occupied the largest and most expensive room at the hotel; that, being the only lodger at the inn, he ordered the best living that the landlord could procure for him, and at dinner-time indulged in the unusual extravagance of a glass or two of wine.

So it was not long before the villagers made up their minds that the quiet man at the inn was without an object. As he cared for nothing which they or their village could offer him, it was plain enough that he had no reason for coming there. But the investigations and consultations of the villagers had a positive as well as a negative result. They proved, without the shadow of a doubt, that this person was a thorough landsman. He did not seem to care for the ocean or anything connected with it; and, on the one occasion when he had gone out in a boat, it was manifest to the skipper and to the mariner who was with him that this stranger knew nothing whatever about navigation, about boats, about sails, about sheets, or even about a tiller.

He did not seem to mind the motion of the waves, but it was remarked, when the subject was discussed that evening, that it was very probable that he did not know enough about the ocean to be aware that people unaccustomed to it were made to feel badly when the sea was rough, and on that day it had been a little rough.

The stranger now occupied a peculiar position in the village; he was the only landsman therein. All the men in the place were nautical, in some degree or other, and there was not one of them over thirty years of age who was not called captain. They had not all commanded a vessel, but it would have been considered discourteous in that region to cast upon a man old enough to be a captain the imputation that he had not attained that distinction. Not to be able to sail a boat would have been considered in a citizen of the village a condition of denser ignorance than inability to read.

But, of course, conditions were different in the case of a thorough landsman: he would not know anything about the sea, but he might know something about the land, and in the inferior sphere in which he moved he might hold a very fair position. Consequently, when it was agreed that the man at the inn was an out-and-out landsman, he rose in the esteem of the villagers. To be sure, he did not know anything about the sea, but then he did not pretend to know anything; such a man they had never seen before.

Many men had come down there in the summer-time who, although they did not know the difference between a sliding keel and a shuffle-board, hitched up their trousers, walked with a rolling gait, wore little caps with visors, and were perfectly willing to take the helm if they should find anyone fool enough to let them do it. These men had always been looked upon with the contempt proper to their pretensions; but here was a man who pretended nothing: a good, honest, square, outright, unvarnished landsman. As such they recognized him, and as such they gave him a position—not a very high one, but one they believed he deserved.

When the season for seaside visitors was over, and when the evenings were cold, it was the custom of some of the captains of the village to gather, after supper, in the large room of the inn and to sit around the great fireplace to smoke and to talk: and now the landsman often found it pleasant to sit there and listen to them as he smoked his cigar. He was not much of a talker, but he was a very good listener, and for this the captains liked him. It often happened that when an old skipper told a tale of adventures in far-away seas, and told it ostensibly to the assembled company, he really told it to the landsman, and all the rest knew it, and the more evidently such tales were directed at the landsman and the better they were adapted to his want of comprehension of nautical subjects, the better they were liked by the rest of the assembled company.

One evening there was a public meeting in the large room of the inn, composed not only of the captains of the place, but of their wives, their daughters, and their sisters. This had been called together for the purpose of considering the establishment of a library in the village. The captains, old and young, as well as their wives and daughters, were always glad to have something to read during the long evenings of winter, and as their stock

of reading-matter was very limited, and as
they had heard a great deal about village
libraries from their summer visitors, they had
now determined to establish a little library
for themselves. So this meeting was called,
and it was hoped that it might result in encouraging subscriptions.

The landlord of the inn, who had taken part
in public meetings elsewhere, was called upon
to preside, and the exercises consisted in
speeches from the more prominent captains
present. These speeches were all of the same
character, they had the same object, and they
were constructed on the same general plan.
They recounted the speaker's love of reading,
which always began in his boyhood; they
told how difficult it had been for him to get
access to books; and how he had always longed
for first-class A-No. 1, copper-fastened litera-
ture; and they all ended with remarks on
the great advantages of an institution which
should supply reading-matter to nautical people, and of the peculiar need of their own village for such an institution.

These speeches, most of them autobiograph-
ical to an extent not required by the subject,
were listened to with great attention, and when

every captain who desired to speak had spoken, it was evident that the audience would be pleased with a continuation of the interesting proceedings.

With this idea in his mind the landlord stood up and glanced toward the landsman. "There is a gentleman present," he said, "who is not a seafaring person and for that reason is not likely to feel as we do about the needs of mariners and their families for books, but he may be able to say something on the subject which will be useful, and perhaps he may get from what has happened to him in his inland life a point or two which may come in well upon an occasion like this. It may be that some of us mariners have got into the way of thinking that this world is all water—that is, all the parts that are good for much—but that isn't the right way of thinking: there are plenty of things which have happened on land that are well worth hearing about. So, if the gentleman would not mind, I am sure we would all be very glad to have him say something to us, something which may come in with the general drift of the public feeling in this village in the direction of a library."

All eyes were now directed toward the landsman, who, without hesitation, rose in his place.

" Mr. Chairman," said he, " I am very willing to make some remarks upon this occasion, but I should prefer not to divert the very interesting and instructive current in which the proceedings of this evening have been flowing. I therefore ask that you will allow me to tell you, instead of a story of the land, which would not harmonize with the tenor of the narrations to which we have listened with such pleasure this evening, a story of the sea."

At this everybody stared in surprise. What could this landsman know about the sea? Of course he might have heard of something which happened at sea, but how could he repeat it? That would be as if one of their townsmen should overhear a couple of Welshmen talking in their native tongue and should endeavor to give the points of their conversation. It was odd, truly, that this landsman should want to tell a sea story, but for that very reason everybody wanted to hear it.

" It was some time ago," the landsman said, " exactly how long I cannot state, that a good-sized schooner was sailing on the Pacific Ocean. It was an American schooner, and was manned by a crew of ten thoroughbred seamen, a captain, and a boy. I don't know to what port this schooner was bound, but I think it very likely she was going to the Sandwich Islands; nor do I know what her cargo was, but that would be of no interest to us.

" Her crew were all respectable mariners; on such a vessel a foreigner would have been decidedly out of place. These men cared not only for their bodies, but for their minds; they would not have been satisfied with enough to eat and to drink, good clothes to wear, and not too much work to do; they must have more than this, they must have food for the mind; they must have reading - matter. Every one of them, including the captain and the boy, was fond of books.

" It may well be supposed that a crew with tastes of that sort would not start out of port without taking along, among their other stores, a store of books, and so this schooner had on board a library. This was a very small one, and was contained in a portable bookcase not much larger than a soap-box; but the books were all in small type—for a sailor who has not good eyes can't be much of a sailor—and, as it takes a long time to read a book at sea where there are so many interruptions in the way of watches and storms and meals, and going to the masthead to look out for whales and sails, the contents of the little portable bookcase had never failed to give the crew all the reading-matter they wanted, no matter how long a voyage might be. Even if a rapid reader had got through with the whole of them before the schooner reached the port to which she was bound, he would have been very willing to begin again and read them all the second time, for they were good books. Consequently great care was taken of this portable library, and whenever there was rough weather the doors of the little bookcase were battened down, so that the precious volumes should not be tumbled out."

At this some of the captains looked at each other; it was all right to batten down hatches when there was a storm, but nobody ever battened down the doors of a bookcase; however, this person was a landsman.

" They had been sailing," the speaker continued, " for some weeks, and, as there had been many calms, the men had had unusual opportunities for reading, and all of them had become very much interested in the books they had in hand. This state of things was pleasant, although not profitable, but it soon came to an end, for one morning just after breakfast a violent wind arose and soon became so strong that the captain was quite sure that a tornado or a hurricane would soon be upon them. He gave orders to take in all the sails, but before this could be done one of the small ones in front was blown entirely away from the ropes which held it, and went whirling out to sea, far in advance of the vessel.

" The wind came from the south, and, therefore, the schooner was soon scudding along under bare poles as if she intended to dash through the water to the region of the polar bears, and, as the captain had expected, this wind-storm grew into a hurricane, and the masts of the schooner, although they were good ones, could not stand it. First the topmast of the foremast went, then the other topmast followed, then the thicker part of the masts snapped off one after the other, just about the middle, and jerking themselves loose from the rope ladders and all the cords which held them, they went off through the air as if they had been birds, and none of them touched water until they had gone at least a mile ahead.

" Now the booms, which held the two large

sails wrapped up upon them, blew away from the half-masts on which they swung, and went up into the air, and the violence of the wind was such that the little cords which held the sails to the booms were broken, and the sails spread out like great kites, and higher and higher they went up into the air, until they seemed like little white specks against the black tempestuous sky.

" Now the ends of the masts which had been left standing broke off with a great crack and disappeared as suddenly as if each one of them had been the flame of a candle when it is blown out, and after them the bowsprit was wrenched from its fastenings and hurled forward like a javelin cast into the wild waste ahead."

At this point the captains, who had been listening with eager interest, looked at each other, and the landsman noticed it.

" That may seem somewhat strange," he said, " but this wind was now acquiring the character of an irregular cyclone, and as it passed the schooner its corkscrew-like movements drew out the bowsprit as if it had been the stopper from a bottle. And now the small boats, which had been so firmly fastened to the irons which held them like pots suspended from an old-fashioned crane in a fireplace, up-heaved themselves and blew away, and when this happened the heart of each one of the crew, including the captain and the boy, sank as if it had been the lead on a line. But there was no need for such mental depression, for those sailors soon saw that they would have been no better off in such a storm as that with the boats than without them.

" There were two of these boats, a long-boat and a shorter one, and the crew gazed with amazement at their behavior. The boats were in front of them not very far away, and for a time did not seem to be blown along any faster than the schooner, but their motions were wonderful. First the long-boat rose high in the air, then it turned bow down and stern up and plunged into the ocean, dipping up a boatful of water and rising again into the air, turned completely over, upsetting its whole load of water upon the other boat which was just beneath it. This made the shorter boat sink, but it soon came up some distance ahead and flew into the air, followed hard by the long-boat, which seemed to be trying to bump it.

" The two rose and fell together, sometimes high, sometimes low, the long-boat always in pursuit of the shorter boat, like a hawk after a pigeon, until at last they came together, with their hollow parts toward each other like the two shells of a clam. The shock was so great that they burst into fragments with a great noise, as if they had exploded, and little pieces of them scattered themselves over the sea like hail. To think of their fate had they been in those boats was enough to make that crew shiver.

" Now the wind grew stronger and stronger; it was a real, full-grown tornado, and every man of the crew, including the captain and the boy, was obliged to lie flat upon the deck and hold on to some ring or bar to keep himself from being blown away. They did this none too soon, for in a few minutes the wind began to blow the bulwarks off that schooner, and if the stern rail had not lifted itself a little as it flew over the schooner and out ahead, it would have wiped every man off that deck as neatly as you would peel the skin from a banana."

The captains did not look at each other now, but they stared steadfastly at the landsman;

even their wives, their daughters, and their sisters were impressed with the intensity of the storm that was being described. Their nerves were in a state of tension; ·if one of their hairpins had dropped, it would have startled them.

"On went that schooner," continued the landsman, "faster and faster, before that awful, howling, shrieking wind; it seemed as if the waves behind were yelling to the waves in front to turn and stop the flying vessel so that they might leap on board. The captain, flat on his face on the deck, kept his hand upon the helm, and so steered the schooner that she sped straight forward over the waves and before the wind. Now the whole ocean was boiling under the hot fury of the tempest, and great waves seemed to rise perpendicularly out of the depths, and one of these, coming up under the schooner, lifted her stern high into the air. This was only for a moment, but it was an eventful one, for the wild blast struck the rudder, now exposed to its fury, and tore it from the stern as if it had been the stem of a strawberry. Over the sea now skipped that rudder, as a stone from the hand of a boy skims and jumps over the smooth surface of a mill-pond.

" Now, of course, the schooner could be no longer directed or controlled. On she still went before the maddened gale, but not as before, bows in front and stern behind; but sometimes stern foremost, sometimes whirling around like a top, sometimes brushing broadside over the waves as if she were trying to smooth them down. On, on, still on she plunged and dashed and spun, until the men clinging to her deck were sometimes almost dizzy with the motion, but still the heart of the captain did not falter: ' Hold on, my men,' he cried, whenever the roaring tempest would allow him to be heard; ' we have yet a good hull beneath us and the wind may fall.'

" But now a terrible thing happened. The schooner was down in the trough of the sea, and as she rose, a fierce blast, blowing close to the surface of the water, struck her broadside and turned her over upon her beam-ends: so far over, indeed, that the men clung to the deck as if they had been hanging against the side of a perpendicular wall. She went over still farther, and everyone felt that she was going to capsize entirely. Just at this. moment there came over the sea the wildest and most furious blast that had yet blown, and in one mad whiff it blew off the keel of that schooner."

As the landsman now gazed in the faces of his audience, it seemed as if each one of the captains had been transformed into a wooden image. With open eyes, with close closed lips, and without a sign of emotion upon their rigid faces, they sat and listened. In the eyes of some of the women were tears; others had their mouths open. The landsman paused for a few seconds, and then continued:

" That schooner did not capsize. As soon as her keel was gone she righted and went plunging, bounding, whirling, northward. But the wind had done its worst, there was nothing about that vessel which could be blown away except the crew, and they stuck so close to the deck that the wind passed over them as if they had been mere knobs or pimples on the surface of the vessel.

" Having done its worst, the wind did really begin to fall, and the storm passed away almost as suddenly as it had risen, and before long the hull of the schooner was rising and falling and rolling on the great swells which had followed the tempest. Now the crew could sit up and look about them, but there wasn't much to look at, for everything of wood or iron which had projected from the hull of that schooner had been blown away.

" The captain folded his arms and considered the case. It was a hard thing for him to make up his mind to desert his vessel. Under ordinary circumstances he would have rigged up some sort of a rudder; he would have made some sort of a mast; he would have hoisted sails, even if they had been table-cloths and sheets—he would have endeavored to make his way to the nearest port; but now it was of no use for him to try to do any of these things. You all know as well as he did that when a vessel has lost her keel in the ocean, the time has come to give her up.

" So the captain addressed his crew: ' My men,' he said, ' we must leave this vessel; her keel is gone, and she is of no further use. Down below, with our freight, there is a boat which was shipped in sections; it is a hunting-boat, which can be taken apart and carried over the land when necessary. Of course this boat does not belong to us, but under the circumstances we are warranted in using it. We will get this boat on deck and put it together; there are oars belonging to it, and in it we

will row away to the nearest land. Of course
I don't know how near such land may be, and
I can't take any observations now; but by dead
reckoning; and I have been doing a good deal
of this since I have been lying here on the
deck, I think I have a fair idea where we are.
We sailed on pretty near the same line of
latitude from the time I took my observation
yesterday until the storm struck us this morning, and then I dead-reckoned that that wind
must have been blowing at the rate of sixty
miles an hour, and, although it could not carry
us along as fast as that, it must have taken us
thirty-five miles an hour, and so in the five
hours in which it blew we must have sailed
northward one hundred and seventy-five miles.

" Now, according to the chart as I remember it, there are some desert islands about
forty-five miles to the northeast of us, and it
will not be difficult for us to row to them in
that boat. So, my men, let us get to work
and launch her.

" The men sprang up with a will, and in a
short time the boat was hauled up on deck,
put together, and lowered to the water.

" The crew of the schooner now got down
into the boat, and as they did so it seemed

doubtful to the captain whether or not the little hunting craft would hold them all; but
they crowded in until they were all aboard except the captain, who, of course, would be the
last to leave his ship. They were packed tightly together, barely leaving room for the oars-
men to move their arms, but there was still a
vacant space at the stern which had been left
for the captain.

"But this good man, instead of descending,
stood on the edge of the deck and looked down
into the boat.

"'Hurry, captain,' said the first mate, 'and
come down; we have got a good way to row
and we ought to be starting; there is room for
you here.'

"'I see that,' said the captain, 'and I have
been considering that vacant space. Hold on
a few moments; I will be with you directly.'

"Now the captain hurried down into the
hold, but soon reappeared carrying under
each arm a box. These he placed on the edge
of the deck and stood between them.

"'My men,' he said, addressing the crew,
'I have calculated that if I sit with my knees
drawn up, there is room in that boat for one
of these boxes, and as that is all the additional

load which the boat can carry, it will not be possible to put both boxes into her. Now one of these is a box I have always kept packed, to be used in a case of emergency like this; it contains condensed food of various kinds, sufficient to last us all for some days. As to water, I don't think we shall suffer for that, for I see it is going to rain. The other box is our portable library; it contains our precious books. Now, my men, we can take but one of these boxes, and I leave it to you to decide which it shall be. Please come to an agreement among yourselves as quickly as possible, and I will lower down to you one of the boxes and then get in myself.'

" The men in the boat now held a consultation; it was an earnest one, but did not last long. The first mate rose in his place and spoke for the others.

" ' Captain,' said he, ' we have made up our minds. If it is only forty-five miles to the nearest land, we can easily row that far without eating. When we reach the island, even if it should be a desert one, it is not unlikely that we shall find some sort of .food, berries, birds, or bread-fruit, and almost certainly some fish in the adjacent water, but there is no reason to suppose that upon such islands we shall find books. Therefore, we have unanimously agreed that we will take with us our library. There's not a man among us who is not interested in a story or in a historical volume, and to leave our books behind would be a wrench, captain, which in all deference to your opinion, if it be otherwise, we truly think we ought not to be obliged to give ourselves.'

"In a faltering voice the captain spoke: ' My men,' said he, ' you have chosen wisely; I will lower the library to the boat.'

"When this had been done, he got down himself and the boat pushed off from the hull of the schooner and rowed away to the northeast."

The speaker ceased. For a moment there was absolute silence in the room, but on the face of every captain there seemed to be a shadow which grew darker and darker as grows the sky before a storm.

The landsman, who appeared to be possessed of a certain amount of weather wisdom, advanced toward the chairman of the meeting. "I have told my little tale," said he, " and now allow me to make this contribution to your library fund, and to bid you good-evening."

Laying a bank-note on the table before the presiding officer, he bowed and withdrew. After which, without any motion being made to that effect, the meeting adjourned.

There was a great deal of talking as the people went home. Some of the captains who were in the habit of refraining from swearing in the presence of their wives, their sisters, and their daughters, now swerved from their usual custom.

"Do you suppose," said Captain Ephraim Smolley to Captain Daniel Yates, "that that confounded fool came here for nothing else than to get the chance to spin us that all-fired yarn?"

"Dunno," said Captain Daniel, "but as there wasn't nuthin' else that he could have come for, it must have been that."

Miss Amelia Brindley, a young woman with a high color and a quick step, who was to be the librarian of the library when it should be founded, said to her mother when she got home: "What nettles me most, is not thinking of the story he told to us to-night, but thinking of the story he is going to tell about us when he goes somewhere else; they say he has ordered himself driven to the cars early in the morning."

FRANK R. STOCKTO

CHARLES SCRIBNER'S SONS, Publishers

> " I have been reading him now a good many years, wi
> an increasing pleasure which his constant public seems
> share, and I am more and more certain that our literatu
> does not know a more original or originative spirit. I dou
> if any author of our time stamps his personality so distinc
> on his work."—WILLIAM DEAN HOWELLS.

THE GIRL AT COBHURST

12mo, $1.50.

" Delightfully Stocktonian, just as unique, as fresh, as original, as Stockton had never done anything else in similar vein."—*New York Time*

" 'The Girl at Cobhurst' will grow upon you as you read, and that is quality in any book, whether novel or other sort. It is a story cast in the wh and quaint fashion of plot for which Stockton has become so justly cele and which in its essence approaches more closely to genuine humor than th of any other American writer to-day."—*Brooklyn Eagle.*

A STORY TELLER'S PACK

Illustrated, 12mo, $1.50.

" His gift is one of the most characteristic that has yet appeared in our ture. The fact that it is humorous and light must not make us oblivious original quality."—*The Outlook.*

" Here is that quizzical vein of serious humor, that droll inventiver incident, and that adroit suggestion of character which aie prominent cha istics of Mr. Stockton's books."—*Philadelphia Press.*

Lightning Source UK Ltd.
Milton Keynes UK
UKHW02n0935120218
317657UK00002B/205/P